# A FLOWER'S FATAL THORN

JORDAN DUGDALE

Interior art by Etheric Designs

Cover Art by Jules @ coversbyjule.s

Map by Andrés @ aaguirreart

Careful. Cut off a wolf's head, and it still has the power to bite.

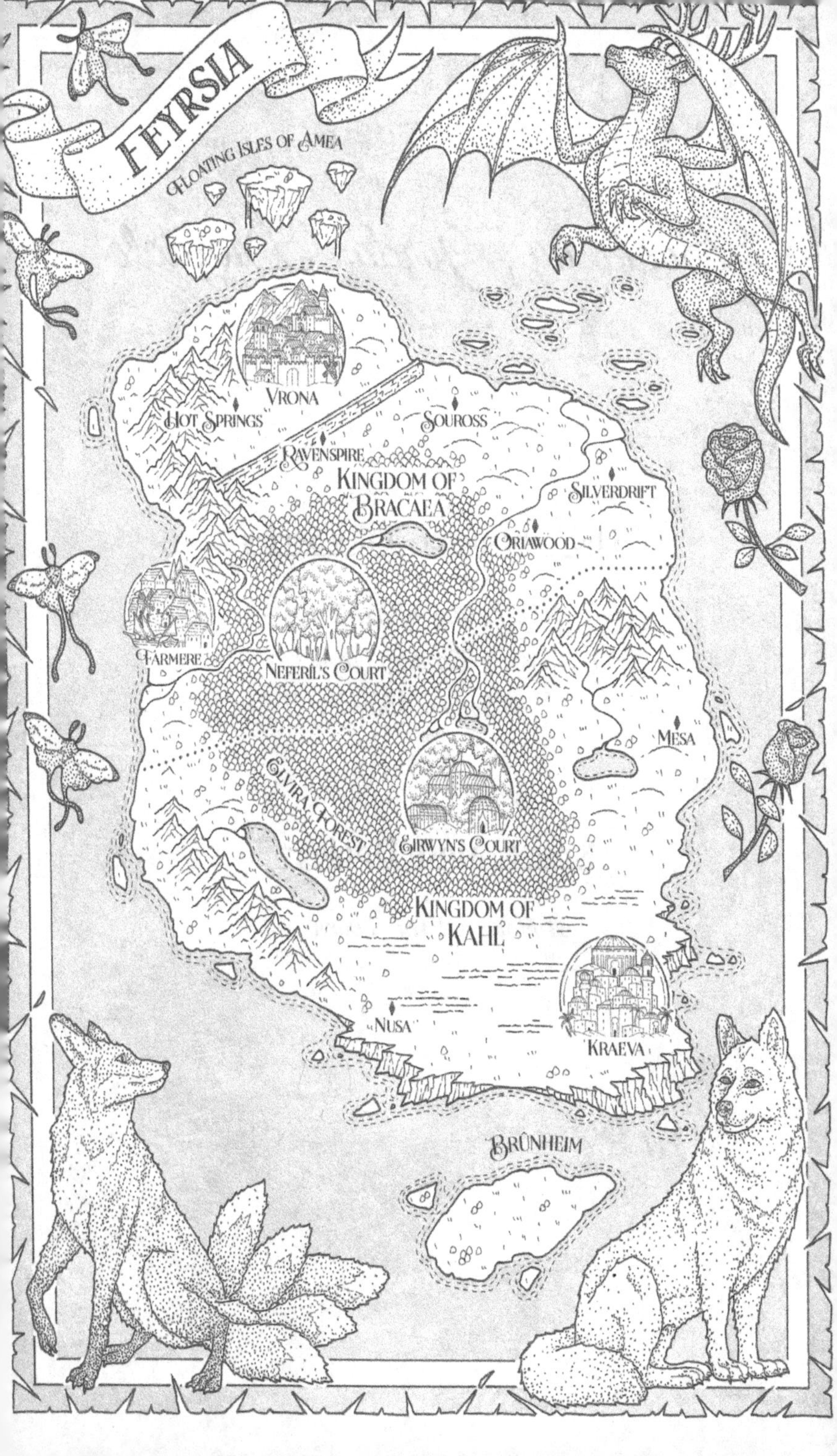
FEYRSIA
Floating Isles of Amea
Vrona
Hot Springs
Souross
Ravenspire
Kingdom of Bracaea
Silverdrift
Oriawood
Farmere
Neferil's Court
Mesa
Elvira Forest
Eirwyn's Court
Kingdom of Kahl
Nusa
Kraeva
Brûnheim

# Books by Jordan Dugdale

## The Whispered Tales Series

*The Tidings of Misfits*
*A Waltz Through Flames*
*A Song of Hope*

## Rose & Moth Duology

*A Flower's Fatal Thorn*

# Content Warnings

While there is no spice in this novel, I consider this book **new adult** due to some of its themes & the age of the characters. I have listed the content warnings for this title below. Your comfort is most important to me.

Body horror (body decay due to a magical rot that plagues the forest) / gore
Depictions of death
Mild moments of panic
Creepy atmosphere
Sibling/Family trauma

# ONE

## *Neferit*

Each time the forest cried out in pain, my anger festered.

The Rot had come slowly. Winter had just come and gone. In my ignorance, I'd thought nothing of the reek of decay in the air. Winter's sleep oft brought the illusion of death, but then spring would come, and the trees would wake.

This time, something was different.

"Another one?"

Rhi nodded, bowing her head. "Yes. Another dead, Your Majesty."

My lips pulled back into a wordless snarl as sharpened teeth elongated and extended in response to my anger. I knew my frustrations would cause much unrest in the forest should I allow it to fester, but it had been quite some time since an unknown illness had plagued my lands.

Another court faerie death did not bode well for my rule.

"Take me to them," I commanded.

Hesitation flickered across the honey-hue of Rhi's eyes. She was a pretty little thing on this side of her glamour, the brushstrokes of her humanity still clinging to her skin. Her hair coiled into curls. Her skin was dark and smooth. Freckles adorned her cheeks, and her smile dimpled, especially when she found a human that had strayed too far into our home. How quickly her sweet smile turned to malice was exactly why she was my right hand.

"Rhi, *take me to them*." My voice flooded with warning.

Rhi's charm did not work here, and it did not work on me unless I willed it so.

Lowering her head, Rhi turned and led me from my throne of vines that connected into a seat worthy only for the queen of the Unseelie Court. I could not recall how long it had been now since I'd taken the mantle, but time in my kingdom moved quickly. A year on the Other Side was mere moments in Elvira.

As I stood, I tapped the arm on my throne three times, calling to the spirit of the wood. A translucent visage clawed out of the wood, vaguely resembling a half-woman, half-tree. Branches crowned her head, and she stared at me with wide eyes.

"Keep watch over the palace while I am away," I whispered, reaching into my pocket and pulling out an acorn. "My gift to you in exchange for your protection. Plant it where a tree has died. Return one of your sisters to the forest."

The spirit solidified, her skin a soft green, her eyes a muted yellow. She grinned, her hair flowing about her face as if it had life of its own. She nodded and took the acorn from me before disappearing in thin air.

"I've noticed the dryads come less and less to our aid these days," Rhi said as we left. The palace itself was carved inside and around a large tree, its branches stretching high and intricately woven through the neighboring trees, and I stepped outside of the palace's front door and down some stairs with Rhi keeping steady pace beside me.

"Yes, well, it does not surprise me. There is tension between us and the wild fae." My people, the court fae, normally held great relations with the wild fae, but the forest had been agitated as of late, turned cruel by its sickness. The Rot had forged tension between the court faerie and the wild fae for some time now, and I knew we would need to be careful once we left my walls.

My court extended beyond the palace. Many of us lived inside the trees, twisted to our visage by our magic. Faeries flitted about attending to different duties, and I made sure to return every smile or kind gesture that was given to me. I loved my people fiercely.

We had high, angular faces, and our eyes were as dark as night. Our tall, slender forms creaked like the trees with every step. We were not much different than the wild fae that had lived in these woods long before the court faeries had come to dwell here. The only difference was our ties to humanity, being the human babies the wild fae stole from nearby towns and turned into fae.

"How did they die?" I asked as we trailed through the court. It was not a far walk to the edges of my court's land, the forest that I held dominion over was vast, but I kept my people close, where I could protect them. Rhi tilted her head back as several droplets of water fell off a massive blue flower clinging to the tree above us, the water hitting her face and drawing a smile to her lips. The queen's question, however, sobered her spirits. She did not answer until we stepped outside of my court walls. There were no physical walls to speak of, but the absence of the wards that kept my palace safe from any form of danger was felt immediately. I suppressed a shudder.

"Strayed too close to the forest's edge. The humans are getting *bold*." The bitterness in Rhi's voice bled into the air, infecting it with rage. Several small trees nearby bent towards her ire and cradled it to their branches. The wind picked up, and their wood creaked.

"*Rhi*," I said sharply. Rhi's anger dampened almost immediately, and the trees resumed their upright positions, no longer reaching out to soothe Rhi's distress.

"I apologize," Rhi said sheepishly. "We had our traps set, Your Majesty. How the humans made it past them and inside the forest while keeping their minds intact, we do not know. I have Kaer and Velki investigating right now."

A headache cradled my temples. It blossomed like a newly forged flower as I sighed, pressing my fingers to the bridge of my nose. "How far?"

"Near the edge. Thankfully the Rot doesn't seem to be straying too far in. I blame the humans," Rhi said.

"You blame the humans for everything." I paused for a moment, then nodded. "Of course they're to blame. I'm certain the forest and the wild fae will require more sacrifices, more babes for us to raise. We'll set up more guards around the border. If anything gets in or goes out, we'll know about it."

Rhi nodded as the conversation died. I had been fighting the humans off for centuries, my kingdom a paradise the humans craved. They were never meant to find solace within the forest, but as time went on, they were growing bolder and more intent on claiming what wasn't their right to claim. I scoffed in disgust; humans were greedy little creatures.

We walked for nearly an hour. The forest was quiet, eerily so. There were no birds singing above, no crack of twigs of nearby deer. Signs of the Rot were everywhere, but tucked away, only noticed by those who knew what to look for. A blackened spot on a trunk, or the dead curl of a rotten flower. It had taken me a long time, too long, to realize it was more than the natural rot of the forest.

The further we walked, the more acutely aware I became that while we were still in my domain, the wild fae called these trees home. A small family of goblins stared out from a cluster of rocks, their ears large and quivering as they stared. A small creature with sharp teeth and a red hat swatted at Rhi's ankle from a brush.

"Blood of a court fae is...oh, *delightful*," the wild fae uttered, causing Rhi to frown and spare a glance at me.

"We are close."

I nodded and remained silent. The wild fae could not touch us, not without a certain level of trickery and wit, not without upsetting the balance of things, but being surrounded by them left me on edge.

"Here," Rhi said, stepping over a fallen log and gesturing to something behind a tree. I sensed it before I saw it–a sickness that plagued the air. It made my lungs constrict, and every feeling in my body urged me to flee. The sky darkened, and I became acutely aware of every bug and movement of the trees in the forest. They all cried out, begging me to do something. A faint clicking sound hit the air at the same moment the smell did, a rancid stench that clogged my nose and made my eyes water. I straightened my back, pursed my lips, and forced myself to step forward.

The body had all but decomposed. When faeries died—court faeries and wild fae alike—their bodies gave back to the earth, rotting away to feed the local fauna and flora. The natural rot was common within Elvira; it was the circle of life.

This rot was unlike any I had ever seen. A black sludge covered the bark of the tree the body was pressed up against, and it had begun to eat away at the trunk itself. Bugs crawled over the corpse, but the other local wildlife avoided the place. I couldn't sense another animal for miles. The Rot wasn't contributing to the natural order; it was all-consuming, an aching void of death that demanded its claim on whatever it encountered. There was no balance to this rot's consumption. Only destruction.

"I think it's Bruk, but the corpse is too far gone to know for sure. He was stationed to patrol this part of the forest, though, and hasn't reported in for days now," Rhi said softly. She stood several feet away, refusing to draw close to the body, and I couldn't blame her. The curdle of fear festered in my own belly.

Even I, the Queen of Faeries, wasn't safe from fear.

"I don't want anyone near here. Please return and tell all of the guards that this part of the forest is forbidden until we can figure out a way to remove the Rot safely."

Rhi nodded. "Will you be accompanying me?"

I shook my head. "I'm going to stay a little longer and see if the trees will tell me how I may be able to help them."

After Rhi left, I found a large round rock a safe distance from the Rot that I could sit on. Crossing my legs beneath me, I let loose a soft, slow exhale. There was so much pain in the forest, that it was nearly overwhelming, a noise I could not escape.

"Your Majesty?"

I peeked an eye open to the approach of a seer. I hadn't even heard her footsteps, but that didn't come as a surprise. Seers were notorious for their quiet nature, even to the court faeries. This one wore a hood that sheathed her eyes, but I recognized her immediately by the curl of her smile.

"Deirdre. Always a pleasure." I took care to keep the formality in my voice despite my aversion to her. I had never liked being around seers. As a child, I had always been terrified of them. They spoke only to invoke fear and confusion and oftentimes just in riddles. After a conversation with them, I'd always left uncertain about what had been said at all. "What brings you to this part of the forest? I thought you liked to stay near your home further north."

Deirdre said nothing as she reached out, the cloth of her shawl slipping. Her nails were cut short and dirtied like she had been digging, but I refused to flinch as she curled her fingers around my wrist and clamped tightly. "I found something. A possible cure for this rot." She spoke plainly today, and my eyes widened briefly before I nodded.

"Tell me."

The seer's eyes gleamed.

*At the edge of the rotting forest, a girl shall rise, her blood a potent elixir of life. As her veins flow with vitality, each drop shed will rejuvenate the land, erasing decay and breathing new life into the ancient trees. A healer, cursed yet blessed shall be the savior of the forest, her sacrifice birthing a realm reborn.*

A chill shuddered through me as the prophecy sank into the air, the seer having willed it into existence. Nausea plagued my belly, but it wasn't so terrible that I couldn't stifle it as I eyed the seer wearily.

"I suppose you don't mean to explain any further? Where can I find this girl?"

Deirdre gave a slight shake of her head. "To walk the path with eyes unclouded will grant you your salvation. Go forth. Find her. Set us free."

I blinked angrily, but she was gone before I could question her further, which was typical for a seer. Absolutely useless, save for one thing: I needed to find the human girl with life magic.

Killing her and using her blood would bring the forest back from the husk the Rot had caused.

I straightened, flattening my fingers against my dress. There was much work to be done.

# TWO

## *Róis*

D AWN BROKE, AND THE shadows of the forest receded.

Rather, that was what I told myself as I paced at the
forest's edge, trying to gather my courage. *They're more
active when the sun goes down. If you lose your way, stay near
running water. Don't go near circles of mushrooms. Don't
eat their fruit. Don't drink their wine. If you hear music, go
the other way.*

I repeated these things until my mantra chased the fear away. After a deep breath, I lifted my foot and prepared to take the first step into the forest.

"Róis, where do you think you're going?"

I stopped even as my will urged me forward. *Go find Sister. Bring her home.* Before she had been taken, we'd been inseparable, and I feared one day I would forget her. I couldn't remember when I had lost the ability to recall her name or when I'd forgotten the shape and look of her face. Her eyes were the only thing I could see clearly in my mind's eye: that deep, impossible green, the same as mine.

I swallowed hard. Thinking of Sister always made my heart hurt, but deep down, I felt it. That thread that tethered us together still forged strong bonds. Something in my heart of hearts told me she lived.

"You know damn well where I'm going, Caolan." *Into the beast.* The forest stood tall before me, dark and terrible. The trees were so large that some of them sailed well above the clouds, their trunks so massive in roundness that it would take days to travel around them. Those trees were situated in the middle of the forest. The edge, though, was dotted with babes no older than a few hundred years. Still, just two of these trees had provided more than enough wood to build the entire village of Farmere, which was tucked between the edge of Elvira and the coast.

"You're not ready," Caolan said.

Turning, I frowned. Caolan stared at me, his face rugged with time and exhaustion. The beard that shadowed his face barely stood ground against his cheeks, and he folded his arms across his slender frame as he looked over at me in disapproval. "You thought you'd sneak away without anyone noticing? Wee Collin alerted me and said he saw you leaving early this morning with your pack and nothing else."

I scowled. I'd shove Collin's head in the mud for snitching. A childish thought that I quelled immediately. I've seen over twenty-six winters. There was no time for childish antics.

Tucking a strand of untamed reddish-brown curls behind my ear, I slumped my shoulders. "Fine, fine. What more do you have to teach me, oh great and wise mentor?" Holding my hands up in surrender, I ignored the twitch of suppressed amusement in Caolan's smile.

"Patience is the only lesson you have yet to learn, and it is one I am not eager to teach you. You must practice it on your own." His smile faltered. "If you go into the forest without your head, you are already lost."

I glanced reluctantly back at the forest but moved away, just as Caolan asked. I didn't need him watching me too closely from now on, but my skin itched with impatience, forcing a restless nature. I grew tired of waiting.

"Do you spew this shite to Father as well?" I asked.

Caolan snorted and shook his head, running a hand over his beard. "The chance to teach your father some patience has long since been buried in the ground."

I smiled but said nothing in response. Caolan was Father's best friend, and other than me, he knew the man better than anyone. Since Mother's death some winters ago, my father had never been the same. My mother had walked into Elvira one night and given herself to the forest. She'd never come back out. Everyone but my father was convinced she was dead. He had never stopped plotting for a way to search for her. Sometimes I'd wondered why he never gave up on my mother, but my sister's death was something he'd made peace with long ago. Perhaps it was because so much time had passed. Questions he'd never answer.

My people called Elvira the Forest of Dreams. Any human who dared attempt passage through it was lost, their mind given as an offering to the queen who ruled at the forest's center. We did our best to stay out of the forest and fall prey to its wicked ways, but it called to us, a soft and gentle song that tempted us into its tree line. Many blamed the fae for such magic. Some went in seeking glory or a child that the spirits of this place had claimed.

Hence some of us had been re-learning the Ways of Olde, those who had been taught a way through the forest and could return with sound of mind. Those who could hunt the Fair Folk.

It was my love for my father that had caused me to devote myself to such a cause, to take up the ways of the *fiagaila*.

"Róis, I—" Caolan's sentence was cut short as something shuffled in the bushes. It was the soft sigh of the wind, perhaps, or the cry of a changeling, a faerie baby that the forest sent to deceive us, to trick us into trading our own babies away.

I glanced at Caolan as the shuffling resumed, and large luminescent eyes dotted the lining of the trees.

They remained under the blanket of the forest, a slave to the darkness as the sun rose high into the sky. During the day, they could not pass the tree line, not unless they wished to watch their skin burn from bone.

My lips peeled back as my heart thundered in my ears. The fae were ruthless creatures, and many times I had laid in my bed, clinging to my dagger and wondering if tonight would be the night they'd come calling for demands of new human babies to be offered up as sacrifice. I would never forget the night they'd come for me.

*"No, no! Please, I beg thee. Do not take her." My mother's cheeks were stained with tears as my small arm was pulled through the darkness by large, grotesque, spindly fingers. The terror I'd felt had been unmatched, but the fae did not care about willing away the fear of human children.*

*"This one is sick. Take her! Heal her like you so desperately want to heal your silly forest." My mother's words caused the faerie to halt, and my soft cries were silenced by a hiss that echoed off the walls of sharp teeth. The faerie moved erratically, its head cocked to the side as Mother offered up the small child pressed to her hip. Upon a pale, sick-stricken face, her eyes wide with fright.*

*"No, Mama," I cried. "Not sibber!"*

I was jostled from the memory by a wet cough echoing through the trees, followed closely by a low whine. It wasn't quite animalistic but not human, either. I glanced at Caolan with mild concern before I slipped the dagger from the hilt at my waist. I didn't go anywhere without it. The blade was made from a rare metal mined from the Voiceless Mountains in the north. It was the only material my people had been able to find that could harm the fair folk.

This blade had been in my father's family for many, many generations.

"Keep light on your feet," Caolan uttered, the air ripe with magic as he called it to him. Mages were rare this far south, so it had been considered a blessing by the people of Farmere when Caolan had arrived to do what he could to help against the constant threat of the forest. It had been a blessing for me as well, for he had been the one who taught me when life magic first started to flow through my veins and manifest itself. I hadn't been able to control it until he'd come along.

"Something is different," he noted.

I tasted it on my tongue; it was foul, like the very fabric of nature was suffering. The hair on my arms stood on end, and I shuddered against the weight of *wrongness* in the air.

A faerie burst out of the trees, its limbs creaking as they bent in unnatural directions. Something was wrong with this one. Despite the sun peeling away its skin, it did not flinch back into the shadows, and the side of its face was infected with some kind of rot eating away at its flesh.

"Don't let it touch you," Caolan warned as I dived out of the way, rolling along the ground. The faerie nearly barreled into me but missed, its claws gouging the ground as it hissed in frustration.

"Come, come. Into the forest where we *rot*." The faerie's words were grating and wet, spoken through a layer of drool that thickened at the faerie's mouth as I turned, my heartbeat roaring in my ears. "Off, off to lose our mind and lose our way. It festers and flounders and fills our bellies with maggots. Oh, please. It *hurts*." The faerie moaned, falling to the ground. I scooted away, the skin on my palm breaking as I scraped it against rocks, but the faerie did not move from where it had fallen, its breathing ragged. The sun burned it away until there was naught but ash and bone. Soon enough, the wind carried that away, too.

"What—" A lump of fear gathered in my throat as I tore my gaze away and found Caolan's, my eyes wide with shock. I'd never seen a faerie act in such a manner before. "Have you ever seen something like this?"

Caolan's face had paled. Green tendrils of magic slipped from his fingers and trailed over to the spot of dead grass where the faerie had fallen. He gasped sharply in pain and jerked his fingers away. Shuffling towards me, he offered his hand. "That is strange magic. You best stay away from it. My magic flinches from it, which means it cannot be good. Not at all."

Strangely, I stared at the spot as my magic did the opposite, tempting me to reach out and touch where the faerie had perished, but I didn't tell Caolan my magic called to it. I took his hand instead, and with his help, I was back on my feet.

Luckily, whatever had happened to the faerie didn't seem to be spreading; the patch of rotting grass contained to the spot where the faerie had fallen. Still, looking at it hurt something inside me—the part that wanted to heal. I had never been a soft child, always getting into fights with the other children of Farmere and protecting my sister from the sharp edges of the world—my soft, gentle sister. Our father had used to call me his little wolf even before I had gotten my canines filed to sharp points as a right of passage when I'd passed my tests and became a *fiagaila d'orla,* a warrior and sworn protector of our little village. I was all tooth and claws when the world angered me. Father had always told me it wasn't right to let my hurt and anger fester inside me, but it had been like a wound had opened when my sister had been taken. Twins were linked, far more than could be rightly explained, and I felt her absence as if a hole had formed in my chest.

"Father might know what's going on," I said. My father wasn't the best of healers, but he was still good enough in the Olde Ways of medicine to be the village's healer. If anyone knew what might be happening to the balance of nature, it was my father.

"This is extremely troubling." My father was a large man, so broad in the shoulders that visitors often mistook him for the blacksmith, not the village healer. There was nothing but kindness that danced behind his dark eyes, but they also brimmed with concern as he knelt at the spot where the faerie had died, rubbing his greying beard with his hand. "Most troubling indeed." The ground had darkened considerably since Caolan and I had left to retrieve my father.

"What do you think it could be, Faergus?" Caolan asked, staring at my father.

"Something new, which isn't good. We need to block this place off and make sure no one comes near it. Róis, go and fetch Sircha. She needs to know of this."

I nodded silently and turned on my heel, hurrying back through the village. Now that the sun was up, people were out and about, and most of the village had collected near the edge of town, speaking in hushed tones as I hurried past. I ignored their curious stares. My mind was a whirlwind of emotions as I pushed through the crowd and nearly stumbled into Sircha, who'd been heading towards the commotion.

"Róis, what is *happening*?" Lines aged her face gracefully, and her whitened hair was pulled back into a loose bun as her fingers gripped her shawl closed. She halted in front of me, her brows furrowed in concern.

"Come, *girda*. It is better if you see," I whispered, taking Sircha's hand and tucking it into the crook of my arm. Sircha did not see with her eyes as most humans did. She had never spoken of how she'd lost her sight. "I never lost it, child. There are more ways to see," she'd said when I had asked her once, many years ago. "I see far more than anyone with eyes." Some whispered she was blessed by faerie magic, with the part of the forest realm that was merciful.

"Sickness trails through the weaves of magic," Sircha whispered, the fog of her eyes trained towards the sky as I led her back towards Caolan and Father. "Something is wrong, little wolf."

A chill rolled down my spine. It took a lot to shake Sircha, but the fear rolled off her in waves, and despite my instincts screaming at me to bolt, I held my ground and urged my feet forward until they had returned to Father's side.

"Have you felt it too, Caolan?" Sircha called out, her voice raspy from sleep.

Caolan nodded. "I have. Something is shifting. I have never once felt anything like it in my entire life." He looked troubled, his lower lip caught between his teeth. "I may need to ride north for this and seek out the guidance of the council." The Council of Maerga was a council of mages that oversaw magical affairs in the realm. Caolan spoke highly of them, but I always thought they cared little for troubles outside of the major cities. If they cared so much, they would have sent more mages to take care of our faerie problem.

I swallowed thickly. "If you leave, so will your protection. The faeries might get bold again." The implications were poor. Faerie hadn't been able to snag babies from their homes unchecked since Caolan's arrival. They were forced to resort to trickery and wit, deceiving parents with changeling babes or convincing children to open their windows and invite them inside. By the time the parents realized something was amiss, their babies were already passing through Elvira to be claimed by the forest. Without Caolan's magic, the faeries would be able to enter the village and claim whomever they liked again.

"I don't think I have a choice," Caolan said sadly. "This is beyond my expertise."

"It is beyond mine, too," Sircha said. "I fear if nothing is done, we will be dealing with far worse than the threat of the fae."

I clenched my fist at my side, my mouth drawn into a hard line. My fear betrayed me as it curled against my chest like a sickness, but I steeled myself against it as I stepped forward.

"I'll go in. I'll face the fair folk and find out what is causing this."

# THREE
## *Róis*

"No. Absolutely not." Father stepped back from the rotting ground to turn and stare at me. The pain in his eyes took my breath away, but I stood my ground, my mouth set in a stubborn line. "I've lost everyone, Róis. *Everything*. I cannot lose you too." The hurt in his voice brushed up against the gaping wound of grief in my chest, making it weep.

I swallowed the thorns in my throat and reached out to take my father's hands, to allow his palms to swallow my fingers in his grasp. "The other warriors have all gone,

Papa. I'm a grown woman now. If Sister and Mother are in there somewhere, someone who is capable of fighting the fae should they go."

"I fear she is right, Faergus," Sircha uttered, her voice nearly lost to the wind. "Someone must find the source of this sickness. I can feel it rotting the trees, even now. The forest cries out in pain. I am surprised you, of all people, do not feel it." She turned to me, her expression pleading. "You must kill her, Róis. She is darkness. Surely she is the cause of this rot."

"Who, Sircha?"

"The queen of the Unseelie Court." Her faded eyes stared up at the looming forest as if she could see far beyond the naked eye. "She is the heart, girl. Kill her, and we'll see an end to this wickedness."

My heart pattered nervously. I wasn't sure what I'd thought I'd greet once I entered the forest, but it hadn't been dealing with the queen. Still, I set a determined expression as I nodded. I would cast this foolish fear away and do what was asked of me.

"I will go with her," Caolan said. He stared out at the wall of trees, his face grim. I had never seen Caolan look so *aged*. I had never asked the mage how old he was—the magic that flowed through them allowed mages to live longer than those with no magic, but the age in his eyes when he turned to lock his gaze against mine was timeless.

"I thought you were to go to the council?" I shook my head. "No. I'll go inside alone."

Caolan's eyes burned into me. "I will send a raven. Another mage will be sent at once. Farmere is within Bracaea's borders; they must send someone, as is deemed within their territory to protect."

Father's shoulders slumped. People remained at the edge of the village, their faces solemn and pinched with worry. Many held on to their children as if their lives depended on it, and I couldn't help but feel for their fear. Farmere had lost much to the wild forest and the fae folk.

"You've been telling me she's not ready," Faergus uttered, rubbing his chin in his distress. "She's too rash, too passionate, not patient enough. Caolan's words, not mine," he said, noticing my anger.

Caolan nodded slowly. "Sometimes life doesn't give us a choice, my friend. Sometimes we must overcome our flaws because we *must*, not because we are granted with the gift of time." He sighed, the weight of his anxiety heavy in the air as he turned back towards the forest, where the glittering eyes of the faeries were absent from the tree line.

"Go and get what you need, Róis, and pack lightly."

I gave a swift nod and squeezed my father's hands once more, forcing him to meet my eyes. "I *will* return to you," I said with as much conviction as I could muster. "The forest won't claim me. I won't let it."

Father's eyes were sad as he tugged me into a hug. He smelled of sage and something sharp; he must have been working in the apothecary earlier, and I struggled to pull away, relishing every moment of protection his warmth provided. I didn't want to leave him, but I knew I must.

"I love you, *aida*," I whispered, pressing my fingers to his cheek as I pulled away.

"I love you too, little wolf."

I took one long look at my father before I forced myself to turn, gesturing to Caolan. "I'll meet you here when the sun is at its highest," I said, pointing to the rising sun. It was just past dawn, and there was much to do.

As I rushed off into the village towards my home, I began to make peace with the idea that I might never return.

"Róis, wait—" One of the villagers followed me into my house, which was little more than a small wooden hut filled with a bed, a table, and a fireplace to cook on in the corner. Father was always trying to convince me to come back home with him, but the notion of returning home left a sour taste in my mouth. There were too many ghosts roaming those halls.

"We both knew this day would come, Sal." My words sounded harsher than intended, and I immediately regretted them as hurt flickered across Salia's face. She'd been my friend for as long as I could remember. A tiny thing, she had more fire in her belly than I did. I would never forget the day some of the village boys had pinned my arms in the mud. I'd fought tooth and nail to get free, but it had been Salia who had saved me that day. She had come out of nowhere, and the boys had never stood a chance. She had managed to knock their teeth out before one of the village leaders pulled her away. Salia had been the first to join the *fiagaila*, but I had joined not long after.

"Let me come with you. Who will make sure you don't do something reckless?" Salia's voice was little more than a whisper. The auburn of her gaze stitched with pain, she reached out to take my hands and drew them away from the pack I was filling with cheese and dried meats. I let her, watching as she threaded her fingers through mine. My heart leapt to my throat, but I always knew saying goodbye to Salia would be the most difficult part of all of this.

"You must stay." I found the courage to meet her gaze and then wished I hadn't. There was so much pain and fierce determination that wobbled in her expression. Her lower lip trembled as the words tumbled quickly from my lips. "I need you here to protect Father and the rest of the

villagers. Caolan is to come with me, and without him..."
I swallowed the lump in my throat and shook my head.
"Without him, I do not know what the fae will do."

Salia shook, her hands tightening around mine. "I cannot force you to stay, but wait, at least, until the passing of the full moon. Let her bless your travels and keep you safe."

I hesitated. The full moon wasn't for another few days, and now that it was happening, I was anxious to go. The restless nature sat in my chest and clawed at my throat. Waiting that long would be agonizing.

But it was Salia who was asking. Anyone else would have gotten my scorn. But not Salia, never her.

Salia threw her arms around me, tugging me close. My heart shuttered and plummeted to my stomach as I returned the hug, burying my face into the trails of her long dark hair.

I couldn't remember the moment I'd fallen in love with her. Even as a young girl, no boy had ever managed to capture my attention—many of them thought I was too wild anyway. I never felt the same desire to lay with anyone; that kind of intimacy was a strange concept to me. It didn't stop my desire for companionship though. Salia's company had been steady through Sister's capture, Mother's disappearance, and the plethora of other chaotic events in my life. Perhaps it was her steadfastness that caused the flicker of butterflies in my stomach. Perhaps it was the soft way she carried herself until she was angry, and then she was as sharp and as quick as a viper. Or perhaps it was something else entirely, something I couldn't seem to place. All I knew was that as I'd grown older, as I'd turned from girl to woman, I'd craved her presence like I was drowning and she was the only source of air.

"Okay," I whispered, my heart aching painfully at the thought of leaving her soon. I would likely never see her again, and the delay would only make that eventual goodbye all the more painful. "I'll stay until after the full moon."

Salia's sigh of relief aggravated the wound in my chest. She tugged away, staring at me as her hands gripped my arms. "You were always the best fighter of us all," she said. "If anyone has a chance of being swallowed by the forest and spat back out, it's you."

I attempted a smile—a weak one. "You and I both know that..." I was cut off as Salia pressed her hand to my mouth with a swift shake of her head.

"No. I won't hear you say it." Her face darkened, an anger sweeping through her quick and without mercy. "I won't. Promise me you won't say it."

Another crack in my heart, another empty promise. Just like the one I gave my father.

Slowly, I nodded.

She took her hand away, sliding the other one down to thread through my fingers once again. "You're going to change things, Róis. I can feel it. Don't lost hope."

"You know how stubborn I am, Sal. If I have to claw my way back to you, you know I will as I have always done." My eyes flickered to her lips, and I thought of kissing her. Oh, how *desperately* I wanted to. It would be so easy to tug her close. Fear stayed my hand. Fear of her rejection. Fear of her kissing me back and feeding the pain of having to leave her. So I didn't. My eyes strayed back up to meet hers, and I squeezed her fingers and pulled my hand away.

"I'll see you tomorrow. There's much to prepare for before the celebrations."

The moment she pulled away, I locked my heart down, my head rebelling against the ache in my chest. I felt like a lovesick fool, and it sickened me. It sickened me so much that I forced myself to turn away and only look back when I knew for certain she had gone.

The loneliness her absence brought still sent me to my knees, and I fought the urge to despair. I would not. I *could* not.

The fate of my people depended on me.

# FOUR

## *Róis*

I PEERED UP AS the sun began its descent over the trees. Three days had passed since I had agreed to stay, and it had given my father three days to try to convince me not to go. Three days for me to war against my own decision. Three days to watch Salia flourish under the preparations for the Festival of Nymera to give praise to the wolf goddess of the moon. My heart broke every moment I realized I would have to leave Salia's side. A sense of relief had washed through Caolan at the suggestion to remain until after the festival as if he, too, believed in the blessing of Nymera.

The village was vibrant with magical orbs of light that dipped and floated between the buildings. The center of town held the main festivities with tables centered around a massive pyre, where gifts were set to be offered up to the moon. At the end of the night, just before dawn, we'd burn the pyre and all the gifts so that the smoke could carry them up to Nymera.

I suppressed a shiver as my fingers grazed the hilt of my dagger for the hundredth time at my hip. It stilled my anxiety as I trailed through town, unable to shake the lingering darkness that danced at its edges. Ever since that faerie had come charging out of the woods, infected with that strange rot, I had been unable to relax. Something in the air was screaming out in pain, and it felt like no one else could hear it.

"I'm glad you decided to stay, if only for the Moon Mother's blessing," Sircha said, taking my hands in her wrinkled ones and pulling me from my worries. "The Olde Ways dictate She always guides us along our path. Show me your crown, child."

I obeyed, bowing my head forward. Sircha laid a wreath of roses upon my head, then dragged two fingers down my forehead and over the tip of my nose. As I straightened, she smiled, the swirling white of her eyes staring past my left shoulder.

"Let go of earthy troubles tonight, Róis. The Moon Mother still has much to teach us. Your father is preparing the teas, should you care to partake."

I nodded silently. Tea brewed from a special herb only grown local to our village was often given at the moon festivals as a way to get closer to Nymera, Moon Mother. With everything going on, I didn't feel comfortable enough to indulge, but Sircha didn't need to know that. Not when her walks with Nymera were so important to her.

"Róis, come dance with me." Salia appeared before me, white lilies pinned into her braids. Her smile was radiant; Salia had always loved the moon festivals and was a fierce believer in Nymera's gifts. "One must honor nature," she'd told me once. "Nature always has a way of rewarding those who love it."

I took her outstretched hand and allowed her to lead me over to where people were dancing. Men and women clapped from their seats as a boy no older than ten winters stood upon a bench and threw flower petals over the dancing bodies. I found myself laughing despite myself as I fell into the rhythm with Salia. I loved to dance. Just another way to let go, to focus on nothing more than the movement. Someone played the flute nearby in tune with the clapping, and I kept my eyes trained on Salia as she led us in a sweeping motion around the dance circle.

"Remember when we were children? You used to hate dancing." Salia laughed, a gentle sound that threatened to be carried away by the music.

I scrunched my nose at her. "That's because I thought it was so silly and only being forced on me because I'm a girl. It's like fighting, though, kind of. Different but just as deadly."

"Oh yes, deadly indeed. Many people have died dancing," Salia teased, and it drew laughter from my lips. I hated how easily she could make me laugh, how giddy and light I felt from her presence. I hated what lengths I would go to see that smile so delicately painted on her lips.

"You know what I mean," I argued. "There's a silent conversation that can go on while dancing with someone. Remember the last festival? Derik was seen leaving with Alisa after they'd danced together all night, and now there are rumors she's with child and they're to take the marriage rites in the coming season."

Salia's mouth fell open. "So soon? They hardly know each other."

"That's what I thought too, but who are we to judge? Life can be so short."

My mind turned suddenly to the forest, the same forest I'd be entering in a day or two, and I halted.

"Ro?" Salia's voice trailed out over the celebrations, and I shivered, forcing myself to meet her eyes.

"Let's go to the cove, hide away like we used to," I whispered.

After a moment, she nodded.

The cove was silent when we reached it, save for the soft crashing of waves against the shore. The cove was small, nothing more than a stretch of beach nestled against a crescent shape of trees. Many spoke ill of going here, fearing the presence of fae so near the wood, but Salia and I had been sneaking away to this cove for as long as I could remember. We'd never seen the fae here.

"I knew if it were going to be anyone, it would be you."

I glanced at Salia as we sat near the shoreline, where the water lapped up against the sand. A chill whispered through the air, and I tugged my legs up to my chest and rested my chin on my knee as I stared out to sea.

"You've been in once already. It's my turn," I said, laughing when Salia pushed me lightly on my shoulder. Tilting my head, I looked at her and watched the laughter etch in the curve of her cheeks when she smiled and the way her eyes lit up. "What's it like?" I ask.

Salia sobered, tucking a strand of hair behind her ear as she stretched her feet out. Salia was tall and lean, her arms well-defined from her constant sparring. She had been the youngest to enter the forest and sent on a small caravan through the edges of Elvira to Vrona, the capital of Bracaea in the north. They'd only traversed the edges of the forest, but nowhere was safe beyond the tree line.

"Magical, like we truly don't know the raw power of life until we step inside. I can see how some are so easily swayed by its temptations to give themselves over to it." She stared up at the full moon, resting her hands on her legs. "It's haunting too, like beyond every tree is something trying to kill you, or take you away, or trick you into some deal you cannot get out of."

Silence fell between us for a time.

"Did you drink any of the tea?" she asked, changing the subject. I was grateful for it. The air was thick with awkward tension, and I was glad to be free of the tea's influence. The trees behind us rustled gently in the wind as I shook my head.

"I'll seek out the Moon Mother's blessing with a clear head tonight," I said. "You?"

She shook her head. "Didn't feel right for some reason. I—" Her words died as the brush in the trees surrounding them rustled again, only this time, it was too strong to be the wind. Salia unsheathed her dagger at the exact moment I did, both of us locking eyes as we stood and instinctively drew near each other. We'd been alive long enough to know when the fae were near.

"You stay low," Salia said softly, and I nodded, keeping my blade flush against my forearm as we pushed forward. We had never been disturbed in our cove, the only haven from the fae since we'd stumbled upon it as kids.

But not anymore.

A faerie burst through the trees on creaky limbs, its scream so high pitched it was nearly lost, a grating ache in my ears that sent chills down my spine. It was more tree-like than human, its arms and legs nothing but bark, its hair twigs standing straight up as it barreled towards us.

It wasn't the only one.

The moment it left the forest, dark shadows of more fae followed suit. Some were solid and nature-like, similar to the first one that had appeared, but some were little more than wisps of shadows, teeth, and claws. Nature died wherever they walked, and Salia and I were surrounded in mere moments.

"Salia," I said, hating the betrayal of fear in my voice. Lashing out with my dagger, I smiled with grim satisfaction when the faerie I struck wailed and flinched back, only to be replaced by another one of its kind. One drew so close to me that I smelled the sharpness of its breath, like a cross between wildflowers and the unnatural nature of magic. It was almost like the smell of lightning and rain. I attempted to flinch away, but it lashed out and grabbed my arm, sending the shutter of a memory slashing through me as I fell to the ground.

*Terrified child screams. A pair of green eyes, round and tear-stricken. Moist air like it had just rained.*

I shuddered as my magic woke like a slumbering beast in my belly. I did not beckon it forth, or perhaps I did in my fear-stricken state, and it blossomed as a soft green light etched against my skin and sank into the faerie's fingers where they were wrapped around my arm.

The strangest thing happened after that.

The sickness that rotted the faerie's skin along their arms began to heal. The rage centered in the faerie's expression calmed, turning to confusion as they pulled away. Life sprouted from their arms, little flowers and vines of such violent luminescent green that I did nothing but stare in shocked silence.

Had I done that?

The thought passed unbidden through me as I lunged forward to attack the fae in its state of confusion, but I wasn't quick enough.

The last faerie wailed as it died, Salia's dagger embedded in its chest. The light of the moon bathed Salia in Her beautiful luminescence. My friend's eyes were wide with fear and triumph, and I looked up at her with such fierce adoration that I couldn't formulate the words to thank her. I'd dropped my own knife in the sand. If she hadn't cut in, I would've died.

"Ro—your arm," she said softly, her gaze trailing down to where the faerie had grabbed me. I tore my gaze away from hers and peered down, sucking in a breath of horror at what I saw.

Small mushrooms unfurled from my skin where the faerie had touched me. A dark rot flourished up my arm. It didn't go past the handprint left on my forearm, and it didn't hurt, but the sight of it was so raw and wrong that I couldn't stop the whimper from pressing against my teeth. If the faerie had healed from whatever was rotting them, why was it now infecting my arm?

I moved to rip the mushrooms out of my skin, only to howl in pain as the mushrooms clung stubbornly to my arm. It was like I was pulling out my hair, and I jerked my arm away. "Stay away from me. I don't know what they did. I don't know what's going to happen." There was no pain, not yet, save for the sensitive area around where I had been trying to pull the mushrooms out, but my mind immediately went back to that faerie that'd burst from the woods, moaning in pain.

Will that happen to me?

The thought died as I glanced up, and my fingers tightened around the hilt of my dagger. "Salia!"

My words were spoken too late. I locked eyes with Salia as a faerie shot out of the woods, covered in black ooze. This faerie was winged – only, the translucent part of its wings were diseased, with splotches of gray mold blossoming across them. One of them was broken and hanging limply as it tackled Salia, and both went stumbling onto the beach. Salia slashed her blade up, attempting to jam it into the faerie's side, but the faerie was too quick. A shrill scream filled the air as it pinned Salia's wrist to the ground, leaving her defenseless.

I stumbled to my feet, baring my teeth as I grabbed my dagger from where I'd dropped it and ran towards them, but I wasn't fast enough.

Salia's eyes met mine as the faerie plunged sharp, needle-thin fingers into her chest. Something inside me broke, and by the time I was barreling into the faerie, my dagger in its side, all sound had fled the grove, save for something akin to a hundred angry bees.

I didn't stop stabbing until I felt the faerie go limp beneath me, my rage coursing through me with ill-concealed greed. My hands were bloody and shaking as I pulled away. The faerie deteriorated at an alarming rate as rot spread from its corpse, attempting to cling to the sand but failing as it was washed away by the water.

"Sal." My voice was warped like it was far off, and I turned immediately to where Salia lay.

I hurried to her side, but she was already dead.

A sob lodged itself in my throat, and I choked on it, collapsing next to her. I dropped my knife beside me, then pulled her into my arms. Her chest was ruined, torn apart by the faerie, and her face was stuck in an expression of terror as her eyes stared at the woods beyond. As I brushed her hair out of her face, anger swept through me, chasing away my grief, chasing away the guilt for having not been fast enough. The strange rot the faerie had left on my arm began to burn in the light of the moon, but I ignored it as my anger was flung towards the sky, towards the moon who had not protected Salia from the creatures of the forest.

I sat and wept with her until I could not see, until my throat was raw, until a headache pierced through my skull. Her blood soaked my skin, and it wasn't until my breath shuddered that I started to think about how the moon festival was not far away. If the faeries were getting so bold as to attack places they had not attacked before, perhaps the magic that was holding them out was growing weak. I needed to warn the rest of the village and demand that something be done.

Setting Salia gently on the ground, I pressed my lips softly to her forehead. A wave of regret flowed through me. I'd never told her how I'd felt. There had never been that chance for us because of my fear. This regret fueled my grief, and I forced myself to my feet before my body decided to not get up again.

*You must. For the others, you must, Róis.*

I repeated that in my head as I picked up my dagger from the ground. I looked over at where the faerie had died. It was nothing but rotted ground now, dead grass that had somehow grown over the sand and died.

I couldn't bear to look at Salia again as I passed her, my hand shaking as it gripped the hilt of my dagger tightly. I would need to travel through a shallow part of the woods to return to the festival, and the trees suddenly seemed malicious, standing tall and dark and full of shadows where faeries could be lying in wait. As I pushed into the forest, I was relieved to see no glowing eyes in the darkness.

I made it through without coming upon another faerie, but I hesitated at the wood's edge. People were still dancing, laughing, and enjoying the festivities. Several lay in the grass, having taken the tea Sircha had brewed to get them closer to the Nymera. The town was untouched by the devastation that I had just gone through with Salia. A sob rattled in my throat. What if they had heard our fight? What if help had come and Salia had been spared from the cruelty of the forest?

I stared down at my arm, at the rot the faerie had left on my skin; it was a reminder that all this hadn't just been a horrible hallucination. If the others saw the mark, they'd never let me go into the forest. They'd likely send someone else, and I needed answers. I needed answers more than anyone.

"I'm sorry, *aida*," I whispered mournfully as I kept to the edge of the forest. "I'm so sorry for everything."

# FIVE

## *Róis*

I MANAGED TO MAKE it to my house without anyone stopping me or seeing me. I shoved as much food into my pack as I could carry, then changed into tighter clothes that would be less likely to snag on branches. I paused at the threshold of my door, exhaling slowly and taking one last look at my home. I didn't expect to see it again.

My mind was a whirlwind of anger and pain, the vacancy in Salia's eyes haunting me like kindling to a flame. Throwing my pack over my shoulder, I left wordlessly and without hesitation. I barely registered arriving at the edge of the forest until it stood before me, dark and menacing. My thirst for revenge kept the fear at bay, and I entered quickly. There was no room for hesitation. No room to wonder if the forest would simply claim me.

The moment I stepped inside, they came for me.

The fae were quick, but I had learned to be quicker, attacking before I could be struck down. I slashed out with precise aim, severing limbs and stabbing critical points until the faerie dropped. One pulled at my arm, but the moment they touched the place where the rot had infected my skin, it spread through their fingers like wildfire, and the faerie screamed and shot away. The rot had been slow-moving when it'd been touched by the other fae, but this one died in under a minute. The surrounding faeries hissed and pulled away, the glow of their eyes leering in the darkness. I didn't give them a chance to retreat as a snarl peeled back my lips, and I pushed forward. I dropped them more quickly than I could count.

One crashed into my side and knocked my dagger from my hand. I hit the ground hard and exhaled sharply as the impact jarred my lungs. I groaned, raising an arm to protect my face as the faerie bit me, the pain sharp and unyielding as I howled. I slammed my fist into their head. They let go, and I dove for my dagger, curling in on myself and rolling so that I bounced back on my feet. I heaved, shoving my blade through the faerie's mouth, satisfaction singing through me as it gurgled and died. Blood welled at the wound where it had bit me, but I ignored the pain as I whirled. Exhaustion and fear mingled within me.

Several more crawled through the trees, the trickling light of the moon the only way I saw them coming. I was cold, so cold, my anger burning out as soon as I realized I was going to die. There were too many.

A beam of light shot through the trees, and the fae instantly fled, hissing and darting away. Some couldn't get away quick enough, though, and the light tore through them, exposing their sick and alien bodies. They died shrieking as Caolan stepped out from behind a tree, his gaze bristling with rage.

"I had it," I said bitterly, refusing to look at Caolan as I leaned down to wipe the blood off my blade and onto the moss. My hands were shaking alongside the beat of my thundering heart. I felt his anger; it soaked the air, thickening in the space between us.

"Do you have a death wish?" His words cut through me, and I whipped around quickly, a gut-wrenching sob tearing itself from deep within my chest.

"Salia is dead."

I regretted the words the moment they left my lips. Saying them made it real. It reminded me of her eyes, large and unseeing, back at the grove. It was supposed to be safe there, the only place of solace in a world of darkness. Now it was forever tainted by Salia's blood, and my shoulders shook as I fought back tears. My chest ached, burdened by grief, and I wanted to claw it out of me, to dig it out of my chest so it no longer sat there and festered.

Caolan's face fell to a sadness all its own—his more contained than mine—as he reached out his hand to rest on my shoulder. "I'm so sorry, Róis. Salia was a lovely girl. I know the two of you were close."

I jerked away from his touch and his words of comfort. They felt poisonous, a pity I didn't want nor need. "If you're insistent on coming with me, just know I do not intend to return."

"What happened to your arm?" Caolan asked, his tone sharp.

I looked down at the rot infecting my arm. The sight of it threatened to make me ill, but I didn't try to hide it. Not now. "It's why I decided to leave tonight," I said softly, showing Caolan my arm. "Salia and I... we were attacked." My voice had wobbled at Salia's name, but I did not cry again as Caolan's expression remained unreadable. "It's why I thought it best for you to stay with the village. Now there's no one to protect them. No one that I trust."

"Where?" Caolan raised his palm to his mouth, whispering magic into his skin. A blue wisp rose out of his hand, dancing like it was a flame that sat just above his fingers.

"The cove," I said. "Where you caught Salia and I sneaking off to when we were kids."

Caolan murmured quietly to the wisp, and it darted off, disappearing back towards the village. I had seen Caolan use wisps from time to time to send messages, but most of my people still feared them. Wisps in the wild often meant faeries were nearby.

"The wisp will instruct Sircha to send word north. Another mage will take my place guarding Farmere until I return with you." Silence encompassed the both of us. Vrona and the mages of Ravenspire did not care, not truly. They sent one mage to keep us safe, and where had that gotten us? Babies were being taken so often that people feared having them. Had the royal family abandoned us? Most days, it felt like it. Still, it was not Caolan's fault, so I shouldered my bitterness silently, and tears spilled over as the reality of what had happened crashed down on my shoulders. It hurt worse than when I'd lost Sister or my mother, hurt worse than anything I'd felt in my life. Salia's death was fresh, raw, and struck me without mercy. My rage boiled away as sobs wracked my body, and I collapsed, my fingers digging into the moss and dirt of the forest floor.

I knew I needed to be quiet, and I knew the faeries would return if I continued to cry so loudly. A part of me wished they would so I could instill in them a hurt like the one that grew inside me. Their cruelty, their malice: I hated them. I hated this forest. I hated the moon goddess Nymera for abandoning us when we needed Her the most.

Caolan's face swam in front of me as he knelt, cupping my cheeks and wiping my tears away. The tingling sensation of his magic sank into my skin, and I hiccupped as the grief dampened. It wasn't gone, but my cries quieted, and I was able to breathe.

"Which way do we go then?" I asked, dejected, my voice void of emotion. I was numb, and Caolan was right. I had no idea which way I was supposed to go. I'd be lying to myself if I said his presence also wasn't providing some sense of comfort and safety. My skin crawled like eyes were still on me, but I ignored it, already knowing full well we weren't alone. One was never alone in the forest.

"Further in. The way to their Court is near the center," Caolan said. Wind sailed through the trees, crafting noises that prodded at my paranoia, but I forced my breathing to steady as I nodded and stood.

No matter how quiet we were, I knew it mattered little. The faeries would be able to hear our heartbeats and taste our scent in the air. Still, the steady motion forward was a comfort. My mind wandered to stories I'd heard of the southern cities and their good relations with the fae there.

"What is it like in the southern cities? Have you ever been?" I watched my feet while we walked. The forest was wild and old, with gnarled roots and hidden burrows that would easily trip us if we weren't too careful.

Caolan nodded. "Far different than here. I've only been once when the kingdoms weren't at war." It was a moment before Caolan continued, his fingers grazing the trunk of the trees as we trailed by. "The elf king and the royal family of Kahl have some sort of delicate treaty, so it's not uncommon for the fae to visit. They are…" He paused, glancing over at me. "A lot different than the fae that I've encountered in the north."

It was difficult to imagine. The only faeries I had ever known were the ones that came at night: large, spindly, terrifying, and quick. They snatched children mostly, a penance for some old belief that our ancestors had wronged them. Many of the elders believed we were paying for our sins, paying for having betrayed a treaty we'd had with the spirits of the forest. It was difficult to think of a time when there had been peace between humans and fae.

Silence passed between us, and we walked for a better part of the night. We made camp as the sun began its ascent when we knew we would be safer from the faeries, and immediately began to walk again in the early afternoon after I pulled some cheese and dried meats from my sack, and we had a quick lunch at a bustling stream in case more fae came. One of the first things Caolan had taught me was the fear the fae had for running water.

"I couldn't tell you why," Caolan had told me some years ago. "But they do not cross it. If a fae gives chase, find a stream to cross."

As the world grew dark around us again, even Caolan's magical wisp did little to chase away the shadows etching the trees. The trunks had grown larger than the younglings at the forest's edge, and I eyed Caolan.

"Perhaps it would be safer to camp?" When he didn't respond, I asked, "Caolan?"

I blinked, and suddenly I was on the ground, unable to move. It was like the paralysis I sometimes suffered when I woke from nightmares, and I stared about the forest as panic sank heavily in my chest. *When did I fall asleep?* A low clicking echoed through the trees, the creature it belonged to tucked out of sight in the canopy. Off in the distance, a wisp danced through the trees. It was either Caolan's or a warning: there was a faerie nearby.

"Róis…run," Caolan's voice caressed my ear, and I moaned softly as I ripped myself out of my state of paralysis and stumbled to my feet. Caolan was nowhere to be found, and fear blossomed in my chest as it curled around my heart and squeezed. I unsheathed my dagger as something tackled me from behind before I could bolt through the woods.

I hit the ground hard, the air rattling around my lungs as I gasped. Something—a knee, perhaps?—pressed into the middle of my back, pinning me down. It was by some miracle I had kept hold of my dagger, and I snarled as I was flipped over. I lashed out, my dagger hitting soft flesh. The moment the weight was gone, I dug my fingers into the supple moss and kicked off, bolting into the darkness of the woods.

I barely reacted when a thin branch whipped me across the cheek. My heart pounding, I thanked Nymera for the grip on my dagger as I ignored the clicking and screeching that was coming from behind me.

I just needed to find running water. If I found a creek or, better yet, a stream, I could evade them. The forest still felt the breath of lingering winter at night, but I'd bear the cold and wade to the middle where the fae could not get me.

I just needed to make it there.

The soft calls of water sounded somewhere to my right, so I veered towards it despite my lungs screaming at me to slow down. I ignored them; if anything, the sounds of faeries giving chase behind me spurred me to go faster.

But I was too slow. I couldn't hope to outrun the fae in their home.

Something grabbed my ankle, and my dagger was wrangled from my grasp before I could slice out with it. My cheek scraped against the ground as I fell, and I cried out, trying to get my arms beneath me so I could push up as whoever had grabbed me pushed me down into the earth.

I was going to die. In that moment, I relaxed. I could be with Salia again. The haunting memory of her cold, dead eyes wouldn't be a burden anymore.

The faerie's weight disappeared from my back, and then I was being flipped over.

Impossibly green eyes caught my gaze. A strangled sob of disbelief left my lips. "Sister?"

My world slanted.

# SIX

## *Róis*

M Y SISTER'S NAME HAD slowly faded away with time, just as the memory of her face had. The endless sea of green—her eyes, however—had remained. They'd haunted me, swimming at the edges of my vision as they did now.

"Is it really you?" Sister's voice was hushed, her eyes wild and lingering. Tears cascaded down my face as I wrapped my arms around her and tugged her close.

"Everyone thinks you were dead. *Father* thinks you are dead." I pulled away. I needed to look at her, needed to make sure the forest wasn't playing some twisted, cruel trick. But no. She stood, pulling me with her, and it was her. It was really *her*.

She was tall now. How different things might have been if the faeries had not taken her as a child? Would Sister have survived the constant illnesses that had plagued her when she lived in Farmere? Would she have seen past twenty-six as she did now? I loathed to think the forest had saved her, but it was a relief regardless.

She was slimmer than I was and fairer in the face, but I was still surprised to find her lack of...change. I would have thought the forest had claimed her, twisted her into its own image. Instead, she looked as I did, as if she had grown up in Farmere as I had.

"Your arm," she said softly, her eyes trailing down to where the rot festered against my skin.

"Oh yes," I said, attempting to tuck my arm behind my back. "I'm not sure what happened—"

"It looks like this," she whispered, gesturing to the forest as it bent and transformed around us. Rot festered against the trunks of trees, with leaves curling in on themselves, and everywhere was a heartbeat of pain...the forest crying out, begging to be healed.

"I've been trying to find a cure," she cried. "I've been searching for so long. All the faeries avoid me, but they're the only ones who can help."

"What do you mean?" The words soured my tongue and fueled my rage. Salia's dead eyes stared up at me.

"Come, come. I know the way. Follow me. Please—" She took off, and I darted after her, fearful I would lose her again.

"Sister, wait!"

She was too quick as she darted through the trees and was soon swallowed up by the darkness. The forest was quiet now save for the soft chirping of birds and my sister's occasional soft calls. Rays of light pooled through the trees, bathing the forest floor with a soft, ethereal glow as the sun started to rise, and I was rejuvenated, kicking off the roots and running faster. Somewhere in the blanket of trees, the soft melody of a flute played, tempting me to seek it out and swaying me to dance. I resisted, knowing if I started, I would not be able to stop.

"Sister, please," I called out.

A low sigh sounded to my right, so slight I heard it too late. Something brushed my leg, and I looked over to see two large golden eyes in the dimness of the trees staring out at me. I groaned as a chill rolled down my spine. Several fae had surrounded me, their faces burdened with hatred.

These fae were different than the ones I was used to. Most of them looked vaguely human, with the barest hint of nature elevating their features. Glamours, the Caolan in my mind warned. *They are master illusionists and will use their old faces to trick you.*

A wild, untamed thing inside me rattled against the prison of my rib cage. If they thought to subdue me, I would not go so tamely into the dark.

One moved towards me, and my fist flung out quick as a bird. Pain licked up my arm as I contacted with their chin. The fae was strong and quick, but I had prepared myself and knew I had to fall back into the most primal, instinctual parts of myself to survive.

Reaching down into my boot, I pried a smaller dagger from the sheath tucked against my ankle. It was not as strong or as sharp as my main blade, but I lashed out with it regardless, my lips tugged back to bare my pointed canines. The fae howled in pain as they collapsed, and I grinned savagely in sick satisfaction.

The fae cursed, their language low and beautiful as they rolled back onto their feet. I danced out of reach as it attempted to grab me again, and three more luminescent eyes appeared in the darkness behind it. Two of them appeared female, the other a male, and all were breathtakingly beautiful. I knew the illusion willed it so, that there was nothing but monstrosity beneath. They all wielded swords made of shaerva, a metal of white gold that grew within the forest. It was sharp and wicked, a common metal used by the fae to carve their weapons.

"Lay down your weapon…" It was like a sigh in the wind, a simple murmur in the breeze, only it echoed, bouncing off the trees as if I was standing in a ravine.

Wild, breathless laughter passed my lips. How could I understand them? I recalled drinking water from the creek the first time Caolan and I had made camp, but that should not have granted me the ability to understand them. Was that why Sister had not come home? I had heard of faerie food and its effects on humans, but I did not think it extended to anything found in the forest. My chest tightened with fear, and my world threatened to slant once more.

Was I stuck here?

*No time for fear now*, I thought as I tucked it behind a wall and tightened my grip on my dagger. *Or they'll kill me.*

"I'm not the one in danger here," I growled, flashing my filed teeth again.

I moved just as Caolan had trained me, just as the wolves of Brûnheim were trained. When they came for me, I darted away with grace. But I was only human. Moving faster, the first faerie pierced my shoulder with her blade. The pain flourished through me like I'd pricked my finger on a thorn. I hissed and flinched away, and they did the same, noticing the rot on my arm.

Their hesitation spurred me to lash forward, to direct my arm so that it kept the faeries at bay. I cut down the first faerie that had struck me, their death spurring on my lust to see them all struck down by my blade. Another faerie went down, secreting a sap-blood from her wounds, and I slid my dagger across another faerie's throat. Soon it was only the first faerie that had found me that remained standing.

My chest heaved as I moved to strike out at the fae, but they had me pinned onto my back, their fingers pressing my wrists to the ground before I could blink. I stared up into glittering black eyes, their glamour bleeding away to something with a long, angular face and blonde hair.

"Careful, wolf girl," they breathed, their words tickling my ear. "Savage hearts can still shatter like glass." Their voice was barely higher than a whisper, fading with the wind as they pulled me roughly to my feet. Laughter trickled through the forest, and my knees and palms were smarting from where I'd hit the ground.

Where had Sister gone?

*Think, Róis. They cannot take you into their realm. If they take you there, you don't stand a chance.*

But there was nothing to be done. My dagger was wrangled from my grasp, and then the faerie struck me across the head with the hilt of my own blade.

*The fae will try to deceive. Do not fall for their beauty. It all but masks the monstrosity beneath.*

Caolan's words washed through me as I slowly came to.

The faerie that had knocked me out came into focus, and I scowled as I tried to flinch away, only to realize they had tied my wrists together with rope, and they held the other end of it a  few feet away. They hissed at me, their head bobbing as they tugged me forward, and I stumbled to my feet with no choice but to follow. I had no idea how much time had passed.

Dew pattered off leaves on the trees as if it had just rained, and I stared, mesmerized by how otherworldly the forest suddenly seemed. A small, winged being flitted about a bush nearby and smiled when I drew close, revealing razor-sharp teeth.

"When I touch the Other Side, will it change me?" I asked, tearing my eyes away from the little sprite as she flitted away.

The faerie ignored me and tugged at the rope that tied my wrists together, dragging me forward.

We reached a strange half-circle of branches bent to forge a tunnel. It stretched until there was naught but darkness, and the faerie eyed me for a moment.

"Wait, no—" I said, but the faerie tugged me down the path nonetheless.

I didn't know how long we'd walked, only that it'd seemed endless. I despaired, knowing that I had found my sister only to lose her again. How cruel a fate that was.

Just as I feared we were doomed to walk the trail forever, the trees opened up, and the forest changed. Instead of a forest of spring, this forest was bathed in the vibrant colors of autumn. I looked behind me, but there was no longer a path like it had disappeared the moment we'd walked through.

I stared up at the kingdom that sat before us. Giant mushrooms grew on the trunks of trees that looked like they would take days to traverse around. The caps of the mushrooms were bioluminescent, bathing the kingdom in a soft light. Half of the kingdom was nestled against the ground, their homes carved into the roots of the trees.

The other half grew alongside the mushrooms up the sides of the trees, with bridges woven around the trunks and thrown across canopies to allow quicker passage from tree to tree.

*It's beautiful.* I allowed myself to think mournfully before smothering it. I couldn't let my mind be swayed by the deception. The creatures that lived here were coveted by their malice.

The faerie tugged on my bonds, forcing me forward, and I obliged as dusk settled, the last dusting of the sun's rays piercing through the canopy. Several faeries sat nestled between the trees, their eyes glowing in the coming darkness. They shuddered between their glamorous state and their true one, a deceptive human and a true faerie. It was eerie, watching them shift, watching their face rot and peel back to reveal a monster of mushrooms or vines. They were of all shapes and sizes, as beautiful and as terrifying as the forest they inhabited. Nearby, a faerie with fluttering dragonfly wings paused to stare.

"Where are we going?" I asked, but the faerie leading me ignored me as a soft chittering slipped from their lips, a clacking of teeth that was responded to by some of the faeries in the nearby trees.

I cocked my head towards the center of the city, where a palace was carved out of multiple trees. The size of it was lost on me as the roof spiraled up into the tree branches, disappearing among the leaves. The air was crisp here, and I took a deep breath as we approached the palace. The stairs were guarded by two large griffins whose heads were adorned with deer antlers coated in moss. Small pixies flitted about, like the one from before, and they decorated the trees with faint gold flecks. Small goblins with rock heads and squashed noses leered at me from the base of the palace's trees.

The faerie leading me darted towards me, reached out, and pushed my head down, forcing my eyes away from the griffins. My jaw pulsed in irritation as we passed, and the faerie released my head.

The palace stood glittering before me. It shined like it was made of magic with hanging golden lanterns that swung aimlessly in the trees and flickered with a golden flame within.

As we neared the front door, my eyes flickered up and up and up... The doors were massive, with ornate woodland creatures carved into them.

The faerie didn't let me admire them as they knocked erratically on the door and dragged me inside the moment one opened.

# SEVEN

## *Neferil*

IT WAS NEARING NIGHTFALL. The forest was quiet, experiencing a blanket of calm that had recently been robbed from Elvira; the trees did not whisper their words of turmoil. I was grateful for that. Perhaps the forest would purge the Rot on its own.

In my heart, I knew that line of thinking was foolish. Too many faelings had died, and too much of the forest had been ravaged by the sickness. I remained on edge as I sat on my throne of vines, picking at an armrest in agitation. Several dark moths flitted about, landing on my arms and shoulders, and I sighed as Rhi approached and gestured down the grand hall.

"Kau has returned with a human girl."

Hope sang through me, tempting me to smile. Perhaps we had finally discovered the one that would cure this wicked sickness infecting my land and my people.

"Let them come." My voice called out among the vast hall, and the faerie guards at the door pulled it open to grant the faerie and their human captive entrance. Kau was as solemn as ever, their face unreadable. But the human? I was almost gleeful at how easy it was to read the girl's face. Patterns of expression always flickered across human faces like a betrayal. She was angry. She reminded me of a wolf backed into a corner, her reddish-brown hair wild and untamed as it curled around her face. Her eyes were bright as she drank in her surroundings, her chin turned up in spite.

*Smart,* I thought. *She's looking for an escape. Too bad she will not find one here.* My smile turned wicked as the soft patter of their feet carried them ever closer. Kau stopped the girl at the foot of the stairs that led up to my throne. I stared down at them for a time, silent. Kau knew better than to speak before I permitted it. They'd made that mistake only once when their humanity had still forced them to rebel against the nature of the forest. I believe they still carried the scars from that day. Rhi had not been merciful. Mercy was not afforded in Elvira. Not if one wished to survive.

"What have you caught in your web, little spider?" I cooed, one of my taloned fingers digging into the arm of my throne. I sat in my true form in an attempt to frighten and intimidate. Tall and ethereal, my wings shimmered, mirroring those of luna moths, and my eyes were dark, black voids that pierced through anyone who dared make eye contact. My skin was dark and hard, like the bark of a tree, my face angular and thin as I sat in a beautiful blue dress forged from spider silk. "Did a fly come too close to your web?"

"I believe this is the one that sickens your land, my queen." Kau's voice was low and commanding, spoken with conviction. "Her arm rots, as does the land surrounding her." The girl's nose flared in defiance, and she looked ready to bolt at any moment, her gaze wild and bright.

My eyes slid to her arm, where I recoiled and hissed in rage. "Why have you brought her inside the walls if she is plagued with *Rot*?" I asked, pushing myself to my feet. "Have you lost your mind?"

Kau stilled, and I turned to Rhi. "Take her above, then escort Kau down below."

Rhi's face brightened the moment Kau's paled. The roots of the palace was where the punishments were dealt, and the action of Kau bringing the Rot within the walls, no matter how small, would not go unpunished.

"I shouldn't be –" Kau started.

"Stay your tongue," I hissed, my limbs creaking like wood as I leaned forward. "You have no power here. Your fate is mine and mine alone to decide."

"But Your Grace," Kau said, their jaw clenched with rage. I tasted their ire in the air, and it was delightful. I nearly shuddered from it, at the way it wafted and curled around me seductively. "I only wanted –"

"*Silence.*"

They bit their tongue, and my eyes sought out the girl's. She clearly understood what danger she was in; it bled into her expression and the tense way she held herself.

Rhi and a few guards flinched as the girl whipped around. She ducked sideways as Kau attempted to lash out and grab her, reaching for a dagger they had on their hip. They managed to tear it from their waist, but the blade clattered to the floor, so the human girl dropped down to grab it. Kau kicked her with such force that a resounding crack echoed through the halls as her nose broke, and she reeled back, howling in pain. Blood gushed down her face as she fell back, and Rhi rushed forward, grabbing Kau as the guards grabbed the human girl, taking care not to touch the Rot on her arm.

The girl's glare was hard and unforgiving as she met my gaze, and it bore into me long after the guards led her to the prison cells above.

"Do you think she is the one?" Rhi asked, her voice thick with desire. One might not take Rhi for someone prone to violence, her appearance and voice soft and deceitful, but it was a foolish notion. I had watched Rhi perform at the height of her bloodlust. Crossing paths with a faerie that hungered for humanity was a dangerous one.

"Even if so, she is claimed," I said, and Rhi frowned, her lip falling into a pout.

"By who, my queen?"

I eyed her sharply. "She is *mine*. It is my land she desecrates." I smiled wickedly, brushing my fingers gently across Rhi's cheek. "I will have the honor of tasting her blood first should she be guilty."

Rhi lowered her head. If she was at all offended by the reprimand, she did not show it. "Of course, Your Grace."

"Whoever is responsible for this Rot will pay," I promised, my voice softening as I cupped Rhi's face in my hands. "We will find a way to lead the forest out of this darkness. Do not fret." I could not help but remember my softness when it came to Rhi.

Rhi nodded, her eyes full of such adoration and devotion that my heart squeezed painfully. I loved my court and my people and would do anything to save them.

"Now, please. Leave me. Let me linger with my thoughts." My demand was heeded, and all the other faeries left, and I collapsed into my throne.

My fingers drew to my forehead as another headache threatened what little patience of mine remained. I didn't have time for such trivial pain, but it was insistent, prodding at my temples with little mercy.

If the Rot continued to spread as it was, I'd have to enlist Eirwyn's aid, something I wanted to do only if the situation grew dire. The king of the south sat high and mighty on his throne, and our relationship had been tense and growing tenser.

My fingers closed into a fist. No, I would stop the Rot before it came to that.

A moth landed on the arm of my throne, capturing my attention. It was small for its kind, its fuzzy legs moving as it attempted to stabilize itself. Large round circles of cream color dotted its wings, and I cooed quietly as I reached out a hand. Moths were terribly misunderstood, their tenaciousness towards their love for a flame naught but something to be admired. Sometimes, I felt the same pull towards things dark and forbidden.

*Oh, Neferil, you fool. You are just like this moth. One day, you'll fly too close to the flames.*

The moth climbed over the back of my hand and settled there to rest for a time. I waited patiently, watching its antennae flick to and fro before it took flight and fluttered away, heading towards the door that led to the prisons.

I sighed.

Time to go and pay the human a visit.

# EIGHT

## *Róis*

THE FAERIE THAT THREW me into my cell sneered, his fingers dark with the stain of my blood. I hit the ground hard, a soft exclamation leaving my lips as the shock from the fall radiated up to my broken nose. I touched it tenderly, hissing through clenched teeth as my eyes watered from the pain. It was definitely broken. Pain pulsed as I slowly exhaled and closed my eyes. Magic was fickle. It did not come unless it wished to, but I called to it now, imagining a healed nose in my mind's eye. A moment or two later, the pain in my broken nose was replaced with an insistent itching. A small *pop!* sounded, followed quickly by relief. I tentatively raised my fingers to my nose. I let out a sigh of relief; there was no pain.

Unlike human dungeons, where we took the damned to the deepest parts of the earth to rot until their judgments were made for them, the faeries took me high into the trees, where cells were carved straight out of the branches, with one side open to the forest below with no window or railing to stop you from falling. My stomach rolled as the branches swayed gently in the wind, and I wondered if any of them had ever snapped. At this height, I'd plummet to my death.

Still, being this far off the ground, I couldn't help but admire the beauty of the faerie realm at night. It was deceptive, with a sparkling glow of dancing orbs keeping the forest from being sheathed in endless darkness. It was like a dream, and had there not been dark things lurking in the shadows, I might have been tricked by its charm.

I scooted to the middle of my cell, and the branch stopped swaying. I sighed with small relief. I could only imagine how many had fallen to their deaths trying to escape. My heart pounded. My mind begged me to throw myself off the side of the tree, to demand my death be swift. Sitting here, doomed to contemplate my fate, was agonizing.

I shivered. I would likely die from the stubborn clings of winter as it flitted through the cell and brushed against my bare skin. At this rate, I would freeze to death before they came to sentence me for whatever crime they were painting me with.

Wrapping my arms around my legs, I ignored the throbbing in my nose as I assessed the situation. My thoughts ran to my sister, and a sob settled in my throat, making it difficult to swallow. *Where did you go?* I wondered, and I despaired. I had not imagined returning home once I'd plunged into the forest—I would have been foolish to hope—but I had not imagined this fate.

My thoughts turned to Caolan. Where was he? Had the fae taken him? Killed him? My mind still repelled the reality of what had happened in the forest when I'd last seen him. One moment, I was speaking with him; the next, he was gone. My heart cried out, but I shoved it away. I had to hope that, somehow, he was okay.

Sorrow clung to the edges of my mind, threatening to encroach on me with its bitter hopelessness. I knew the faeries would not show me mercy, but I wondered what they would do to me. I shuddered to think they might turn me into one of them.

Clenching my fists, I ground my teeth together in rage. The hopeless nature of my thoughts did not mean I would go calmly into the night.

They had claws? I had teeth.

My fingers ached for my blades.

A low cry pierced the air, and I raised my head to listen. I could not tell if it was a fellow prisoner or some creature of the night making the noise. It sounded both close and far off, and I shuddered. The animalistic clicking it produced was strange, but I knew some fae could make such a noise in the deep darkness of night.

I looked up and flinched. The queen stood before me. She stood on the other side of my cell in a silent, contemplative manner. She was glamoured this time, her skin dark and almost luminescent in the glow of the moon. Small braids hung from her head and draped around her shoulders, and though she was tall and slender, her bare arms were laden with muscle. She wore a blue dress drenched in silver embellishments, and her lips, pressed in a line, were full and colored with some sort of red stain.

She was beautiful.

The admiration sent a thrill of disgust and awe through me. I had never felt the desire to be fully intimate with anyone, but I could not deny the beauty in people. I had seen it first in Salia, and the queen of the forest stood before me now, radiating so much beauty I nearly lost sight of where I was or why I was here.

*Get it together, Róis. You must kill her, remember?*

My stomach rolled in fear as the branch shifted. I was going to fall to my death if I wasn't careful, but the shift was all I needed to break whatever charm the queen had placed on me, and I lunged forward, my teeth bared.

The queen was as still as a stone as my arm shot out between the bars of my cell. She stood just out of my reach, which only fueled the fire burning in my belly. Still, I would not give the queen the satisfaction of rattling me, so I pulled myself away and settled with a glare.

The queen spoke, low whispers of words that sifted through the air. There was almost a musical lilt to them as they caressed my ears and compelled me to lower my head in respect. Her words were foreign, and I blinked, wondering why I couldn't understand her. Had I just imagined being able to understand that other fae before? The queen's lips twitch in amusement.

*I cannot understand you*, I thought sullenly. Not that it would matter. Faeries were notorious for their tricky ways; the queen would find a way to condemn me whether I was able to defend myself or not.

Despite my instincts screaming at me to never turn my back to an enemy, I did just that, tearing my gaze away as I turned and settled on the ground.

The queen radiated so much power that I knew the exact moment she left. The life of the forest shifted in her absence as it begged for her attention, and it was some time before I found the courage to turn back to where the queen had once stood, noting she'd left something behind.

A small wooden plate sat on the branch just outside of the cell. Blackberries overflowed from it, tucked on top of each other in a small mound. They gleamed in the soft glow of the fireflies that bobbed above, and I stared at them hungrily, my stomach rumbling in protest. When was the last time I'd eaten?

*Don't eat the fruit. Don't give them your name. If they chase you, find running water.*

"If you eat the fruit, you'll understand what they're saying."

I looked up as Sister appeared, standing where the queen had just stood. She gestured to the fruit, her mouth twisting in a cruel line. "Eat the fruit that comes from the forest, and you'll be able to understand them for a time."

It was strange seeing her again after a lifetime of wondering what she'd look like. She looked just like me except, perhaps, her eyes were a darker green. Her skin was also paler, still bearing the sickly complexion it had when we'd been younger.

"I thought you weren't working with them?" I accused. "And what happened to Caolan?"

Sister's lower lip trembled. "I don't know. I saw no one else but you."

Not the answer I wanted, but Sister seemed genuine, and I knew better than to underestimate the magic of the forest. Perhaps Caolan had never entered to find me in the first place.

"Why did you run away?" I asked, crawling closer and changing the subject. My hand reached out to her, and she collapsed to her knees, threading her fingers through mine. The hole in my soul that had formed when she'd left repaired itself, and a tear rolled down my cheek.

"I thought you were right behind me. It was important that we made it here. You need to convince the queen that taking you to Graeir is the way to cure this wicked rot."

"Who's Graeir?"

Sister gestured with a free hand to the forest. "He is the god of this wood. His sacred grove is tucked away in these woods somewhere, but only the queen and king in the south know its location." She squeezed my hand and met my gaze as she coughed, the noise sick and wet as it rattled her lungs.

"I'm sick, so is the forest, so are you," she said, her gaze trailing down to where the rot infected my arm. "The Forest Father is the only one who can help us now. He is our only hope."

"How am I to convince the enemy of this? Why hasn't the queen thought to seek out their god if it is his forest that's rotting?" The questions rolled through me, assaulting me from all sides, and I frowned. "I do not know—"

"You must. I don't know all the answers, but I do know he is the one who can liberate the forest from this plague. I have to go. They will kill me if they see me here." Both of our gazes flickered to the side as a sound crashed against the tree nearby, and she pulled her hand away. The absence of her ached, but by the time I looked back to where she'd stood, more questions on my tongue, she was gone.

A battle raged inside me as I stared down at the mound of blackberries. A part of me urged my hand to reach out and take the fruit, to gain some understanding of the crimes I was being charged with, to try to convince the queen of the things my sister had said. The other part of me knew that in doing so, I would give part of myself to *them*.

I turned my back on the berries but snaked my arms through the slats of the cage behind me. The last thing I wanted was to fall off the opposite edge if sleep took me.

Not that I could sleep despite the way my eyes grew heavy and my head lolled.

Perhaps it would be wise to sleep, to reclaim some of my wits to prepare for whatever the queen had planned.

I fell into it fitfully and dreamed of nothing but the yawning darkness of the void. There was no light, no objects. Just nothing. I came to gasping, my stomach plummeting as if I feared falling. It took a few moments for my mind to catch up (why was I so frightened?) before I remembered that I was in an open-faced cell where I could very easily fall to my death.

Something wasn't right, but I couldn't place it. No one had come while I'd slept, not that I could tell. My cage was the same as I had left it, and the bowl of blackberries still sat in front of my cage on the branch.

The sun rose as I heard someone approaching from below. If I wanted to understand them, as Sister had suggested, I needed to act quickly.

My fingers closed around some of the blackberries.

# NINE

## *Róis*

T HEY CAME TO COLLECT me moments after I popped the blackberry into my mouth. A part of me longed to hate its taste as I bit into the fruit, but I'd be lying if I didn't admit to enjoying it. It was the best damn blackberry I'd ever had, and I swallowed hurriedly. Its magic sang through my veins. I threatened to sway, overwhelmed by my new senses. It was like lightning was coursing through me, making everything vibrant, and the two faerie guards approaching me suddenly did not seem so dangerous.

I couldn't tell their gender, tucked away behind bark and bioluminescent flowers that unfurled straight from their skin. If they had closed their eyes and not moved, I would have easily mistaken them for the nature that surrounded them. They walked with a graceful fluidity despite their rigid bones that creaked every time they moved.

"The queen says she has the fighting spirit of a wolf. Do not underestimate her," one said as they approached the cage. Their dialect was strange, like the creaking of wood, and they stared at me with a cruel expression, their eyes dark and alien.

"Get up," the other hissed, poking me with the end of a stick through a slot of the cell. The end of it that poked me was innocent enough, a blunt end, but the other was forged into a wicked blade that shone in the morning light.

I forced my chin up, my brow furrowed in rage as I pretended not to understand what they were saying. Scowling, they opened the door to my cell and guided me out with their sticks as I bared my teeth.

"Such a pretty little thing. The queen demands her blood, but a tiny taste should go unnoticed..." one said, their long, thin fingers too close to my skin. If they came any closer, I'd bite them off.

"No," the other snarled, tugging the first one's fingers away. "The queen will show you no mercy if you defy her."

The fae grumbled, but didn't try to reach for me again as they led me down the branches. Scowls and glowing eyes of the other faeries stared me down. Perhaps I could fight one or two of them, but I was in the center of their home. I couldn't hope to escape. Plus, Sister's words weighed heavily on my mind. I needed to learn more about Graeir and see if I could really help cure this sickness.

They led me down through the castle, back to the throne room where I'd first met the queen. This time the room was empty save for the queen and another faerie, a small woman with dark skin and coiled curls. Both faeries were tucked behind human glamours, and I openly stared as the guards led me over to the table where they were sitting.

The queen moved gracefully. Silver and blue-stoned beads were woven into her braids, which dangled to her waist. Two massive moth wings unfurled from her back, proudly on display.

"Rhi, pour the human some tea," the queen said. "I wish to sit and speak for a moment." She gave a vague nod to the two faeries that had brought me here, her face melting into a warm smile. "Thank you for bringing her. You may leave us."

The faeries nodded and left, and I stood here rigidly, wondering what they'd do if I tried to bolt.

"It would be foolish to run," the faerie called Rhi said as if she could read my mind. She eyed me with a cool expression as she stood and poured tea into a small porcelain cup, her eyes shielded behind ill-concealed curiosity. "There are hundreds of faeries between you and the forest's edge. You'd die before you even left the castle grounds." Her smile was sweet as dimples cratered both of her round cheeks, her eyes glittering in challenge. "It would be fun to see you try to outrun me."

"Rhi." The queen's warning cut through the air, but Rhi only laughed, waving the queen away as she slipped onto a stool. She had wings too, hers small and dainty, like a dragonfly's. They were translucent, a shimmering blue that sparkled when the light hit it right. They reminded me of the faerie that had attacked Salia and I in the forest, but their wings had been limp and rotting.

I swallowed thickly, my mind consumed by Salia's dead, unseeing eyes.

"By your command, Your Grace," Rhi said, raising her cup to her lips.

If the Rot was killing the forest, perhaps it would kill them too. My rage about what they had done to Salia overtook my desire to help heal the forest they called home, so I lashed out suddenly. Perhaps I could infect the queen before they killed me.

Rhi caught me before I reached her as if she had been anticipating the attack. I'd lost count of how many times I had been put on my back by a faerie. Rhi's glamour was gone, and the glittering face of nature sat above me. Her fingers were long and thin, like twigs; her eyes were glittering and black. Her skin was like bark, and when she opened her mouth, a high-pitched noise echoed from the void past her lips.

She wrangled me to my feet, and I lashed out with my arm, exposing the Rot. I knew the fae feared it –they would be fools not to– and Rhi flinched away, releasing her hold on me.

The queen was upon me before I could flee, and she pinned me to the ground, the cloth of her dress bunched up in her grasp to slam my injured arm against the floor. "Why did you enter the forest?" she asked, any amusement in her face now absent as she stared down at me.

I could answer her. Sister told me I needed to convince her to take me to Graeir, whoever he was, that it was the only way to save the forest. My heart was in my throat as

I stared up at the queen I had been tasked to kill. Desperation clung to her eyes, refusing to hide behind the blank slate of her face. I knew I couldn't trust her, but how was I to get to the sacred grove without her? What if killing her did nothing? Sircha may have been the seer of our village, but what if she was wrong? If the queen was dead and the rot still flourished, the journey into Elvira would be for naught. Plus, she'd given me blackberries in hopes of communicating. Perhaps I should try and speak...

My silence pried a sigh from the queen's lips as she pulled away. Returning to the table, she reached out to grab a pastry, which she plucked apart with her fingers.

"Let us bleed her," Rhi cooed, leaning forward. "Perhaps her magic, if she truly has it as Kau thinks, will sing for us after some coaxing."

*My magic?* Were they talking about my life magic?

"The human has already bled on our floor, and there are no signs." The queen's stress bled through her words. "If the Rot reaches Graeir's grove, then we will truly be lost." The queen bit into the pastry and gestured to the middle of the throne room. "Get rid of her. She is useless." Her wings fluttered as she lowered herself back onto the stool.

My brow furrowed even as my pulse spiked at Rhi's approach. They were worried about the spread of the Rot too? I cursed myself. Of course they were; it was the faeries that were being infected, not humans. If I hadn't been so scared of them, I would've realized that. I stared down at my arm. It still flourished with the Rot, but it hadn't moved or spread. Not like it did when it infected the faeries.

"I need you to take me to the Sacred Grove."

My words caused both faeries to pause. Rhi's face broke into glee, her eyes shining with danger. "Oh! She speaks!"

The queen stared at me silently, and though a smile crossed her lips as well, her voice was deceptively quiet. It tangled around me, rooting me in place.

"And why would we take you to our most sacred grove?" The queen laughed, her gaze seeking Rhi's. "Humans aren't allowed in such hallowed places."

My throat constricted in panic. "Please. You have to take me there. The Forest Father is the only one that can save your home."

The queen sneered in dismissal. "The Forest Father has abandoned us. Only a human girl with his magic in her blood can save us now." Her stare cut through me. "Can you wield such magic?"

"Sometimes, but it's unpredictable. I—"

"Show me, and if your power wields true, then I will take you to His Grove." Her words washed over me, and I lowered my head, begging my magic to manifest. It shivered through me, like I was rousing the sun from its slumber, but I could not get it to draw forward as I had in the past.

My magic was failing me.

"I thought not. Guards!" The queen's voice carried throughout the long hall, and the faerie guards returned, their long fingers pulling at my arms as they dragged me to my feet.

"Take her to the courtyard and have someone fetch my sword."

# TEN

## *Róis*

T HEY LED ME DOWN the spiraling staircase until we stood at the bottom of the tree. It appeared as if the whole kingdom had arrived to watch my sentence, and I frowned but kept my head forward, ignoring the fearful twist of my belly. My nose ached but less so than last night. The delicious taste of the blackberry still stained the inside of my mouth.

*Stay calm, Róis. If you panic, you'll stumble. If you stumble, you'll die on your knees.*

Faeries jeered at me from all sides, maintaining their distance while my guards led me down a path through the kingdom. Some children watched from a tree branch above me, their features still bearing the vague resemblance of human children.

*It's because they were human once*, I realized with disgust. *They're children from home.*

Despite my compulsion to turn away, I kept my eyes trained on the children, ignoring their cries. One called me a monster, which made me sneer. Humans were never the problem, never the ones stealing children from their cribs or ripping them from their mother's side.

The queen stood in a small clearing. She looked radiant in a sweeping black dress embellished with gold. A crown made of golden flowers and thorns sat upon her glamorous head.

Rhi stood beside her as if she had done so her whole life, her eyes trained on the queen with adoration and pride.

"Make her kneel," the queen commanded as we approached, and a hush fell upon the faeries as I narrowed my gaze and knelt of my own free will. I would die before they forced me to my knees.

The queen's nostrils flared as a breeze coursed through the trees, bringing unease. Trepidation soaked the air like honey, and I shivered as the queen stepped forward, leaving Rhi behind. Her smile was sweet, but I saw the poison hidden there.

"Despite your stubborn wit, you took my gift. You ate the fruit of the fair folk and learned our tongue." Laughter expelled first from the queen's lips, then soon echoed throughout the rest of the watching faeries. "It matters little. Your crimes have been shown to me."

"What crimes?"

A hush fell on the clearing as my question rang throughout the trees. My head tilted up, and I studied the queen intently.

"For lying. Your arm is coated with the Rot that plagues our lands, yet you do not suffer from it. You are the cause." Shadows crept along the trees, blotting out the sun as they accompanied the queen's rage. "You seek to kill my people and destroy my forest. A prophecy has been spun about you, little human."

I would have laughed if the shock of the queen's words hadn't stolen my breath away. My heart thundered, a betrayal against my ribs. I knew the faeries could hear it. Wicked, mischievous creatures, their hearing went beyond what humans could comprehend. They'd be able to hear the way my breath caught, the way my heart threatened to burst from my chest. Many of the faeries that danced at the edge of the clearing drew closer, their eyes luminescent.

It was the only part of the faeries that bled through their glamour, where humanity could see their visage twisted. That had been the first thing Caolan had taught me when I'd come to him, desperate to brave the forest of the fae.

*If their eyes glow, they are deceiving you. If their eyes glow, they are a faerie.*

I forced my chin up, my rage festering, sitting proudly on my face. No matter what I did or said, the faeries would not believe me. They would not hear my claims, and I would not beg for my life.

A tree rustled as the queen drew forward. The faerie beside me offered her a sword, and she unsheathed it slowly. It was a long, beautiful blade with a cross guard and hilt that looked like luna moth wings. Moths and starlight decorated the metal of the hilt, and Neferíl towered over me, meeting my gaze as she pointed the tip of the blade towards the soft ground.

She said nothing, and my silence matched hers. The queen was tall and regal, beautiful and cruel, and Rhi stood behind her, unable to tame the grin that crossed her face.

I didn't want to die. My body compelled me to fight, to grab the blade and use it against its master. I'd been training for nearly fifteen years for this moment. I wanted to plunge a dagger through the queen's heart and free my people of the forest that continued to take everything from us. This wasn't going at all as I'd imagined, but there had to be a way out. My eyes darted from the queen's to the clearing surrounding me. Everywhere I looked, I caught the gaze of a faerie, of their sneering grin that beckoned their queen to liberate my head from my shoulders. My gaze fell on Sister, situated behind a faerie, her fearful gaze tucked against the trunk of the tree. Oh gods, would someone see her?

A faerie began to turn, as if Sister had made some sort of noise, and I lunged forward on my knees, attempting to crawl to my feet. I kicked out a foot as a guard reached out to restrain me, and clawed at his fingers as they curled around my shoulder, pushing me down. My eyes met Sister's, who remained safely hidden in the trees. My relief was immense; I couldn't protect Sister when we were kids, but I could now.

"Let me have the honor of at least dying on my feet," I said, tearing my gaze away from Sister and meeting the queen once more.

The queen smiled sweetly. "Humans do not deserve such respect."

The cruelty and malice of the queen's expression met my anger, but There was nothing I could do.

The queen raised the blade, but I refused to shut my eyes. I wanted her to look into my gaze as she killed me. Despite the fear that pounded in my throat, despite the desperate itch of my fingers seeking my blades, I'd keep the queen's gaze until her sword swung true.

But the sword never swung.

A bloodcurdling scream echoed across the clearing. The queen's nostrils flared as the guards rushed forward to restrain me. She turned as Rhi danced away from a darkness that was trailing slowly through the grass.

I had seen the natural order of nature, the death that crept along the trees. I'd stepped over rotting logs and had seen flies infesting the corpse of a fox. I knew the beauty of nature and the balance it demanded.

This felt different, yet it whispered at the edges of my mind and beckoned towards familiarity. As the grass curled, browned, and died, the faeries scrambled to flee its touch, but I couldn't help but stare. It was the same rot that had infected the faeries back home, the one that had rotted at my feet when Caolan had been attacked. The same that had attacked Salia and I. Fear crawled up my spine much in the same manner as the rot moved: slowly and with purpose.

My fingers tingled at the sight of it, and I looked down as green magic wove from my fingertips, causing flowers and grass to grow beneath my knees. Magic flourished through the clearing as if to combat the rot, but my magic died upon touching the places where the rot infected the forest.

The queen's eyes flashed. "You were telling the truth." She stepped forward, only to stop as Rhi stumbled nearby. "Rhi!" the queen cried out. "Your arm."

Guards wrangled me to my feet. I tugged my arms against their holds; with the queen distracted, perhaps I could free myself and grab a dagger. But their holds on me were too strong.

Rhi looked down at her arm. Sores blossomed across her skin, weeping yellow as pieces of her skin flecked and rotted away. She did not scream, not really. It was more like a sharp inhale of whistling air as it thickened around her, and rain began to fall in soft trepidation.

"She's marked," one of the guards whispered behind me.

"Get away from her. Do not let her touch you," the other guard screamed, his hold loosening on my arm.

The clearing deteriorated, falling into chaos. Faeries scrambled away as the rot continued to grow, consuming the clearing. It was astonishing how quickly the beauty of the place fell prey to desecration. The color was leeched from nature as brown and black replaced it. The air buzzed with insects. Rhi clutched her arm as she shuddered away from the queen.

"Do not come near me, Your Majesty. It is not safe."

The guards were distracted, which granted me the perfect time to strike.

Throwing my body backwards, I ripped myself from their grasp.

I fell between them, landing on my back, and the air left me with a painful gasp. I quickly kicked up, arching at the waist, and my feet met one of the faeries square in the chest. They were too strong; the attack barely made an impact on their momentum, but it gave me enough time to roll out of the way as they tried to snatch me.

"Filthy human," they sneered, grabbing me by the back of the legs as I moved to crawl away. "I grant you honor for your courage and determination, but it matters little." They leaned over my back, pressing me to the ground as I grunted in pain from their weight. "Your blood smells delicious."

Something pried the faerie from my back. Their screams rang in my ears as I scrambled away. Faeries brushed past me, and their words began to jumble, a mixture of my language and theirs. Perhaps the effects of the blackberry were already wearing off. The world began to dim, and a headache settled at my temples.

One faerie slammed into another, tossing her to the dying ground, and the Rot seeped into her entire right side. It was slow to grow and did not kill her immediately, but the sickness blossomed against her skin as she rose to her feet, and all the other faeries gave her a wide berth.

"Kill her," someone shouted, but I turned away before I could see if the demand was followed through.

Taking off through the trees, a branch struck out at my cheek, and I shot through the brush, only to get tackled to the ground.

"I don't think so, little human." The queen's breath was hot in my ear as she flipped me onto my back. Her eyes were bright with rage as her fingers dug into my skin, and she pulled me to my feet before thrusting me up against a tree.

I slammed my heel down on her foot, and she howled, but the pain only seemed to fuel her as she drew forward, her face a twist of manic glee. "I won't—"

She disappeared from me more quickly than I could follow, replaced by Sister. The world darkened around us. A sob tore at my throat.

She was rotting. Just like the other faeries, just like the forest.

Skin flaked away at her lips and nose, and half of her right cheek was caved in, held together by thin strands of muscle. Her right eye was fogged over, and when she bared her teeth, they were black and rotten. It all faded as she shuddered, pulling her human face back over her rotten one. The Rot on my arm burned painfully.

"Sister, you must kill her, but you must do it in the Sacred Grove. Only killing her in the Grove will cure this land of this rot. Will cure me. Please—"

A snarl echoed through the woods as Sister's visage faded, and the queen returned, her braids flying about her shoulders as she slashed her sword towards me. I ducked, and it embedded itself into the tree behind me. I darted out from beneath her, prying my dagger from her hip as I went by. It felt like a long-lost friend had come home, and I gripped it as I turned and shot back towards her.

We were evenly matched. The queen was a good fighter, and though she had the advantage with her sword and speed as a faerie, I was able to block her attacks, and neither of us were able to land a strike. Until she did.

I hissed as pain sang up my arm, and then I was pinned to a tree, with the bloody edge of the queen's blade pressed to my neck.

"Wait," I whimpered. I didn't want to die. I didn't want to *die*.

The queen's eye refocused on my arm, and she pulled away. "There it is again," she uttered, much to my confusion. I looked down at the tree, where my blood ran down it, and small white flowers blossomed there. My eyes trailed to my arm, where the Rot had begun to heal. I lashed out with a last effort. If I could touch the queen with my arm, perhaps I could infect her with the rotten thing that ailed her forest. But as my arm brushed up against her, nothing happened.

The faerie queen matched my shocked expression. Why didn't the Rot ail her?

A shrill screech pierced the air, and we both stopped and turned as a faerie barreled through the trees towards us. It was sick, touched by the Rot, and it wailed as several more infected faeries followed it.

"They say you were not supposed to know until she was dead," one cried. "Dead and rotten. Festering, *rotting*, dead." The faerie grabbed the queen, its eyes wild with panic. "Kill her so we can all rot." Her words rang out in a hiss as her skin peeled away, black and decayed.

The queen stared down at the rotting faerie, her face contorted in fear. The Rot crawled down the faerie's arms, towards where her fingers clutched the queen's. The queen would get infected and become a rotten twisted thing like the rest of them if I stood here and did nothing.

Sircha's words rang through my head. *You must kill her. She is darkness. She caused this rot.*

Instead, I pounced forward, throwing all of my weight into tackling the queen and ripping her from the sick faerie before the Rot could touch her.

Flowers bloomed all around us, flowers of gold and red and purple. My hand dug into the dirt as life rose up around us, and the sick faeries wailed, unable to come near.

*Wait.*

The ground was sinking. The queen was bound to me, unable to tug away as it began to swallow us. Panic set in as I tried to claw free, but the earth drowned my arms in the dirt, and I closed my eyes as darkness rose to meet us.

# ELEVEN

## Neferit

THE MOMENT WE HIT the ground, I knew something was horribly, horribly wrong. The forest we fell into was dark and damp, the twisting of tree branches overhead menacing and black. Moss hung from their limbs in thick blankets of dark green, and I only had a moment to gather my bearings before I was thrown onto my back and a dagger was pressed to my throat.

The human girl's eyes were alight with fury. I had made the mistake of underestimating her, and now we were in this mess. My heart squeezed at the memory of Rhi rotting away, and I nearly despaired if not for the human girl leaning closer, baring sharpened canines at me.

Her hair was chopped in uneven layers, a mess of reddish-brown that hung around her shoulders in thick curls. I looked into her eyes full of hatred as the dagger pressed more firmly into my neck.

"Why save me if you're just going to kill me now?" I asked, my head swimming with confusion. The human could have easily let that sick faerie contaminate me, but she had tackled me at the last minute. Why?

The girl spoke, but I could not understand her. The human's language was harsh, with quick, rolling words too foreign for me to grasp even though I'd known them once. Her movements were erratic, and if she dug the dagger any deeper, I knew she would draw blood.

*Good*, I thought. *I'll bleed on her. Make her skin boil.*

Staring up at her calmly, I said with a wickedly sweet smile, "I cannot understand you."

The girl hesitated, but it did not quell the fire in her expression. Thrusting my hips upwards, I caught the human by surprise long enough for me to shift my weight. I rolled her over and pinned her to the ground. I dug my knee into the crook of her elbow and wrangled the dagger from her grasp.

Pressing her dagger to her throat, I ignored the sting of the metal from her blade and widened my smile. Her dagger may have been forged by the dragonsteel of the Voiceless Mountains, the only metal known to hurt the fae, but it would be more difficult than that to kill me. The girl did not stop struggling, and I had to offer her some credit. She was prickly. *Like a little thorn.*

That was what I'd call her until I could wrangle her true name from her. Little Thorn.

"Yield," I hissed, pressing the dagger into the girl's neck hard enough that a tiny bead of red ran the length of the blade. "I am stronger, faster, older, and wiser than you. Yield." The last word came out in a growl as I leaned down, my face hovering inches from hers.

Even though the human couldn't understand me, which I knew because I could no longer understand her, her survival instincts must have taken over, and she went limp. The hatred did not leave her eyes however. Her brow furrowed as she waited to see what I would do.

*What should I do?*

Now that I knew she was the girl from the prophecy, I couldn't kill her. Not until I got her to the grove, the heart of the forest, where her blood could purge the Rot from my home.

Pulling the dagger away, I kept my face close to the human's. Spores spewed from my lips, blue-black luminescent dots that hit the girl's eyes. She struggled for a moment, but it wasn't long before her eyes fluttered shut and she fell asleep.

The moment I felt the human's limbs go completely limp, I pushed myself away. Now that she was asleep and all the lines had relaxed on her face, the human looked young and defenseless. She was no child—I was familiar with the human children that had grown up in Elvira, but I had lived hundreds of years, and this pup could not have seen more than thirty winters. I stared down at the purple flowers that had bloomed on my arm. The human must have done that. Had she portaled us here too?

Somewhere off in the distance, a twig snapped, and I remembered that we were no longer in Elvira.

I peered out into the darkness so long my eyes hurt, but I heard no more movement as I growled in frustration and pulled the human into my arms. She was so warm, her heart fluttering like a little bird, but her breath was even, and she did not struggle. I had to resist the urge to lean into her.

A soft giggle sounded somewhere off to my right, but instead of frightening me, it sent anger spreading like a forest fire through my veins. I was not some meek child waiting to be devoured by the dark. I was not a human, bumbling through the brush with no regard for the dangers of the wood. I was Neferíl, queen of the Unseelie Court. I would not bow to whatever evil stalked me.

I moved through the woods, my eyes peeled. The northern part of Elvira had always been home to me. I couldn't remember where I'd come from before, when humanity still etched itself a home in my bones. I couldn't even remember my name before the forest had claimed me, before the blue spirits had tricked me into following them into a circle of mushrooms. The forest had demanded me be their caretaker and queen then, and ever since, I'd felt a connection to each tree, to the roots that rested beneath my feet. I felt love for every goblin, pixie, hag, and fae creature that settled in my court. My court had flourished beneath my rule, but a lot had changed since the Rot had come. A lot had darkened.

But here, these trees felt different, their weight foreign. The revelation did not frighten me though. Pockets into other worlds existed all over Elvira, with our forest weaving into their reality as if it were the natural order of things. Still, it was important I figured out the quickest way back home. I shifted the human girl in my arms, then laid my palm across the trunk of the nearest tree. I felt the steady pulse of its heartbeat beneath my fingers, and I was relieved to find it strong and healthy. It was so unlike many of the trees in my own home as of late.

It began to rain the moment I found a cave. It wasn't a deep cave, by any means, but it would serve as a good resting place out of the elements. I was not gentle setting the human down, and I scoffed in disgust as I studied her. She did not look to be someone capable of creating a rot that would destroy the forest nor as someone capable of curing it, but a faerie knew better than anyone how looks could be deceiving.

A thought came over me, a wicked, dark thought, and I couldn't force the grin from my face as I returned to the forest and found whatever little twigs I could. I returned to the sleeping human and got to work knotting the twigs into her hair. A harmless prank, but one that brought me great amusement as I leaned back on my knees and studied my work. She would panic, thinking she was turning into one of us. And afterwards, it would take her ages to get all the sticks out of her hair.

I let out a laugh as a flash of lightning cascaded through the trees, bathing the forest in a fleeting light as rain began to fall. My stomach twisted as I stood and made my way to the mouth of the cave. I could not see any fae of my court out in the trees. I could not feel their heartbeats, could not sense their soft steps. I was alone with the human. A bitter sigh passed my lips as all of the earlier amusement washed away with the rain, and I ran a hand over my face.

With one last glance over my shoulder, I decided the girl wasn't going to wake for a time, so while I stayed nearby, I went on the hunt for some berries. My ability to turn regular food or drink into faerie food was a magic reserved for Eirwyn and me and one I didn't use lightly. I knew humans were particularly prone to it, gifting them with temporary fae sight and understanding, but the consequences were dire. The more fae food a human ate, the more it twisted them into the very thing they despised. But I had questions, questions only the human could answer: was she the one responsible for sending us somewhere else? This wood was old, that much I sensed from the size of the trees and the way the magic settled in their roots, drenching the earth in a subtle hum. The magic felt different here, too.

It took only a few moments to find a bushel of blackberries near the cave. I barely noticed the rain as I knelt and inspected the berries, noting they were, indeed, blackberries and not something poisonous as I began plucking them from their branches. My thoughts soured as I recalled the rotting faeries that attacked me.

*You were not supposed to know until she was dead.*

Know what? Conflicting emotions echoed through me. It was obvious the girl's life magic was present. I had seen it with my own eyes. Was I led astray, thinking I needed to kill the girl? Why would my seer lie to me? Maybe killing her would free her life magic to heal the forest.

*Or maybe it would murder the one thing that can save us.* A thought made itself present at the forefront of my mind, one I didn't want to entertain. Entertaining it planted a seed of doubt in my mind, a seed I did not wish to water.

My mind turned, unbidden, to Rhi, to the Rot that had flourished through her. The sight of it had struck me with such horror and grief that I did nothing but stare, even as Rhi backed away. It had been a small spot, a tiny speck of black against the back of her hand, but I knew Rhi's death was an eventuality if I did nothing to save her. That memory alone was enough to reinforce my desire to kill the human, but I knew I needed to wait.

*Her blood must fertilize the ground of my home.*

I turned back towards the berries. My magic came to me easily. Just a passing thought as I manifested my desire to fill the berries with faerie magic. A small light drenched my fingers and darted into the blackberries before fading. A human wouldn't be able to tell the difference between these blackberries and non-magical ones, and I rose to my feet with them in grim satisfaction.

I still needed to kill the girl. It was the only lead I had to cure the Rot. I needed some information from her first, though. I couldn't hope to harm her while we weren't in Elvira. What if killing her here did nothing for my home? No, I needed to figure out if she was the one who had transported us here so we could return to Elvira, and I could end this once and for all.

A low clicking sounded in the tree line as I made my way back to the cave, and my head jerked up, cocked towards the noise. I tucked myself beneath my glamour, smooth, dark skin settling over my bark-like features as moth wings unfurled from my back. They were beautiful—soft as velvet and a dark slate grey with black circles near my spine. I quickly set the berries down by where the human slept and then padded back towards the mouth of the cave.

With a quick flap of my wings, I shot out of the cave and up into the air, pushing through the top of the forest and into the night sky. The rain obscured my vision just enough that I couldn't see too far off, only that I was certain I did not recognize what forest we'd been tossed into.

The clicking sounded again, followed by a low, guttural moan. Off in the distance, a blanket of treetops rustled. Something moved through the treeline, and it was coming straight towards me.

Blinking water out of my eyes, I descended, weaving through the tree branches to reach the ground. Tucking my wings against my back, I sensed the dark presence of something nearby. Baring my teeth, I moved slowly backwards towards the cave.

But I never reached it as the thing came crashing through the trees.

# TWELVE

## *Róis*

I WOKE SLOWLY, MY brain a mess of fog that I was forced to swim through. I couldn't even groan, my energy focused on reorienting itself. Where am I? My heart pounded in my chest, but I did not know why I was afraid. Only that the darkness I'd woken to seemed to whisper down to me, begging me to get up.

*Get up. Get up. Getupgetupgetupgetup—*

A strangled sob left my lips as I ripped my eyes open and forced my limbs to move. It was a terrifying notion, wondering if I was truly conscious now or if it was merely another trick. I used to have nightmares when I was a child where I would wake, unable to move. The fear had paralyzed me so fiercely I'd wanted to cry out, only to find that I couldn't. My mind had begged me to simply move as luminescent eyes had stared at me through my bedroom window, its clawed fingers pressed against the glass. The eventual release had always been bittersweet, and my chest heaved now as I willed my eyes to adjust to the dark. My fingers pressed against the cold stone. I was in a cave, and, to my knowledge, I was alone.

A rock bit into my palm as I scrambled backwards, away from the mouth of the cave. The darkness would not be much of a shelter should the fae come looking, but as it blanketed me, I felt a sense of relief. Wrapping my arms around my legs, I tucked myself into a ball, willing away the cold. The place we'd fallen into was strange. It had been early spring back home, but here? I shivered against the cold that wafted from the mouth of the cave.

A twig snapped, and my head shot up as fear blossomed across my chest. Perhaps I should run, meet whatever was at the mouth of the cave, and fight. At least whatever taunted me then would not corner me like an animal. My limbs were unwilling to move, though, and I stayed rooted in place as something shot into the cave, quicker than my eyes could follow. It was on me before I could scream, and only when a hand clamped down over my mouth did I notice that it was the queen. The revelation did not comfort me.

"Shhh. *Ashtala hukta.*" The queen's warning lodged my scream in my throat, trapping it in silence. I still could not understand her, but the tone of her voice was clear enough to heed her warning.

She was surprisingly warm as she pushed me further into the cave, pressing me against the wall. The cold stone bit at my back, but I leaned as far into it as I could, my hand searching for a loose rock with which to hit the queen. *She is dangerous. She will kill me the moment she has the chance.*

A smaller, darker question formed unbidden. *If she wanted to kill me, why is she protecting me?*

I swallowed that question and killed it before it could burrow. Questions like that would tear down my defenses and get me killed.

Off in the distance, a high-pitched screech shattered through the deceitful calm. I tensed against the queen as the tree line rustled as if someone was running through the branches. I willed away my fear. Fear would not help me here.

Something stepped up to the entrance of the cave. A low clicking echoed in the hollow of the creature's throat. I couldn't see its features in the darkness, but I could tell it was grotesque and tall based on its outline. A wet cough echoed over stone, and I closed my eyes as the creature's soft footsteps drew closer, the clicking of its tongue against teeth grating against my courage.

The queen breathed deeply against the cusp of my ear as the creature screamed and lunged. Then I was alone again as the queen left my side. The darkness hid their fight from me, but I still heard it as the queen made contact with whatever was hunting us. Its cry of surprise and rage echoed through the cave as she slammed it into the wall.

I sank low to the ground as the scuffle continued, my hands moving against the cool stone of the cave's wall. I couldn't find a loose rock and I didn't have my dagger—the queen did, and my fear returned as a lump in my throat as I edged towards the mouth of the cave. If the queen didn't silence whatever she was fighting quickly, I knew more would come.

My finger passed over something slick against the wall, and I blanched away from it, narrowly avoiding the queen and the creature as they slammed into the wall next to me. The sounds that echoed through the cave sent shivers down my spine and then the quiet reached up to meet me all at once.

"Is it dead?" I asked, my heart pounding as I failed to see for myself in the dark.

The queen's eyes reflected in the black. She said something I didn't understand, but her voice was tinged with arrogance and a sarcastic sweetness as she tilted her head and stared at me, so I assumed that was a yes. The predatory look in her gaze, however, reminded me I was not safe just because the creature was dead. The queen craved the taste of my blood just as much.

Kneeling next to where I had been sleeping, she retrieved something, but it was too dark to see until she tossed them at my feet. Without taking my eyes off her, I lowered myself to the floor and curled my hand around whatever it was that landed there. It was soft, and as I drew it close to my face, I realized what it was: a blackberry.

The urge to throw it away washed over me, and I raised my hand to do so, only to hesitate. Was it more faerie food, and if so, how much more would I have to eat to be barred from leaving the forest? I knew faerie food was dangerous; eventually the magic would tangle into the very essence of your soul, and you could never leave Elvira. Still, I knew I wouldn't make it out of wherever we'd ended up alive if I couldn't understand her.

I popped the blackberry in my mouth, and the magic was instantaneous. It shuddered through me, sinking into my bones, bringing color into the night. I saw as clearly as I would have if it were day, and the heartbeat of this forest was strange. We weren't in Elvira anymore. I wasn't certain of it until now.

"Why didn't you let it kill me? You were going to kill me anyway." They were questions I didn't get an answer to as her silence bred a heavy weight in the air. The darkness seemed to curl in around us, and I craved the touch and safety of dawn. How long would it be before it came? I didn't know, and my fingers reached up to touch my hair. Fear struck me. Was I already falling prey to change? Did the faerie food work so quickly? As I felt about my hair, I was relieved to find that wasn't the case; something or some*one* had woven my hair around some twigs.

"Did you do this to my hair?" The trickery and mischievous nature of the fae were not lost on me, but anger still overcame me regardless.

Ignoring my anger, she drew closer. She was in her glamoured form, the dark curl of her hair falling around her face in coils. Silver and blue beads still decorated her braids, and she drew so close I could see the dusting of freckles that crossed her cheeks.

My lips peeled back over snarled teeth as I backed away, my palms scraping against the floor of the cave. Pain smarted my left palm where part of the ground dug into my skin, but I ignored it as the queen moved forward with me, denying me space.

"I can taste your fear, little thorn."

My rage was swift, overpowering my fear. I lunged up and forward. My fingers edged the hilt of my dagger at the queen's hip before I was on my back, once more pinned beneath the Queen of Dusk. Her face decayed into the woodland realm she commanded as her glamour bled away.

"Such spirit. Humans can be so full of it, their blood singing songs of their tales. It always tastes better when we break you, when the spirit is gifted to us and our realm," the queen whispered, drawing close. I knew she said these things just to scare me, but they really did as I wiggled beneath her grasp.

I had known fear intimately since I'd been a child, since the fae had first come out of the forest. It had sat with me, festered within me, and I had learned to wield it. Fine-tune it into a weapon. Let it light a fire in my belly and help me fight when I need it.

I growled, breaking a hand free, and raked my fingers across the queen's face before she could slam it to the floor. The queen hissed, much to my satisfaction, and her blood dripped onto my cheek. It sizzled and burned as it met my skin as if it were acid, but I refused to cry out. Tears smarted the corners of my eyes, and even though the pain was excruciating, I thrust my hips to buck her off.

The queen was strong, though, deceptively so. She held me down with ease as the cuts on her face closed. "Shhh, little thorn. Your struggles will only tire you out, and we cannot stay here."

"Why not just kill me?" I breathed, my chest heaving. I was defenseless; it welled in my chest, a betrayal I had fought hard to quell long ago. I knew humans were vastly weaker than the fae—one could only outwit them with trickery or relentless nature. My mind went back to our fight when her sword had met my knife, and I realized that the equal footing I'd thought we'd been on during that had been nothing more than her toying with me. Since then, the queen had proven time and time again that I had no idea how to deal with the fair folk. It suddenly made sense why most, even those among the *fiagaila*, rarely made it out of the forest.

"Because –" She hesitated as if she didn't quite know the answer herself. As soon as she glanced away in thought, I threw all my weight against her. She toppled to the side, and I managed to wrangle my blade from her hip. I lashed out with it in quick succession, making two shallow cuts along the queen's arm. The howl that escaped her lips was high-pitched and grated against my ear drums. My dagger stuck out again towards her neck, but she was ready this time, dodging with ease and pushing me through the mouth of the cave.

I landed on the ground hard, the air leaving my lungs as she pried my dagger from my hands. Her breath was heavy in my ear, her body warm against my back, and a breathless laughter left her lips.

"It is faerie law that I owe you a life debt, human. You saved my life, so I shall save yours by taking you to where you wish to go. You seek the Sacred Grove? You think it can save us all? Fine. I promise no harm from me shall come to you until we step foot inside the Forest's Father's domain."

Her words wove magic into the back of my head, and the hair on my nape rose. I knew she spoke the truth; faeries couldn't lie, and my heart sang at the implications. If I could get to the Sacred Grove, I could find a way to save Sister, to save my people.

So I would go to the Forest Father. And after he healed the forest, I would kill the queen. Even if I didn't return, I owed my people the chance to try.

"What say you, human?" she asked, pressing my face into the soft dirt. It had stopped raining. I could feel and hear the slow patter of the trees, their heartbeats thundering in my ears. The magic here was strong, or perhaps it was because of the food the queen had given me, but I felt like I was living alongside nature here, like I was one with the wind and the small creatures hiding in the bushes.

"You swear it?" I asked her.

The queen went so still I would have thought she'd gone had I not felt her pressing into my back. "I do." And then she liberated me, and I shuffled away, pressing my back against the corner of the cave.

"Stay the fuck away from me," I warned, my voice ringing out through the cave.

The queen sighed and pushed my dagger over to me. I quickly grabbed it and held it protectively against my chest. Its presence in my hand comforted me, and I gripped it tightly as the queen held a hand up.

"First, we need to figure out where you have sent us, little thorn."

I bared my teeth at her accusation. "I do not know what you are talking about." Everything had happened too quickly for me to follow.

The queen took a step forward, her smile radiant. "Oh? Well, we are not in Elvira anymore, that I am certain. It is not uncommon for Elvira to bleed into other worlds, hence our ability to venture into your villages, but we were not near any mushroom rings nor did we fall through any tree holes. So go on. However, you got us here, take us back."

"I do not know how," I said uncertainly. "I thought that was fae magic." I eyed her suspiciously, refusing to cower as she drew close. She ignored the wound on her arm despite it not healing, and I watched it with small satisfaction. Iron against a faerie always dealt slow-to-heal wounds.

All amusement faded from her face, replaced with a troubled expression. "Unfortunate." She clicked her tongue against the roof of her mouth, and her hand darted out towards my head to tug out a twig she'd stuck there. *Don't flinch.* Her words swore an oath; she could not harm me until we were at the Grove.

"Only druids have the ability to walk between worlds; they carry the magic in their blood to forge portals." She sneered, her teeth blinding against her dark lips. "Your human world has several of these portals. They tend to look like circles of stones, mushrooms, or flowers."

I shook my head. "No druids for a very long time. Their magic is all but lost." My back was pressed against the cave, and I raised my dagger threateningly even though I knew I could not lash out at her. "Keep away from me."

"Such a prickly little thing," she cooed, ignoring my threats. "If you don't find a way to return us home, I will use your dagger to bleed you slowly the moment our oath is fulfilled." Her voice turned low and seductive, her eyes lighting with promise. "It is your blood that is valuable, not you, little thorn." Her gaze burned to liquid obsidian. "Return. Us. Home."

Before I could respond, a low voice called out to us through the trees, "You two are making entirely too much noise. You're going to bring the wrath of the forest down upon us if you don't quiet down."

The queen paused, and both of us turned to meet the massive gaze of a goblin.

# THIRTEEN

## *Neferil*

**M**Y ARM ACHED, THE wound the human had inflicted on me refusing to heal. The metal in her dagger was poisonous to the fae and sang through my skin like butter. It would take days for the wound to heal.

The goblin that stood before us had not stopped twitching since the moment he'd intervened. Brutal little creatures, the goblins back home were mischievous, even for my court. They held their own politics, woven with my own demands, and often kept to themselves. They thrived on patrolling the forest's edge and snatching humans that strayed too close.

"Come, come," the goblin said, waving his hand to follow him back into the cave. He was short, shorter than the goblins I was used to, his skin was a very pale green, and his massive ears bounced atop his head as he hurried into the mouth of the cave. "Quickly now! Before the sun comes up!"

The human's jaw was clenched, and she still eyed me wearily, her stance tense. "Go on," she demanded, earning a glare from me. Who was she to command me?

I stared at her for a moment before I followed the goblin deeper into the cave. My shoulders tensed as I sensed the human's dagger behind me, but I did not turn, refusing to give the girl any sort of satisfaction as she followed us.

"What is your name, goblin?"

The goblin sat on the ground and stared at me with a confused look. "Ain't no goblin. Don't know what that is. 'M a myrlír, a wee spore from the forest that serves under our caretaker. Name's Olbi."

"Your caretaker?"

Olbi nodded. "I can take you to him when night lifts."

"Who is he?"

Olbi glared up at me. "You ask too many questions. I quite prefer th' human's approach. Hasn't said a word to me since we met."

I held my hands up. "Apologies. I'm going to go and look for something for my arm." It throbbed painfully, and I retreated back outside to find some moss to slather over it. I wasn't certain what was safe in this world and what wasn't, but the simple moss that littered the ground should be safe enough.

I leaned down, pulled some away from a tree, and pressed it against my wound. The relief was immediate, and I sighed, sagging against the trunk. Now that I knew the human was the one I needed to kill, I was going to have to be careful. I would protect her until we got to the Eldertree and then I would kill her there.

Anything for my home.

After a moment of composing myself, I washed away any ire I had held before and planted a soft smile on my lips. The Rot could be gone soon.

*Keep her safe until you need her, Nef.*

Olbi and the human were talking among themselves when I returned, and a fire had been built, but Olbi's laughter died off the moment I stepped foot into the cave.

"Is that wise?" I asked, gesturing to the flames.

"Will keep the dark at bay, keep us safe," Olbi said.

"If we're going to be traveling together, I must know your name," I said to the human, ignoring the way she scowled at me. "Unless you'd like for me to continue calling you little thorn?" I batted my eyes at her teasingly, and she shook her head. She'd taken all the twigs out of her hair while I'd been gone, but her curls were still a mess.

"Róis."

"Row-sh." I tested the name on my tongue; the strange way she spoke made it difficult to pronounce. Still, I thought it to myself until I could speak it, knowing she'd given it freely because human names did not hold the same weight faerie ones did.

"What about you?"

I raised my head and offered a curling grin. "Your Majesty will do."

Róis glared, and I held my hands up. "Fine, fine. Neferíl is my name." Not my true name, not one the little thorn could use to control and deceive me with, but one I'd chosen after I'd lost the memory of my human one. One I had grown to love.

"Well, Róis, I promise to uphold my end of the oath should no other harm come to me. If that dagger so much as pricks my skin, all promises are broken," I said.

Róis said nothing for some time and then nodded. "Deal." The magic shuddered through the cave, fortifying the oath, and I sat down near them, my arms cradling my legs as satisfaction sang through me. I'd secured my safety until I could get the human to the Grove, where I'd bleed her to save the forest. Now...we just needed to get back to Elvira.

"This caretaker. Can you tell us more about him?" I asked Olbi with a kinder tone. Perhaps this caretaker was the answer to our return home.

"This forest is wicked and dark," Olbi said, quivering. "It has old magic and because of it, there are wicked and dark things that watch from the shadows. The Caretaker has built a safe haven from the darkness, so we go to him as soon as light touches the trees."

Róis stared out into the darkness, the flames of the fire reflecting off her face. "I filled Olbi in on what happened to us. He said his caretaker might be able to tell us how that happened."

I nodded. It was becoming clear that this 'caretaker' was going to be the answer to all our problems. A part of me was relieved at the prospect of being able to go back so soon. Rhi's fear-stricken face haunted my mind, and I couldn't bear it if the Rot had taken her. My stomach twisted at the thought, so I turned my mind to the prophecy instead and the girl who sat beside me.

She didn't look like someone who was able to cause or cure a plague. She barely looked old enough to wield a blade, even though she did so with impressive skill.

"He's not from this realm either," Olbi admitted. "I do not know from where he hails, but he walks the roots between worlds. He decided that he wished to heal this forest from its wounds. He's been trying for some cycles now."

"What wounds this place?"

"Old hurts," Olbi whispered as if the world could hear him. "The creatures of this forest remember when gods walked here. There was a great war, and now the gods are all gone, slumbering or dead beneath the earth. I am afraid..." He paused, his voice drawing even lower. "I am afraid my caretaker fights a lost cause. The wounds are too deep."

It made me glad for our troubles, for they were small and easily cured. Meddling gods? Ancient wounds? I feared our forest's plague, but I was determined we would find a cure. The troubles of this world sounded way worse.

Róis said nothing, her chin resting against her knees, and after a time, the warmth of the fire lulled me to sleep.

I woke with a pounding heart as I rolled to my feet. No danger was present as Róis sheathed her dagger to her hip, and she eyed me wearily, keeping her distance as Olbi put out the fire and urged us into the forest. Dawn began to break among the trees, and the world woke. Wherever we were was beautiful, a beauty rivaling that of Elvira's.

"Come. Quickly, quickly," Olbi urged, taking off through the trees. It did not speak of the dangers he'd spoken of the night before, but I knew better than to doubt the deceit of a forest. Anything could be lingering around the trunks of the trees whose size matched some of those in Elvira.

At one point, I glanced over at Róis to find her dark eyes trained on me. Her fingers rested against the hilt of her dagger, but they did so loosely, almost lazily as we walked, and I raised a brow as if begging her to do something.

She did no such thing, and as we walked with Olbi, the darkness seemed to shirk further away.

It was midday before Olbi stopped. Róis had asked him a question, a question I could not understand, which meant the food I'd graced her with had worn off. Olbi responded to her in kind. I asked what she'd said to him in our tongue, but he didn't care to explain.

Olbi led us towards a collection of trees that were tightly woven in a circular pattern. The trunks were larger than the ones surrounding them, and their branches were woven in a protective barrier. Olbi knocked his tiny fist against one of the trunks in an erratic pattern.

What was the goblin doing? Drawing on the spirit of the tree for protection? I did not sense any danger.

Róis stood several feet away, her eyes darting about as if she were seeking out the best way to bolt or perhaps searching for danger too.

"Oh, that usually works," Olbi said, his contemplative tone causing my gaze to tear away from Róis. His hand was raised to scratch behind one of his ears and then he attempted again, his fist a blur as it knocked on the trunk in the same pattern as before. "Nasty, tricky Caretaker..."

It was as if the trees heard him. Their soft groans but a whisper in the wind, two of them moved aside in a way that granted the three of us passage. They parted to reveal a large grove, a haven from the evil that soaked the air at my back. The meadow was thick with wildflowers, and a family of otters sunbathed near a trickling creek that bumbled over the rocks. Light trickled through the trees, providing a peaceful warmth to caress me.

It felt like Eirwyn's domain. The Seelie King's court in the south was always bright and vibrant. It oft gave way to his deception, for he was as cruel as he was kind, as merciless as he was hospitable. The similarities made my skin crawl.

"Okay, inside now," Olbi urged, reaching up to tug my hand. I flinched away as my mind threatened to transport me back to when I had been small, a child reaching for the hands of those I'd thought would protect me. Olbi lowered his hand as I tucked those memories away and strode forward.

A young stranger approached, sheathed in a green shawl, with a deer skull hiding his features. White-blond hair cascaded down his shoulders, and he carried a long walking staff that forged flowers from the ground each time it hit the grass. There was no indication of his age; many of the fair folk were that way in nature. They aged as the forest did: timeless should no disease or deadly circumstances come to pass.

I also knew immediately that he was a druid.

"Creatures not of our lands step forth with anger and pain festering in their hearts. What ails them, I wonder?"

The druid's voice was as stern as it was gentle, a soft lilt that carried softly through the wind.

"We know not how we stumbled into your realm, only that we have dire need to return," I said, my heart squeezing painfully at the reminder of what we'd left behind. Rhi's shocked expression as the Rot had infected her arm washed over my memory anew, and my fingers clenched into fists as they shook at my sides. I could not lose my general to this Rot. I wouldn't.

Soft laughter etched the tree lines, alongside lilts of whispering voices that quieted when I turned to look. This realm was strange; my eyes grew heavy, like I was the human entering the fae domain for the first time.

"Where is Caretaker?" Olbi asked.

I turned back to the stranger. This wasn't the man we sought?

The stranger brought his hand to his chest. "All in due time, Olbi. Go see if they're okay," he said, gesturing to the otters.

Olbi ambled over, then ran his hands through their fur. They seemed to love him, chattering softly as they hopped on him. One managed to climb up his back, then curled its lanky body across his shoulders.

"You wish to return?" The druid reached up and pulled the skull mask off his head. His youthful features were as I'd expected: he *did* look like an elf from the Seelie Court. Eirwyn's court was ripe with beauty, but it was a deception, just as the Unseelie's glamour was a deception.

The druid held out a kind hand, but I skirted away, eyeing him warily. Much of the Seelie Court saw my people as monsters, too close to the nature they dwelt in. They scoffed and scorned us, and I had tucked my people and my kingdom as far away from the southern forests as I could because of it. My people would not suffer their judgment just because our true natures were monstrous by appearance.

The druid did not lower his hand, instead using it to brush past me to study Róis. Her guard did not lower either; she took a step back as the druid came forward.

"The wood sang of your arrival, but there is a sickness in these lands. It has festered here since its birth and does not take well to strangers." He held his palm up, maintaining a comfortable distance from the both of us and glanced back at me. "I feel the hatred rolling off both of you. You mean this one harm."

"We have an oath in place to prevent that. We must return home."

"Patience. The Caretaker can get you where you need to go, but you'll have to place a bit of trust in me now," the druid said, gesturing to several stumps where we could sit.

Róis stayed standing, her dagger poised as she watched me like a wolf might watch her prey.

"Listen to the druid," Olbi said. "He knows what he's talking about." One of the otters offered Olbi a rock, and I turned back to study the druid.

For some reason, I trusted Olbi. He did not seem the kind to lie and deceive, not like the goblins back home, so unlike Róis, I brushed my dress aside and sat gracefully on one of the stumps. An easy-going smile crossed the druid's face.

"My name is Elahir. I have lived in these woods my entire life. You are the second to have stumbled upon my domain, to have been able to walk the pathways through the stars."

Róis watched him with simple curiosity for a moment before speaking to him in her tongue. Her voice was quiet and soft, but I could taste her anger as it trickled through the air, thick as smoke.

"You tumbled through a tear, I'd imagine," Elahir said to her, prompting my eyebrows to rise in question. A tear? I had heard of doors being made through toadstools and rock formations but never tears. It seemed...reckless.

"How can we both understand you but not each other?" I interrupted.

"The magic here is strong," Elahir said, reaching out to offer an approaching bird a perch on his finger. It was a little bluebird; its small head cocked to the side as it chirped at Elahir. He listened as if he understood, and after a moment, the bird took off.

I watched it go. The quiet chatter of birds surrounded them, and Elahir stilled as Olbi strolled over, an otter pup asleep in his arms.

The trees went silent, and Elahir tilted his head. The wind stilled, no longer caressing the tall branches. Even the birds no longer sang their songs.

"We must move. Quickly."

As he spoke, an encroaching darkness settled across the tree line.

# FOURTEEN
## *Neferil*

E LAHIR USHERED US FURTHER into the grove, but his expression was calm, giving no indication of whether we were in any sort of danger. The rest of the grove did not share his calm. The family of otters chattered anxiously. The pup in Olbi's arms wiggled to the ground to return to its family. Birds fled their homes.

"Listen very carefully," Elahir said, watching the shadow slink across the trees as if a great storm approached. "There is a witch that lives nearby. Her coven is all but gone—only she remains. Kyrie is the druid you are looking. He is the one who can help you. He went to kill the witch, but he has not returned for a moon's cycle. We must hope for his survival."

Olbi's ears wobbled, his distress a thickness that soaked the air.

"This is the Caretaker?" I asked, turning to Olbi.

As his shoulders shook, he nodded.

I cursed.

I didn't want to search for the druid. I didn't want to spend another moment in these cursed woods. Instead, I found myself nodding, looking at Elahir as he turned towards the creeping shadow.

"Go, go now. Olbi knows the way." He raised his hand as the shadow yawned, a gaping maw of darkness that stretched out before him. "Go while I can hold back this darkness."

So we ran. We ran, and we did not look back, following Olbi as he seemed to follow a trail I could not see. We ran until the grove was no longer behind us, until our lungs screamed and even Róis pressed her hand against one of the trees, gasping for air. I did not know what it was about that shadow that had us so scared, but my heart still pattered against my chest as if I would never feel safe again. The forest was dim and dark, and Olbi was staring down at something on the ground.

"What is it?" I asked, drawing close. It was a thick yellow sap-like substance, almost akin to the blood of my court. It coated the grass, drawing bugs to it from all around, and it seemed to lead deeper into the forest.

"Blood," Olbi whispered, horrified. "Think it be Care-taker's blood. Think I can follow th' trail."

Despite my best attempts not to, my gaze strayed over to Róis. The sun was descending below the trees, casting brilliant red through her hair, and a contemplative expression crossed her face as she knelt near the blood, studying it intently. It was strange how youthful the human looked when her face was free of rage.

I didn't remember taking a step towards her. *Like a moth to a flame.*

Róis' gaze shot up, and her body flinched away instinctively. Her actions sang echoes of my own fears, long since buried by time.

I gestured to the blood, my brow furrowed in a questioning gaze. *What have you discovered?* my expression asked.

Seeming to understand me, she pointed a few feet ahead, where the blood thickened, widening into arcs. Whoever it was had been dragged, and they had struggled more fiercely there. As I approached, I noticed something–a collection of twigs.

Olbi inhaled sharply beside me. "Witch trinkets. Nasty, nasty witch trinkets."

No, not just a collection of twigs. They'd been formed into various shapes and designs that I did not recognize, tied together by twine. When I reached out to touch one, a high-pitched exhale shot through the air–a breath of magic. It licked the edges of my fingers, and they hurt as if someone had poked them with a pine needle. I drew back, my gaze sliding over to Olbi.

The goblin muttered to himself, rocking on his feet as he shook his head, his ears bouncing. The forest seemed at a loss of what to do, kicking up wind before falling still.

"Olbi, does this lead to the witch?"

Róis stood as Olbi nodded, his eyes wide with fear. "The witches of this wood are nasty, vile. They will try to trick us, they will." With a trembling finger, he pointed along a trail of blood, where more of the twig shapes dotted the ground. A soft whisper etched the air as the sky darkened, and the world seemed to elongate, making the trail appear longer than it actually was. My stomach twisted anxiously, but I squared my shoulders and pointed, my voice laced with command and as much courage as I could muster.

"Lead the way then."

The trail through the forest was not easy. The air grew thick as I pushed away branches that seemed to want to claw at my skin. Once, Róis' foot caught on a gnarled root. A flicker of compulsion within me beckoned me to reach out, to catch her from falling, but I refrained. Blood bloomed over her scraped knees and palms as she pulled herself back up. The glare she shot my way when she caught me staring sang a song of both guilt and satisfaction inside me.

We had been walking for days—or perhaps only minutes—but it felt agonizingly long, and I was ready to despair.

"No, no, no. Not that way," Olbi kept muttering to himself, pushing his ears back as he led us through the forest. The way he moved and twitched was most unsettling, but I followed him regardless, knowing he was our only hope.

This forest was so strange. It sank into my skin, softly urging me to stop and rest. It was so subtle it had taken me a while to discern it was there, but once I took notice of it, there was a startling clarity about it, and I couldn't shake it away any longer. A low hum stitched itself into the tree line, and I pressed my palm to my forehead as if that would take it away. I was a creature of nature; this *should not* be happening.

"Forest very old," Olbi said, glancing back at me. He chirped several high-pitched noises in quick succession and reached out to knock lovingly on the trunk of a nearby tree. "Magic very ancient here. Probably the oldest in the world. It will do funny things to ya if you don't stay alert."

The human, surprisingly, did not seem affected by it; her gaze was hard and focused as she watched the tree line in front of us. Nighttime had made demons in the wood where there were none, and I forced my chin high, as I always had. This wasn't the first time I'd been forced into old forests with old spirits bent on breaking my spirit.

"This druid—he knows how to walk between worlds?" I asked.

Olbi shrugged. "Not sure. If anyone knows how, would be him." I resisted the urge to jump as Olbi gasped gleefully while scampering off to the left and disappearing into the brush. He returned almost immediately, a shiny red apple in his hand.

"Olbi *looooooves* apples. Sweet an' succulent, they are!" He shuddered, turning the apple over in his grasp as he wove through the trees. "Olbi would stick someone straight through for an apple."

I locked eyes with Róis and then I laughed. It was the first time I had laughed, truly so, in a long time, but I couldn't help it. The idea of Olbi murdering someone for an apple was too comical. I laughed until I couldn't breathe, but then something shifted in the tree line as if a shadow had stepped behind a trunk and disappeared.

We all went silent. Olbi's teeth grazed the edge of the apple as he slowly pulled away and stared up at the trees, his large ears quivering.

"Oh no," he squeaked just as the sky darkened and the softest of sighs curled against the gentle wind. "She's here."

"Where—" My words died on my tongue as an old woman in rags stepped out from behind a tree. She stood, hooded and cloaked, her smile thick with Rot. It blackened her teeth and mottled the skin around her lips.

"Oh dear. It seems you've lost your way," she rasped, reaching a hand out. "Let dear old Graetha lead you home." She stepped forward, her bare feet sinking into the moss that blanketed the ground.

"Run," I hissed, turning on my heel and taking off through the forest. Olbi had already disappeared into a puff of spores; the apple he'd been eating had fallen against the moss and had rolled several feet away.

I cursed as I remembered my need to keep Róis safe. Turning around, I darted back towards where I'd left her. I found her way before I reached our earlier spot. Despite being a human, she was exceptionally light and quick on her feet, and I joined her as we danced around trees and gnarled roots. The forest grew darker still as Róis tripped over a vine that had snagged her foot.

I cursed and turned back as she curled in on herself and rolled, slipping into a brush of leaves. Before she could react, I was on top of her, one hand lashing out to curl over her mouth while the other grabbed her wrist before she could lash out with her dagger.

"Shhh," I uttered, pressing myself against the warmth of her body as the forest grew still. Fear urged adrenaline through my body as Róis went limp beneath me, her wrist no longer fighting my grasp. I was acutely aware of her shifting weight, and a low electrifying heat coursed through my body. A twig snapped, and I lowered my head to breathe silently in Róis' ear, compelling my magic to me. The forest here did not like my beckoning call, but twigs and vines enveloped the both of us, trapping us against one another. It wasn't ideal, I sensed Róis' tension, but I had to hope my magic was strong enough to hide us from the witch.

The thunderous heartbeat of the forest swelled around us, a deep methodical beating that rumbled against my chest. It nearly drowned out the witch's heartbeat, a small buzzing in a sea of bees. As she drew near, however, the buzzing grew louder, a weak pulse that grated against my throat as I curled against Róis. I had never been more afraid than I was in this moment. Despite our oath, Róis could lash out and strike me down if she so wished, but fleeing would only grant the witch her prey.

Minutes passed like days as the witch drew closer and closer and closer. Her laughter cradled the trees above, and I closed my eyes and focused on the quick and shallow breathing of the human below me.

We stayed this way until the witch's heartbeat faded into the forest, and there was nothing left to hear but the slow thrum of the wood. Olbi hadn't reappeared, and it was Róis who shifted first. I pulled away, the vines sinking back into the earth, to see her gaze burning into mine. I realized just how close we still were.

Peeling my hand away from her mouth, I rolled off her and gracefully rose to my feet. Brightly colored leaves clung to my braids and dress as I peered out into the forest, but it appeared as if the witch had disappeared. The air was thick with trepidation, and I looked behind me as Róis crawled out of the bush, her dagger gleaming in her hand.

Those strange twig formations hung from the trees, shaking in the wind. Olbi reappeared suddenly in a puff of spore-like magic, his ears shaking.

"Hate them, hate the nasty, trickster witches. Must find her home, must find the Caretaker."

Laughter trickled out through the trees, loud and all-encompassing. I could not tell where it was coming from as it surrounded us, and then the witch reappeared behind Róis with a wide smile.

*How*? My anger flourished at having been tricked. I should have been able to sense her heartbeat, but even now, even with her standing right in front of me, there was nothing. It was as if she were dead.

Róis whirled around, her teeth bared in a wordless snarl. Her dagger glinted as it lashed out at the witch, but the old woman was quick on her feet, dodging out of the way and reaching out to clasp Róis' wrist.

Fear blossomed from Róis, secreting in the darkness. It was over me like fog as the witch laughed again, a dark laughter that filled the forest. "Foolish little fawns. It is a very bad idea to anger old Graetha."

Róis tugged her arm away with reckless abandon, spewing insults into the air in her foreign language. Birds took flight from the nearby tree, startled. The witch did not let go, her fingers gripping Róis' wrist with an iron grasp. She pried the human's dagger out of her grasp.

"How delightful," the witch said, her eyes lit with glee. "Such spirit, this one. It will be so fun to break her, just as I did the druid."

"Let her go," I said, my voice shaking. If the witch did anything to Róis, my forest would die. I wasn't scared of much, the world at my fingertips, but the idea of watching my forest rot away without being able to do anything about it filled me with a fear that took my breath away. It had become my home when my old one had scorned me. I could not abandon it to its fate. "Róis, be still."

"Oh, ho-ho," the witch mused, laughter dancing on her tongue. "Dance, dance through the trees, quiver and trot; you all are going to fester and rot." The last word was spoken with malice as she twirled Róis' dagger around and sliced it across the girl's stomach. The wound seemed shallow, but her blood hit the air with a subtle sharpness. My nose flared in response as Róis' expression fell to horror.

Olbi cooed in distress as the witch flicked her hand and dragged a finger across Róis' wound. She lifted her hand and pressed the blood to her lips. The witch shuddered in ecstasy, then snapped her fingers. Róis' eyes fluttered as she went limp and was caught by the witch. I moved forward in rage, but the witch's hood shifted as she raised her chin in warning.

"Not another step, dearies. I'll gut her like a pig."

My glamour bled away as my fear sank into my skin—a betrayal. I could not let the witch take her; I did not doubt the witch's threats. She had no reason to keep Róis alive. Not like I did.

"Take us both," I said.

The witch cocked her head to the side unnaturally fast. She flung Róis over her shoulder as she strode forward. "What's that, dear? Now we want ol' Graetha's hospitality?" She clicked her tongue against the roof of her mouth and shook her head, wagging her finger. "I think not. There's something rotten already weeping inside of you. You would not be all that good to eat."

Her insult cut deep, and I scowled, my heart in my throat as Graetha cackled and snapped her fingers. She moved quickly, too quickly even for my fae eyes to follow, and then she was gone.

Olbi muttered and clung to his ears as I sank to the ground, my fingers digging into the earth. With the witch's disappearance, the world grew lighter once more, the trees shifting in the wind bringing a sense of calm. I knew it was all a lie.

I was all but calm.

"Olbi," I said, staring out at the forest, "take me to her."

# FIFTEEN

## *Róis*

"**W**AKE UP."

I hummed, my eyes shut, my face pressed against the softness of some grass. A gentle buzzing lulled me away from consciousness as I curled my fingers into the dirt, and I ignored the soft prodding of someone's fingers against my back.

"Just a little longer," I groaned, attempting to push them away. "Father, please." I swatted behind me, my fingers sailing through the air. When no response was given,

I cracked open an eye. Rays of sunlight peeked into the grove I was napping in, with soft wind singing through the leaves above. Whoever had touched my back was no longer there, and I sat up suddenly and noticed what surrounded me.

I was sitting in the middle of a group of red and white toadstools. Rings of mushrooms were oft entrances to the fae realm and to be avoided at all cost. I swallowed thickly as the mushrooms hummed a soft, tempting noise that threatened to lull me back to sleep. I fought the heaviness with everything I had, but it was almost not enough.

A stranger appeared before me. He was strange, as Elahir had been—draped in a moss cloak, his face hidden behind the mask of a giant elk skull. In his hands was a gnarled wooden staff. He stared at me as I fought against sleep, the dark brown of his hair gleaming in an ethereal glow against the sunlight.

"Wake up." Somehow, I knew the command came from him even though it seemed as if the words sank into my brain like I'd thought them myself. The grass was soft beneath my fingers, and I sighed. I wanted to be frightened by the stranger in front of me, but I wasn't. His presence was oddly comforting, and I curled into myself, watching him through eyes half-closed.

*How did I get here?* I thought, but no answer came, and I yawned, letting sleep take me.

Eventually, I was able to open my eyes again.

This time, I stood in an ancient forest, far older than any I'd ever seen. The trees were so large I could not comprehend their size, their canopy blanketing the sky. Shallow ponds pocketed the earth, and piles of moss draped over the rocks resting near the water.

Before me stood a massive creature, like a cross between a dragon and a stag.

It was unlike anything I'd ever seen. The dragon's scales were honey-gold with flecks of white dusting its backside. Its wings were tucked proudly against its sides, the center tips pointed upwards. One of its teeth had to easily be the size of me. It lay on its belly, its front legs tucked one over the other.

As the dragon turned its head to look at me, I gasped at the full sight of its antlers. It must have hundreds of points, all cascading upwards in elegant patterns. Its stag-like ears flickered to and fro beside its antlers as it stared at me with intelligent eyes, and a great sadness welled inside me, deep and profound. I didn't know what saddened me, only that the great beast seemed to be in pain.

Holding a hand out, the dragon drew close, towering over me much like an old tree from the forest back home would. It snorted in silent contemplation before lowering its head to brush its nose against my fingers. It was soft as velvet with a comforting warmth against the chill in the air. My breath lodged in my throat as a current of *something* surged through me, planting me firmly on the ground. I didn't know when I'd stood, only that I stood now, and when I looked down, my legs had become tree trunks, my feet rooted firmly in the dirt. Roses unfurled on my belly, across my arms, and over my bare breasts. I was unmade, a child of the earth, and when I stared back up at the dragon, my gaze was lost in the pit of its eyes.

My stomach plummeted as I blinked and suddenly found myself in my childhood room. It looked as it had just after Sister had been taken. My handmade dolls were nestled in the corner, and iron bars sat over my windows. A soft melody from my music box played on my vanity, and I found myself a slave in my own body. *I must be reliving some memory.* My feet carried me out of my room against my will, padding silently through the darkness.

My heart pounded as I reached the front door, and when my hand moved to reach for the doorknob, a child's hand came into view.

*Am I a child?* I found myself thinking as I pried open the door and slipped outside. The cold air brushed my cheeks and bare skin. I shivered, ignoring it as I took off through the grass of my village. No fires lit up any of the houses; the village leaders demanded no lights after sundown so as not to tempt the attention of the faeries.

Grief welled in my chest, a grief that felt simultaneously fresh and old as I wove through the houses, stopping only to hesitate at the edge of the forest.

*No, don't go in there*, I begged to myself as I stared up at the trees. *I remember; I remember.* This was just after Sister had been taken. This was when the grief and anger had roared within me and made me do something entirely too reckless.

Squaring my shoulders, the memory of me took my first step into the forest.

It had been easy–at first. My mother had spoken ill of the forest, had told little me that the moment one stepped foot inside, their mind would be lost.

That wasn't the case though, not as I took a tentative step across the tree line. The tree branches whispered to me, urging me forward, but I was of sound mind as my courage grew, as the forest swallowed me up, and I began to run. If I could just find where they'd taken Sister, maybe I could beg for her back. Maybe they would let me stay. I just wanted to be with her. She was my other half. I was hollow without her.

Tears stained my cheeks.

A pair of luminescent eyes blinked at me from behind a tree.

It was the first time I remember feeling true fear.

I screamed, backing away, but tripped over a root. As I hit the ground, I slammed my head against a rock, and everything went painfully dark.

When I woke, I drifted in a sea of stars.

I was weightless, and I couldn't remember ever feeling such a sense of peace. It was like I was wrapped inside a warm blanket near a fire, my eyes heavy. Oh, if I could just sleep.

But no. There was something, someone, I was trying to save.

My little mind couldn't remember who it was. Why I'd run into the forest. *No, no. You must remember.*

I blinked, and like all the moments I had forced my paralyzed limbs to rip themselves away from terrifying nightmares, I moved, dragging myself into a sitting position. I was in another memory, this one long forgotten until now.

But unlike in the previous scene, my mind was trapped in the past too rather than just my body.

I sat in a void, but instead of the endless black of darkness, it was a pool of white, like I sat in an endless sea of fog after a warm, rainy day. Before me stood that stag-like dragon, its antlers glittering like starlight. Little me had never seen anything more beautiful. Tears welled with simplistic joy; never had anyone woven stories or written tales of such a creature. Who was I to be so honored by its attention?

*Am I dead?* I wanted to speak it, but my mouth wouldn't work, so I thought it instead. The idea of it was so heartbreaking, but peace washed over me regardless. I was only four. That was such a short time to live, but if I were to stay with the dragon now, it wouldn't be so bad.

*No.* The dragon's voice reverberated through me, shaking me to my core. It was like when one of the village cats climbed up onto my chest, and their purrs echoed through my lungs. His words filled me and clung to my essence. Despite my state, I felt so incredibly, achingly alive.

I wanted to reach out to the dragon, so I did, my fingers shifting between the size they were when I was a child to how they were now. Each step the dragon took brought new life beneath his feet. He did not nudge me as he stopped in front of me. His eyes pierced through me, stripping me away until my soul was bare.

*"You were made half then, torn and twisted by nature's malice. Be remade whole now and heal where your twisted half has wrought sickness."*

Only then did he nudge my palm with his nose, and the moment his scales made contact, the life I felt brimming within me exploded outwards. Grass and flowers bloomed, chasing pathways through the water of stars and creating trees, bushes, and bustling creeks. The blank canvas I had woken to was no more, replaced with a lush forest as far as the eye could see.

My throat was constricted with emotion, and I opened my mouth to speak but found myself unable to. I blinked, and I was torn from the memory.

Fear lodged itself in my throat. I didn't know where I was. Underground, perhaps? I was inside a building of some sort, the walls made of soil with no windows to peer outside. Small blue wisps trailed about the room, filling it with just enough light for me to see, and I blinked blearily through the darkness.

I moved to stand but hissed as pain shot through my abdomen. Looking down, I saw my midsection had been wrapped in a gleaming white gauze, a hint of it tinged with red. The sight of it brought back the memory, swimming and hazy through my newly wakened thoughts. We'd been attacked by the witch we'd been searching for. I pressed my hand to my wound, gritting my teeth.

Something creaked and shifted in the gloom of the room, and I threw myself back against the wall behind me, ignoring the pain that brought as my heart thumped fearfully in my chest. I reached for my hip, hoping for my dagger, but not surprised when I didn't find it.

Whoever it was stilled, and I held my breath as I inched forward, desperate to make out any features in the dim light.

It was an elf. At least, it looked to be so. I had only ever seen one or two in my life; they mainly stuck to the southern kingdom. It wasn't uncommon for Seelie Court fae to have offspring with humans, which was how humans could use magic in the first place.

"I mean you no harm," the elf called out, his voice naught more than a whisper. He looked considerably worse off than I did, lying on the ground, with shallow wounds that wept yellow sap-blood along his arms and legs. His clothes were filthy and torn. I suspected he'd been down here for a while.

His hair, long and brown, was matted and covered in dirt and dried blood, and despite being a woodland creature, his breath came out quick and shallow, like he was fighting some kind of disease. "Please... I've been alone for what has felt like so long..."

A cough rattled his throat, and my stomach constricted as I urged myself forward, careful to stay just out of reach should the elf prove dangerous. "Where are we?" I asked. I realized how thirsty I was, but it didn't look like there was any water down here.

"The witch brought you some nights ago," the elf said, struggling to push himself into a seated position against the wall. "I haven't seen her since, but she doesn't stay away for long." He reached forward, his eyes hazy and his mouth pressed into a pained frown. "If she comes back—"

"Stay where you are," I hissed. My fingers ached for my blade, but it would have been a foolish mistake for the witch to have left me with my dagger. Still, an elf was an elf. I had never met one personally, but I imagined he was the same as those from the fae realm.

He paused, his eyes shielded behind a mask of indifference, and a pain pulled through me. I did not recall falling until I was on the floor. I could not reach out even as the elf dragged himself over to me, the rattling of his breath like chains clattering against the walls of his chest.

"The witch must have cursed your wound," he whispered as I moaned, gripping my stomach. I had looked at it just moments ago; it'd seemed like nothing more than a scratch, but looking down, I noticed more red than there should have been for such a shallow wound.

"Her sickness plagues these lands. She means to use us to feed her crops," the elf said, his words haunting me as I stared through the room. There didn't seem to be any way out. There was a door on the other side of the room, the wood infected with some manner of decay, but it did not budge when I tried to pry it open.

Still, that did not defer my determination.

I had survived this long and through worse. If I had to tear this place apart to escape, so be it.

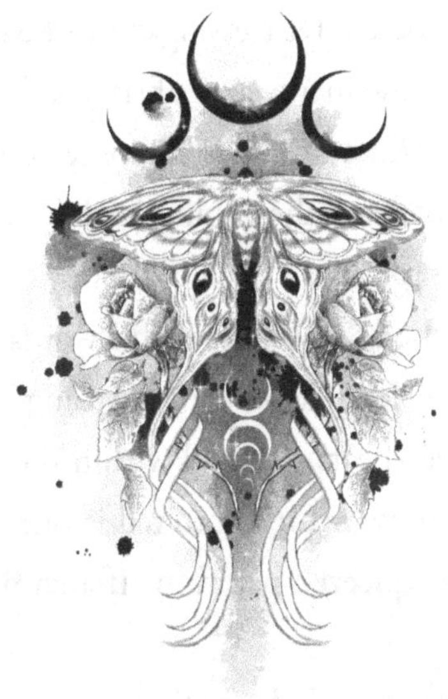

# SIXTEEN

## *Neferit*

"**Y**OU'RE SURE?" I SAT nestled on the outskirts of a small village. It was dark, with cottages made of rotten wood and dead flowers that curled at the top. The air was stale and scented with something vaguely sour, and Olbi shook beside me, his ears pressed back against his skull.

"Yes," he whispered. Distressing chirps fled his lips, and he kept disappearing in a swarm of spores that stayed suspended in the air for a moment before reforming into his body. I could not recall the goblins back home being able to do such a thing.

I took a deep breath. Whatever this woman was, whatever magic she wielded, it wasn't something I was familiar with. Several heartbeats pattered within the vicinity, but they were too far away for me to tell if one of them was Róis'. My heart squeezed painfully. If anything had happened to her...

*No, no, Nef. Do not think like that.*

I inhaled sharply. If Róis was dead, nothing could stop the desecration I would cause upon the witch and her land. The rage that sank through me at the thought made me dizzy, and I looked to Olbi to steel myself. "These witches... you told me on the way here that they are not to be underestimated. Does their magic have a weakness?"

Olbi nodded his head quickly, dipped down behind a bush, and then pointed towards a gnarled, twisted tree. "The witches of this forest are old, old, old..." He trailed off, muttering into his hands. "Ancient, wild magic. Has to have somewhere to pull from. The trees—" He raised his hand, and I stared up towards the trees. "The trees grant them their magic. That one–" He gestured to the gnarled tree again. "That one is hers. Destroy it, and her magic is gone." The pull of magic from the trees was undeniable; I had been caressed by them since we'd found ourselves trapped here. The magic that echoed from the blackened tree was uncomfortable, like the threat of something sharp across the skin. Everything in me begged to flinch from it, but my desire to find Róis won, and I nodded to Olbi.

"Stay here."

He squeaked, his ears shifting up and down as his level of distress grew. "You want me to stay *here*?" He shook his head, his eyes furrowing. "Oh no, no, no. Olbi is a good myrlír. He will be going with to find his caretaker."

Annoyance sang through me, but something told me Olbi wouldn't be stopped, so I ran a hand over my face and nodded. "Fine, fine. But stay close."

Olbi nodded so quickly I almost didn't see it as he ducked behind me. I darted forward, my eyes peeled at the abandoned village set before me. The forest made no sound save for a quiet hum that radiated off the trees, and I pressed myself up against the rotten wood of a desolate home with ease. The house itself was little more than a wooden shack with dark windows and gnarled roots that made up its roof. A dark tree grew above it with bells and more wooden twig shapes hanging from its branches.

The forest's silence was almost overwhelming. Panic clawed in my throat, and if I had been unaccustomed to the way nature stilled from time to time, it might have overcome me. Instead, I took a moment to steady myself, to still the fear that settled in my belly. If Róis was dead...

No. My oath would have told me so. The magic that tethered me to her still stood strong. She was alive.

A bell tinkled above me, and Olbi whimpered.

"She is *coming*," he cried softly, clutching my leg in terror. Another bell rang overhead and then another and then more so until all of them were ringing—tiny warnings in the branches that could not have been caused by the wind for there was none.

"Get down," I commanded quietly, slipping behind some large rocks pressed conveniently against the witch's house. The stone was cool beneath my fingertips, and this time, when I sensed the witch nearby, I called upon my magic to mask my heartbeat with the soft sounds of nature.

Olbi did as I instructed, his ears flush against the top of his head. Footsteps crunched the leaves on the ground, and I went still, my ears straining to hear if the witch came too close. There was still no heartbeat that came from her, not even the buzzing that had infected the air before, and the back of my throat ached for the taste of fear or rage or anything as the footsteps approached.

Olbi's fear wafted over me instead, a flowery scent that hung over my head as I held my breath. The footsteps halted, and with them, the bells stopped ringing, their silence a shock to my ears as they rang with the echoes of their lingering sound. I peeked up just in time to see the witch disappear into her home, and as I glanced up at the tree, its dark branches reaching out across the grove, I latched onto my courage. I wasn't sure how the tree still lived, its trunk weeping sap, with large deep wounds lacerated across its bark, but I knew I needed to destroy it. I just had to find Róis first.

Glancing behind me, I met Olbi's gaze. "Your fear is justified, but do not let it slow you down. We're about to charge into a den of snakes." My stomach twisted, and I took a deep breath as I moved forward. My fear would only fester the longer I delayed.

Rain began to fall, shattering the silence, and I blinked away the droplets as I pondered what to do. I didn't think it was a good idea to go through the front door, not when the witch had just entered that way herself, but I found no other entrances. The small hut was forged against the wicked tree that stood tall over it, with only one way in and one way out that I could tell. It felt akin to the old ways of fae, when we were naught more than spirits that thrived within the wood of trees.

Olbi whimpered again as I pushed open the front door, only to still as the wood creaked in defiance. There wasn't any movement inside, and after a moment I pushed forward.

The house looked abandoned, with dirty plates and glasses littering the table off to the left. There was only two rooms, one leading to a bedroom with a mattress on the floor that had twisted roots growing from its feathers. The air was thick with a musty smell, and I wrinkled my nose as I padded slowly into the house. There was a thickness in the air, a tension that sat across my shoulders. The main room was dark and damp, with roots hanging from the ceiling. A door sat slightly ajar back where the house was nestled up against the tree, and a light flickered off the door, as if beckoning me to come closer.

The witch was nowhere in sight.

That did not bode well. I sensed two heartbeats below my feet, somewhere deeper in the earth. They tempted me to lose reason, to push through the house and anyone in my way until I found Róis. My sword shook in my hand. Something boiled in a pot in the kitchen, the fire dancing beneath it in a quiet, bubbling tune. Animal skulls clung to the walls, their eye sockets filling the air with trepidation, and I moved towards the other door. Róis had to be beyond it. Somehow, I just knew.

"Caretaker down there," Olbi whispered, still clinging to my leg. "Must go down, quick-quick."

"I do not know where the witch went." Her absence had set me on edge. Not being able to hear her heartbeat made her a terrifying enemy, and I swept my fingers across the wood of the door as I pulled it further open.

A quiet moan echoed from the stairs as they twisted and curled before rounding a corner, and I could not see where they went. I glanced back down at Olbi before I descended. If the witch was down there, I would simply deal with her.

The staircase was thin and winding, and the air began to grow stale as we descended deeper and deeper underground until we came upon another door, only this one was closed. The two heartbeats were strong; whoever they were, they were right behind the door.

I tried to push it open, but it wouldn't budge, and there was still no sign of the witch. It was as if she'd entered and left without my knowing, but the skin on the back of my neck prickled as if we were being watched.

"Can you get this open?" I asked Olbi, who brushed past me to knock intricate patterns into the door. Pollen-like magic dusted the frame as the door clicked and swung open, and both of us pushed inside.

The room was small, square, and dim as a few firefly-like lights danced in the air. Róis was on the bed furthest from the door, a male elf on the other. I strode over to Róis, my sword falling to my side.

"Róis," I whispered, my throat constricting painfully. I wasn't sure what the witch had done to her, but lacerations littered her arms and legs, weeping thin trails of blood, and thorns grew from her wounds. She was unconscious, her face pinched as her eyes flickered behind closed lids. I sank onto the bed beside her. She was alive. Wounded and sick, perhaps, but still alive.

"Róis," I said again, louder this time. My fingers pressed into her arm; it was hot to the touch, hotter than normal, and a thin layer of sweat coated her brow as her eyes shot open. She flinched away, her lips pulled back to bare sharp canines, and she hissed in pain. She spoke, her words panicked, but I could not understand her.

"It's okay, I'm here." My words meant nothing to her as her gaze darted about the room, searching for a witch that was not here. I had no idea where the witch had gone, but the longer we lingered, the stronger the tension grew. We needed to leave.

"Caretaker," Olbi yowled, shooting over to the other bed. The elf was chained down, looking considerably sicklier and more taken by nature than Róis. Until he moved, he looked little more than a clump of leaves and twigs, like nature was attempting to claim him. It made me glance down at the thorns growing out of Róis' injuries, a horrified expression crossing my face.

"We must get out of here. *Now*," I said. I ignored Róis' protests as I grabbed her hand and pulled her to her feet. I hesitated when she cried out, but she straightened regardless. Her wounds wept every time she moved. Her heartbeat echoed in my throat, and I searched her eyes for any sign of understanding.

"I gave you my word," I said softly. "You are safe with me until you step foot in the Grove." I squeezed her hand softly as Olbi pried the sticks away from the druid. He muttered quickly in his own quick tongue, and we hurried over to him.

"This is the druid?" I asked, and Olbi nodded without looking away from him, his fingers darting out to brush the druid's face. The elf was awake but only just, his face bruised and dirty.

"If you can get me back to my grove," he rasped weakly, "Elahir and I can rid us of this rot."

My eyes darted around the room, assessing the best way to flee. The druid didn't look strong enough to walk, and Róis wasn't looking too well either. Róis was my priority, but without the druid, I wasn't sure how we'd return home.

"Can get Caretaker if you can get her," Olbi whispered, gesturing to Róis. I stared at him as his head wobbled, his ears dancing about as he disappeared in a puff of yellow spores with the elf in his arms. He reappeared on the other side of the room.

"Take him and go. We'll find a way out." The air whooshed as he disappeared with the Caretaker, and I tugged Róis towards the door.

She mumbled something as another moan escaped her lips. She stumbled, but I caught her, tugging her close. She didn't fight me, and that was how I knew she was truly sick.

I stared down at our joined hands, and a part of me begged to pull away. If it was an infection like the Rot consuming Elvira, I could not afford to get sick. I fought against this idea as I caught sight of the terror in Róis' eyes. For the first time since meeting her, I didn't think the anger and fear in her expression were directed towards me, and it made the seed of my own fear flourish.

"We cannot delay," I said even though I knew she could not understand me. Now that it was just the two of us, the silence was stifling, and I was eager to be free of this strange place.

As I tugged her towards the open door, she stumbled again, and this time, she hit the ground hard, a soft cry peeling from her lips.

Sweeping around, I sheathed my sword and tugged her into my arms, ignoring her protests. She didn't fight me, not completely. Her eyes fluttered shut as she curled against my chest and went limp. I ascended the stairs as quickly as possible, ignoring how light the human was in my arms.

The witch's house was still completely empty, and I didn't spend time looking around to see what might be lurking in the shadows. A whispered breath ghosted my neck, and I turned, but there was no one there. The weight of a presence suffocated the room, but other than the weak beating of Róis' heart, I sensed no other life.

I left quickly.

# SEVENTEEN
## *Róis*

I SHUDDERED IN AND out of consciousness as Neferíl carried me through a strange village. Time felt odd; I couldn't remember the last time I'd seen the queen, while at the same time, it felt like no time had passed. Neferíl was warm. It would have been easy in this moment to reach up and tear her throat out, liberating me from her eventual wrath.

The thought died as something hit us, and the queen dropped me. I cried out as I hit the ground, but then the gentle caress of the grass pressed against my cheek and urged me to sleep. It would be so easy to let go, stop fighting, and seek solace from whatever came next...

"Touch her, and I will tear you apart."

The words sent a surge of life through me, and my eyes shot open as the queen stood above me, her wings out on full display. She stood with her back erect and her sword drawn, and the power that coiled off her was so intense that a violent shiver shuddered through me.

I curled against myself as the witch from before stepped forward, shuttering in and out of sight as she used magic to step through pockets of air towards the queen. The grass was so soft against my skin, and as the witch drew near, the pain in my stomach seized up, and I screamed. My blood was aflame. The thorns in my wounds grew larger, peeling back my skin to demand room. I nearly passed out, but fear kept me from slipping into the void. The air was thick with sickness, a wrongness to the magic that soaked into the trees and ground. My own magic seemed to flinch from it, and the witch laughed, a low grating sound as she approached the queen.

"It's not nice to take what isn't yours, my dear." Her voice had changed, thickened into something dark and wet like she was struck with a cold. The witch had drawn much closer, and I whimpered without meaning to. The world kept getting leeched of its color, graying where it shouldn't. Something inside me woke, shaking away the sleep as it dashed through my limbs. My fingers tingled, and I looked up as I met the queen's eyes.

Her glamour bled away to long, sharp features and pointed teeth. Her dark eyes glittered with rage, and the scream that fled her lips was so high-pitched that it hurt my ears as she lunged at the witch quicker than I could follow.

I was left alone in the middle of the village as the queen ripped the witch away from where she stood. Stand up, I begged myself desperately. My strength had all gone, and the pain in my skin was almost making me blind. Stars dotted the edges of my vision, and I wept in frustration.

*I don't want to die*, I thought just before the darkness took me.

*Waves crashed against the shore of the beach where I stood. The water lapped at my feet as the sun peeked over the horizon, bathing the world in brilliant oranges and golds. A chill ran down my spine as I turned. I was immediately tackled to the ground, and Sister pinned me there with a dagger to my throat.*

She pressed so firmly that a trickle of blood ran down my neck. Sand scratched at my arms and back, and I glared up at her in shock and betrayal as she leaned close, her lips peeled back in a gleaming snarl.

"You took everything from me," she whispered, her voice cradling me as she brushed my hair back with her free hand. No longer was my sister staring at me with fear or love as she had when I'd found her in Elvira. No longer was she tinged with the sickness as I'd seen consuming her before. Rage and darkness pierced her expression as she leaned close.

"I can't even remember my own name. Do you know how terrible that is, Róis? My own name. My identity. My life. Everything was given as tribute to the forest. All of its pain, its malice, its anger...I feel it all." She whined, the pain beneath her gaze endless and deep. I sank into it, my heart roaring like I stood beneath a massive waterfall and I cried, tears falling from the corners of my eyes as I relinquished myself to it.

I'm sorry. I thought the words but did not speak them. I knew she would not hear it. I knew I could not take back the horrible thing our mother had done even though I would have gladly taken her place all of those years ago.

"You will learn. Soon, everyone will pay." Her hand tensed at my neck, and I knew she was going to kill me. I bucked my hips, catching her by surprise. I hissed as the blade sliced a part of my cheek, but I managed to throw her off me before it could slice my neck. The absence of the blade against my skin sent a course of adrenaline running through me, and I scrambled away as Sister stood. My heart breaking, I turned and threw myself at her with everything I had.

My sister was dead. Truly. I knew that now. She'd died when the forest had taken her.

It was a mantra I repeated to myself as I fought her. As I tried to wrestle the knife from her grasp.

"Why?" I cried. "I don't want to hurt you."

Sister's grin was twisted. "Well, I want to hurt you."

I wasn't quick enough to avoid her blade this time.

A gurgle of surprise passed my lips as she shoved the dagger further into my gut and twisted. The pain that swept through my abdomen was chilling, like the touch of winter. I looked up and drowned myself in the impossible dark green of her eyes.

"I'll enjoy seeing those insides rot, sweet sister," Sister whispered, prying the dagger out.

I woke screaming, sweat coating my brow as my eyes tore through my surroundings. My abdomen was on fire, and my arms were coated with thorns and Rot. Someone grabbed my arm, but I tore away, forced myself to my feet, and took off through the clearing I was in.

"She cannot leave this place!" someone shouted behind me, but I ran as fast as I could, ignoring the pain as I wove around a tree and slipped through the brush. It was daylight now, sunlight peeking through the dense cover of the canopy.

Someone tackled me before I could get very far, and they twisted so that I landed on top of them. The air left my lungs, and I attempted to tear myself away, but the pain from my wounds betrayed me. Whoever had a hold of me was too strong, her words attempting to comfort me as she cradled my body, taking care not to touch my arm riddled with the Rot.

I knew it was the queen before she sat us both up. Her fingers grazed my arms as she spoke softly to me in her language. It came out in a quiet lilt, almost akin to a lullaby, and I was dragged back into unconsciousness before I realized what was happening.

I did not dream this time, and when I woke, I came to slowly and more peacefully than before. Whatever my head was resting on was soft, and voices of conversation carried on above me. I didn't open my eyes, lulled by how comfortable and warm I was, and for the first time since being injured by the witch, I was free of pain.

"Yes, she'll live," a voice said, decidedly male. "The witch's curse ran deep. Despite our healing, she'll carry a scar on her belly as a reminder. She might feel it from time to time too, but she wields strong healing magic of her own. It's nothing like we've ever seen."

I force my eyes to open, my surroundings a blur as the corners of my eyes tingle in weakness.

I locked eyes with the queen. Her gaze flickered with relief and a sense of conflict before she tucked her emotions away behind a mask. I sat up, my brow furrowed, wondering why she'd come back to save me. Was she truly capable of honor? Her oath bound her, as was the logic of the fae, but it was the first time I believed her when she said she would not harm me. That trust scared me.

Unsettled, I pushed away from the group, tucking myself against the trunk of a tree as Elahir and the druid from the witch's basement eyed me silently. The dark-haired elf looked significantly better than when I'd seen him last: his cheeks were fuller of color, and his wounds no longer bled. He had cleaned himself, and his eyes shone with life as he watched me intently.

"Your wounds have healed remarkably," he said, his voice free from the rattling sick sound that had encompassed it before.

"Truly," Elahir agreed, brushing his hair back from his face. "I have never seen anything like it. You fought off a plague like your magic was meant to do so. It's absolutely breathtaking."

"It's strange," Elahir said, eyeing the wound on my arm. "I could not do anything about that. The roots of it go deep into your arm, and it appeared as if the witch's curse has urged it forward. My magic could not untangle it."

"Ask her," I snarled, jutting my head in the queen's direction. "Her court forged this plague to bring an end to my people and then forced the blame on me when it turned on its creator."

Neferíl eyed me silently, her expression ever vigilant. Her unyielding calmness was infuriating, grating on my panic as I dug my fingers into the grass beneath me.

The dark-haired druid turned to Neferíl and spoke quietly to her.

Neferíl furrowed her brow and tossed her braids behind her back, raising her chin defiantly. She laughed, a pretty sound that echoed about the grove, and her eyes flashed dangerously as they darted between the druid and I. The wind shifted, and I shivered as the wound around my midsection ached, a ghost of what it had been before the druids had healed it.

"She sings a different song," the dark-haired druid said finally, holding a hand out for a small bird to land on. He cooed at it softly, uttering to it in gentle tongues, and it took off as the druid leaned forward, his expression contemplative.

"Elahir and I have been watching for some time." He eyed Elahir before continuing, "It has been some time since I was in Elvira and I have made a home here in these woods, but it seems whatever is happening in your world is bleeding into this one."

"You mean to say that this wood suffers from a rot similar to the one back home?" I asked.

The druid nodded. "I believe so. I spoke with Elahir while you slept, and I think I will accompany you and see if my aid can soothe whatever pain your woods suffer from."

"Olbi comes too." A small form shot out from behind a rock and clung to the druid's leg. It was Olbi, his massive ears trembling as he stared up at the druid with large eyes. "Olbi keep Caretaker safe."

The druid brushed his fingers against Olbi's face, softly caressing his cheeks as adoration blossomed across his expression. "If Elahir wills it so, I wouldn't dare go anywhere without you. You saved my life, Olbi. I owe you a basket of apples."

Elahir grinned, the blue of his eyes twinkling. "I do not see why it would be an issue."

I stared at Neferíl, trying to discern what she'd told the druid about the rotting forest. My mind was a war of conflicting emotions. The recent nightmare of my sister stabbing me resurfaced. *I'll enjoy seeing those insides rot, sweet sister.*

What if... no.

It was just a dream.

But Nef had put her life at risk to save me. She could have left me to die at the hands of the witch. A part of me wondered what the queen's role was in all of this. The forest here showed signs of Rot...could its origin be here, and not from the queen's court at all?

Not to mention the queen was clearly against the Rot and the infection. My mind went back to the rotting faerie that tried to kill the queen just before I saved her and accidentally sent us through a portal. The queen had clearly been attacked, which meant some of the fae were warring with one another.

My mind rebelled; the fae were more complex than I ever could have imagined.

The queen nudged the side of my leg with her foot. My first reaction was to lash out and grab her, but I refrained. She had saved my life. I met her gaze, and she gestured silently with her head towards the druid, who had stood with Olbi on his heels.

*Time to go?* my expression read, and after a moment, the queen nodded.

I struggled to get to my feet, and several times I noted Neferíl shift in the corner of my eye as if she wanted to help but refrained. The pain had gone from my wound, and though I felt lightheaded and unsteady on my feet, I managed to stay upright. Shaking my hair from my face, I longed desperately for a brush and ignored the tingling in my fingertips.

"Now that everyone is awake, I feel it best for introductions." the dark-haired druid said. "You can call me Kyrie."

I gave him my name at the same time the queen did.

"I should be able to return you to your homeland now," Elahir called out as he swept along the edges of the grove.

He held his hands out as if testing an invisible magical barrier. "But it would be wise to stay close to Kyrie. The forest has grown different in its sickness."

I shuffled close as Kyrie offered me a small glass bottle. It gave off a faint glow, its contents a golden hue, and it was small enough to hold only a mouthful of liquid.

"For the dizziness," he explained, meeting my questioning expression. "No need to fear it. I would not go through all the trouble of healing you if I was just going to poison you after."

I eyed him wearily as I uncorked the bottle and raised it to my face. It smelled of wildflowers and something sharp, a scent I couldn't place. I had grown used to identifying different herbs and flora that went into potion-making due to my father being the town healer, but this one was foreign. Still, Kyrie was right. He had no reason to poison me. I wasn't sure if the rule where fae couldn't lie applied to his kind, but I tipped the bottle back and downed the liquid.

The taste was sweet, almost sickeningly so. I frowned as it rolled slowly down my throat. The effects were almost immediate. The tingling went away in my fingers, and warmth curled against my core, like it was burning away the blood loss and exhaustion. I felt almost normal within moments, and I smiled briefly at Kyrie.

"My father was...*is*..." I frowned at the mistake. It wasn't as if he was dead. "He's an exceptional healer, and even his potions don't work that quickly."

"I've been practicing for a very long time, and Elahir here has been a great teacher." Elahir bowed his head in acknowledgment as Kyrie thumbed his chin. "Sometimes there simply isn't a cure, or sometimes nature will tell you where the balance lies. That potion, for example, would make Olbi very sick." Olbi disappeared through the brush as we left the grove and ventured back into the woods. I did not know how long I'd been unconscious while healing, but the woods seemed lighter, as if dark magic had been lifted.

"Nature is our guide," Kyrie continued. "There is much we can learn from our elders." He smiled fondly as he laid a hand across the trunk of a tree, and I frowned.

"My people used to think that as well." My words came out bitter and harsh. "Despite our best efforts, we've become deaf to the teachings of Old. Some of my village still practices the Old Ways, but I can see it dying around me. The cities of the north no longer cling to tradition."

"Knowledge can be re-taught," Kyrie said.

I shook my head. "Knowledge can be lost if there is no one there to seek it out. I remember stories of my people and the spirits of the forest living side by side in harmony, but so much anger and pain has occurred between both sides, I don't ever see it returning to those ways."

Kyrie paused, pulling his hand away. His gaze shifted to something over my shoulder, and I turned to see Neferíl regarding us with some interest.

"Never say never, Róis. It is that same pain and anger that has caused this plague to fester. Forest rots occur because of stubborn despair."

I gritted my teeth together and went silent. Kyrie could not know of my people's trials. Even if he was a fae from my world, he did not know how my people suffered, how deep their wounds ran. Their pain could not be so easily stifled.

Neferíl spoke as a breeze sifted softly through the trees. Kyrie laughed, and my stomach rolled suspiciously as Neferíl's mouth twitched as if she were suppressing a smile.

"Apple? Olbi found it nice and shiny," Olbi said, reappearing at my side. The apple in question gleamed a vibrant red against the light green of his fingers as he offered it to me, his gaze solemn.

"Are you sure?" I asked. "You love those apples."

Olbi nodded and shoved the apple into my palm. "Does your home have apples?"

I nodded as I turned it about in my hands. This place was foreign to me; would fae logic deem this apple was unsafe for human consumption? It was in pristine condition, with no bruising to make note of, and I studied it closely before glancing over at Olbi. "Yes. Great big ones. They're not in season right now, but if you're still in Elvira with Kyrie come summer, you'll see them growing near the edge of the forest."

Olbi's eyes glittered. "Will have to ask Kyrie to stay until summer."

A stab of grief tore through me. Memories surfaced of Salia having dragged me to the edge of the forest to collect apples for her pies, and my lower lip wobbled as I nodded, then offered Olbi the apple.

"Take it. I'm not too hungry after all, and it would be a shame for it to go to waste."

"Wait," Kyrie said, tossing a hand out to stop us. It was only now that I noticed we'd been wandering through the wood for some time. The grove was no longer in sight; the trees were dark and foreboding as they hung over us. Somewhere off in the distance, something laughed, a small and wispy sound, and a chill rolled down my spine.

"Where are we going?" I asked, comforting myself by touching the hilt of my dagger. I watched as Neferíl did the same with her sword.

"The way back is about half a day's journey from here." Kyrie stared over at us, his mouth pressed in a thin line.

"But the woods of Daesthara hold no mercy. You think your wood is cruel and full of malice? These trees stood as babes at the birth of this world and carry a pain greater than any I've ever seen. One day, I might tell you the story Elahir told me of how the gods fought one another and of the scars their bloodshed left behind."

Kyrie's words sank into the air, and I looked up as the forest shivered around us, the branches swaying in the wind. Shadows darted between branches out of the corner of my eye, and I stepped on a twig. It snapped, and the sound echoed as if we were standing in a great ravine.

Neferíl spoke, and Kyrie nodded. "The witches were only a pocket of this forest's dangers. While we travel, we need to remain alert. The birds have begun to sing of ancient warriors shaking the sleep from their bones and heeding a call to the north, and I can assure you..." His gaze darkened. "You don't want to run into the dyrvak."

"What are they?" My curiosity burned, endlessly unchecked.

Kyrie bit into an apple Olbi offered him.

"Spirits of the forest," Kyrie said finally. "They've been blessed by the great serpent that claimed this planet. Mighty warriors, they are the bottom half of elk or deer or sometimes moose, and their upper bodies are that of man.

The antlers 'pon their head have been blessed by the great serpent, the dragon Mot, and are as hard as dragon scales."

I had never heard of such creatures, but it didn't sound all too out of league with the sort of creatures that resided in Elvira. They sounded closest to the southern wolves of Brûnheim, but even then, their forms shifted from beast to man, not always sharing both forms at once but rather drifting between the two. It was difficult to picture, but the sound of them seemed less than pleasant, and I was more than content with the idea of imagining them rather than seeing them in person.

"We do not want to run into them. They tend to fight in war parties, and they kill without question. If we're lucky, they'll remain mere stories to you." Kyrie went silent as he moved forward, his eyes trained on the tree line. He bent quickly, darting to the side to use a tree as cover. "Get low," he hissed, and both Neferíl and I complied without hesitation.

Neferíl pressed herself up against another tree as I knelt behind a bush, careful not to rustle the leaves and cause any noise. I didn't see anything out of the ordinary, but the wood grew still. It was almost eerily so, the constant wait like the world was holding its breath. I pried my dagger from its sheath, careful to remain silent, and gripped it with bated breath.

I opened my mouth, ready to ask what we were waiting for, when a herd of...*something* came barreling through the woods.

They were massive. Giant creatures of various woodland mammals with the upper halves of men. Some of them bore many pointed antlers, while others had no antlers at all, and they all carried various weapons varying between glaives and swords. One of them had an intricate pattern painted across his chest and face, and every single one wore their hair long and braided. The painted one seemed to be their leader, and he shouted in a harsh tongue. The very fabric of their language made every hair on my arms stand on end.

I looked at Kyrie, and he nodded. These were the dyrvak he'd been describing, and I could see now why he wanted to avoid them. There were dozens of them, all armed and massive in size. I could say with confidence that I could probably bring down five or six of them before they killed me, but there were simply too many.

The realization felt heavy on my shoulders. I was in a different world full of creatures who were nothing like the faeries I'd fougdht and killed back home. Perhaps I wouldn't be able to take as many as I'd thought. I was in over my head.

I forced my breathing to slow as it lodged in my throat and the world grew dizzy. Panic swelled in my chest, and my palms grew sweaty, threatening to lose grip on my dagger. I clung to the blade as if it were my only source of protection as the dyrvak wove through the woods, their low voices chanting in a way that thrummed against my bones.

We stayed still and silent until long after they passed. My knees had long since begun to ache from kneeling for so long, but the dyrvak had scared me enough to pause, so I'd stayed as still as I could.

"Come," Kyrie said finally, pushing away from the tree. "We must move quickly." Neferíl and Olbi followed, and I stood, ignoring the biting groan that cradled my lips as my stiff joints screamed in protest.

Neferíl spoke quietly and quickly to Kyrie as I fell into step with Olbi, who seemed nervous. His eyes kept darting about, and he wrung his hands together as small chirps escaped his lips.

"Are you okay?" I asked quietly.

Olbi shook his head. "Dyrvak sleeping and dead for very long time. Their return can only mean bad, nasty, unkind things for everyone. Do not know why the world whispers and beckons them, but it's not good. It's not good. It's not *good*." He continued to mutter to himself as he grabbed his ears and tugged them down against the sides of his head. My stomach lurched at the implications, but I comforted myself with knowing that this wasn't my world. Somewhere out there, the dyrvak mustering for whatever darkness may be coming was a problem for someone else to deal with.

I had my own trials to overcome.

# EIGHTEEN

## *Neferil*

T HE DYRVAK'S APPEARANCE must have rattled Kyrie and Elahir because we moved quicker after that. They also went silent, their focus on getting us through the forest. I was thankful for it; the dyrvak had rattled me too. I'd never seen anything like them.

My gaze kept seeking out Róis', but her eyes kept scanning the forest around us and making sure nothing was sneaking up behind us. It left me prey to my own thoughts, and I found myself wondering if Rhi was okay or if going back for Róis had doomed her.

My heart plummeted at the thought, and I chased it away before the fear could grow. Despairing now would not change her fate.

"We're here," Kyrie said after hours of walking.

I looked around, my brow furrowed in confusion. We stood before a great lake so vast in size that trees grew straight out of the water and grassy trails rose above the water's edge, only to slip beneath it again. There was no sign of a doorway, no circle of mushrooms or cluster of rocks.

"Forgive me, but I don't believe you," I told him.

Kyrie gave me a sidelong glance. "If it were obvious, there would be creatures traveling between the realms all the time, and traveling between worlds is extremely dangerous."

I sniffed. "The spirits of Elvira pass through to the mortal realm all the time."

Kyrie shrugged. "The veil between Elvira and the mortal world is thin. If I don't make the proper preparations, your human will go insane the moment we take the walk. It's a miracle she survived the journey here."

I opened my mouth to protest. *She's not* my *human*, I wanted to say, but I didn't as I turned to glance behind me. Róis had knelt to carve apple slices with her dagger and was now handing a them over to Olbi. Our eyes met, and she gave a faint nod. She'd heard what Kyrie had said, and I noted the fire in her expression. She wasn't frightened. Not that we had a choice.

"How long do you all need?" I asked. He and Elahir led us over a trail towards the center of the lake, where a clearing lay before us. Daisies poked up from the ground, the only beautiful thing in the clearing as darkness and shadow etched the forest in growing night.

Kyrie moved about the clearing, sending Olbi off to find perfectly round rocks while he himself gathered sticks and Elahir circled the clearing, trying to gauge something as he dragged a foot through the dirt and whispered to himself. "Sunrise will present the way to us. Elahir and I will need to meditate all night, so I need you and Róis to guard us from any danger that might come near." He looked up, his expression serious. "We will only have a few moments to get through, so if something comes for us, take care of it quickly."

He stared at the both of us until we agreed and then he started to create a circle of stones from the pile Olbi had collected. He dropped the sticks in a strange runic pattern in the middle. It almost looked like the symbols the witch had had hanging in her tree, and I watched on with a fair bit of weariness.

He did this until he created a large circle of runic symbols. He and Elahir then stepped in the middle, sitting in a cross-legged position.

"Olbi is the only one who can safely pull us from our meditative states, but it is of the upmost importance that we are not interrupted. Doing so can have serious repercussions." He hesitated, his eyes darting out towards the growing darkness. "Doors that open to other worlds create large magical vibrations. Many will come, whether they are curious or malicious. Olbi can keep some of them out with his magic but best be on guard."

Olbi nodded quickly as he moved about the clearing. He waved his hands erratically, and at first nothing happened. The world was still and deceptively calm. Kyrie and Elahir checked all the runes they'd forged. Then all at once, the pull of Olbi's magic took my breath away as it soaked the air. It was like a tangible thing that sat on my tongue and weighed against my mind, beckoning me to bend to its will.

I steadied my breathing and strengthened my bonds to my own magic as Róis replaced Olbi in traversing the edge of the clearing, her brow furrowed in attention. She moved like a wolf prowling for danger, her strides long and graceful as she stalked about. She held her dagger poised, ready to lash out should something slip out from the trees, and I unsheathed my sword as well. Would the witch come? Would others? The air was still, eerily so, and a whisper etched the trees, trailing through the air.

*"Stay alert."*

"It's time," Kyrie said, resting his hands on his knees and shutting his eyes. Across from him, Elahir did the same wordlessly. Green spores of light ascended from each rune in the circle that surrounded them, and a small humming noise cradled the trees. I found myself drawn to Róis as Olbi muttered to himself and worried over the borders.

"Stay close," I whispered, only remembering Róis could not understand me when she glanced over with a blank expression. I scowled in frustration; I'd never thought the language barrier would prove to be such a problem.

I gestured to the space between us as something shuffled in the brush nearby, then stilled. A small animal, perhaps? Whatever it was, it didn't slip into the clearing. Olbi whimpered quietly as the world grew a shade darker.

"Can already feel the weight of darkness," Olbi whispered, sparing a glance in our direction. His lower lip trembled. "Going to be a long night."

Róis spoke to Olbi, her face drawn with worry.

Olbi shook his head. "Olbi must do this on his own. Will help by keeping nasty darkness away."

They waited in silence after that. I couldn't speak with Róis and had the feeling she wouldn't want to speak with me anyway. She still flinched when I drew too close, her hand tightening on the hilt of her dagger, and the dormancy of my own monstrosity woke in response.

I stilled as the first wave of shadows sailed through Olbi's defenses.

They weren't corporeal, not wholly, and had sharp teeth and claws. Some of the most painful parts of Elvira bore such shadow, a manifestation of the forest's pain, but these shadows were heavier, strangling the air as they floated towards where Kyrie and Elahir sat.

Róis shoved her dagger through a shadow, twisted, then pried it out. She fought with a precise and stubborn focus as she moved from one to the next. They evaporated in wisps around her. Watching her fight was a marvel, and it became clear how she'd killed so many of my faeries before they'd brought her in. I studied her in calm calculation, learning her moves.

A high-pitched whistle pierced the air behind me. I turned just in time to avoid the wrath of a set of claws. Ducking low, I struck out with my blade. The shadow crumpled and faded away, and it went like this for a while. I lost count of how many shadows we banished, and where I persevered without tiring, I could tell by a couple of close calls that Róis' wound was beginning to affect her fighting. I lashed out at a shadow that came too close to raking its claws across Róis' back, and later, she flung her dagger over my shoulder, hitting a shadow in the mouth and sending it hurling backwards.

Finally, a reprieve was given.

The human's arms trembled as she pried her dagger from the ground, and Olbi collapsed, pulling up blades of grass as he hummed softly to himself. Kyrie and Elahir remained in the middle of their circle, eyes closed, and still as stone. Despite the wind blowing, it never reached the druids, who looked as if they were tucked away from the elements.

"What are they?" I asked, kneeling down next to Olbi as he stared out into the darkness. No more shadows came, but that did not mean we could let our guard down. I sensed Róis patrolling the other side of the clearing despite her exhaustion. Now that we were no longer fighting, even I felt the strain of exertion.

"Forest spirits," Olbi said. "They trail the forest in small packs, mhmm. Their calls mimic the sound of rain falling. Usually quite peaceful." He pressed his fingers to his head, his eyes narrowing as he watched the tree line for any signs of movement. "They only turn into those when they've been angered. Been angry for long time."

"It sounds like home," I said sadly. "Humans think my people come out of the wood and steal their children to turn into monsters, but we're not the monsters that tore down the trees and killed the wildlife. We're not the ones that forged metal into teeth and wielded it with cruelty. Who are they to blame us when they murdered the trees and then cried for mercy when the forest retaliated?" Bitterness struck my tone, and Olbi reached over to press a hand to my arm, his eyes full of sadness.

"A lot of pain everywhere. Pain and anger. See it even in Caretaker sometimes, and Caretaker holds everything in balance, he does. Balances it all in his hands and his magic." He glanced at Kyrie. There was a peculiar look in the myrlír's eye, something ancient and lingering. "Think there can only be solution if there is forgiveness and change."

"Why would we forgive when we were the ones wronged?"

Olbi shrugged, staring down at his hands. They were long and thin, and some of his fingers bore shiny silvery scars. "Someone has to, or one day, everything will be dead, dead, gone."

Anger swept through me like an old wound, one that caused my hands to tremble as my brow furrowed in disagreement. I pursed my lips and did not reply: Olbi didn't understand. It wasn't his fault. *It isn't anyone's fault, and at the same time, everyone is to blame.*

Memories bubbled to the surface, undesired and stubborn, of twig-like fingers that pulled at my skin while the forest chattered above me with terrifying noises. I shoved them away before the panic of those memories plucked at my control. Still, my hands shook, remembering the human girl who'd found herself sacrificed to a forest that would demand so much from her.

"Maybe one day things will be different," I said, staring down as I clenched my hand so tightly into a fist that my nails dug into my palm. I had fought my way to royal standing and now? Now I would do whatever I needed to ensure the safety of those I'd once seen as an enemy. My gaze found Róis as she continued to patrol the clearing, her lips pressed in a thin line.

The human had to die.

But something about her was just so *intriguing*. She was every raw edge of humanity, every sharp tooth and passionate emotion. I found myself drawn to her despite my best efforts to avoid her flame. I knew, when the time came, it would test my will to scorn her.

Róis finally noticed me watching her and bared her teeth at me. I noticed she did that whenever she felt threatened, and I found it interesting her canines were filed to points. If I hadn't sarcastically nicknamed her little thorn, little wolf might describe her better.

I held her gaze, challenging her as my brow quirked in a silent question: who would turn away first? I thought I'd feel satisfied when she lost, her lips pulled down in a scowl, but though my mouth tugged up in a smirk, the victory felt hollow.

"What—" Obli's question was interrupted as a dyrvak burst through the woods.

It was even more massive up close, its hooves easily the size of my head. Its hair was dark and long, braided intricately to keep it free from the creature's face, which twisted in rage. Deer antlers grew out of its head. I counted five points as it raised its spear and prepared to throw it, its eyes glued on Kyrie.

"Keep focusing your magic," I told Olbi quickly, twirling my sword as I darted towards the dyrvak. "Let us hope it has not brought any friends."

# NINETEEN

## *Róis*

A s THE DYRVAK BARRELED into the clearing, the hair on the back of my neck stood on end. I ducked, narrowly avoiding a spear as it sailed through the trees and planted itself not far from where Kyrie sat. It was too close, and I twisted just as two more dyrvak appeared. They were terrifying up close, much larger than I had given them credit for, and one stomped its cloven foot and shouted in a language that grated against my psyche. Their very presence demanded attention, and I fought against the urge to kneel as I shot forward, my dagger clutched tightly in my left hand.

Across the clearing, Neferíl fought one silently and gracefully. Despite the dryrvak's otherworldly speed, the queen was beating it back at every turn, her sword slicing one wound after the other. One of the two new dyrvak ran past me to help his bleeding ally. The other one charged at me.

Magic drenched the air, and it was strange; it tugged at my skin and beckoned at a panic that sat lodged in my chest. It pried and plucked at my soul until I felt raw like the underside of my skin had been scrubbed clean. I'd never felt a sensation quite like it in my life, and I suppressed the urge to shudder as I met the advancing dyrvak, the blade of my dagger gleaming in the light of the full moon. *Nymera, grant me strength.*

The dyrvak was quick. I lashed out with my dagger, but the creature pranced out of my way and then thrust its spear out. Luckily for me, I was quick too, and I dodged around the spear and struck out, quicker this time. My thrusts were shallow but numerous. The dyrvak's grunts of pain were a song to my ears. I ducked under its underbelly and stabbed my dagger into its soft skin. Blood splattered across my face, warm and thick and...yellow? I groaned as some hit my tongue, its taste sickeningly sweet, but I didn't stop stabbing until I dodged to one side, and the dyrvak fell over, dead before it hit the ground.

Breathing heavily, Neferíl had finished taking care of the two she'd been fighting, and we were safe from whatever darkness had come to stop the druids. She stood elegantly without any blood covering her, but her chest heaved in the same manner mine did: the dyrvak hadn't made it easy.

Olbi waddled up, his face scrunched up in disgust.

"Olbi can clean blood off you when he doesn't have to worry about Caretaker."

"Don't worry about it, Olbi," I said, waving him away. "This isn't the first time I've been covered in blood."

Olbi gulped and nodded frantically. "Olbi familiar with blood too."

He ran off, and I couldn't help but think oddly of the goblin. A sense of fondness warmed my belly, a fondness that simultaneously disgusted me. I had only had a few interactions with goblins back home. They were harmless for the most part, obsessed with mischievous pranks and stealing trinkets from human homes to add to their collection of shiny things, but they were still *fae*. Olbi was making me question everything. He didn't seem all bad.

I looked down as my hands shook. Kneeling, I wiped the blood off my dagger and onto the grass. Neferíl approached, but her eyes were on Kyrie and Elahir as they silently mediated. I wasn't sure how much time had passed, but the sky was beginning to lighten, hinting at the coming sunrise, and my shoulders sagged with relief. Soon, we'd be in Elvira, which was one step closer to home.

The queen spoke, and I turned to look at her, noting she had been watching me. For how long, I didn't know. She gestured to my arm. I stared down at the tiny pockets of exposure where the Rot had feasted on my skin. It was quite the wound, and I held my arm up for closer inspection, granting Neferíl the chance to look too.

She stayed an acceptable distance away, and a part of me wondered if it could be contained and used as a weapon against the fae. It didn't seem to infect humans, not like it did faeries, so perhaps it could be used to save my people and future generations from the wrath of the forest once and for all.

My stomach twisted in disgust.

It didn't feel right, though. Not now. My eyes skirted to Olbi. Would the weapon kill his kind too? The thought made my heart ache at the thought of Olbi dying. *I don't want that*, I realized.

Neferíl's head cocked to the side ever so slightly, a questioning expression crossing her face. I couldn't discern it, and my constant frustrations at not being able to understand her returned, like a persistent headache. Consequences be damned; the next chance I got my hands on some faerie food, I was going to eat it.

A sharp inhale came from Kyrie as his eyes opened, and the rune circles surrounding him glowed brighter. He leaned over and vomited. His shoulders shaking, he waved away our concerns.

"We're just about ready," he rasped, composing himself and wiping his mouth with the back of his hand. Olbi hovered nearby, his lips drawn with worry, and I gazed around curiously. Would it be like the path I had taken to get to Elvira?

Neferíl spoke softly, and Kyrie shook his head. As they conversed, I trailed my gaze around the clearing's edge, looking for any more signs of movement or enemies. The last thing we needed was to be attacked when our guard was down.

But no others came. The forest was quiet, and soon Kyrie stood and offered his hand. "Come, Róis. You must come with me."

"Why?"

"Olbi is going to go at the same time as Neferíl. You're going to need a guide through the roots. Losing your way out there is not like losing your way here. Trust me."

A sharp noise pierced the air, so high I nearly didn't hear it. Olbi definitely did, though, his ears twitching to and fro in response as he pressed himself against Neferíl's legs.

"We must hurry and go! Must hurry and go before more arrive," he said.

"What about you?" I asked, turning to Elahir.

A smile peaked at the corner of his lips. "I must remain. There is much to be done in this forest. Much to heal. Many to prevent from following you all through. Now go."

I nodded, steadied myself, and took Kyrie's hand.

As he dragged me through the circle, something curled low in my belly and tugged so hard I nearly vomited. I might have passed out had my willful stubbornness not demanded I remain conscious. By the time I found myself planted on solid ground once more, tears trailed down my face. We stood upon a massive gnarled root, so large I could hardly comprehend it.

Kyrie's hand tightened around mine as he stood tall next to me. "Do not, under any circumstances, let go of my hand."

I complied, though my hand began sweating immediately. I stared out into the world around us and realized with startling clarity that it was an endless sea of twisting roots, a labyrinth of paths. Beyond the tree root paths was a void of cosmic brilliance. Sometimes, during the right time of year and in the right place, the sky in my world lit up with trails of brilliant blues and greens and sometimes purples and golds. They danced and wove across the sky like it had been ripped open to reveal the color behind it. I'd only seen it twice in my life, and the endless stretch of nothingness beyond the roots here looked very much the same.

"How do you know how to navigate through here?" I asked as we began walking forward. Kyrie walked easily and with purpose as if he'd done this many times before. The path we walked on looked sick, as if the Rot had reached here and claimed this path for its illness. Dark, blackened mushrooms grew on the edges as we walked, and I pressed close to Kyrie, eager to stay away from them.

"I come here often in my dreams—the world between worlds. All of these paths lead to another plane of existence. Another planet. Another reality. Whatever you wish to call it." He went silent, and when I looked at him, he was staring out at the ocean of color. "I usually only ever come here when I dream. It is an honor that I get to lead you through the roots back home."

"And Olbi knows the way too?" I asked.

Kyrie nodded. "He knows the way just as well as I do."

I stared out at the root system. It was so complex, with so many twists and turns that disappeared behind clouds and trunks, that I grew dizzy trying to comprehend it. I settled with the knowledge that I couldn't, and that where I stood now was so far beyond my understanding that I shouldn't even begin to try.

"Luckily, your world is but a small travel away from Vilanthris, which is where we just came from, so we should be arriving shortly." I clung to Kyrie's arm as the root bridge beneath our feet grew narrow. My foot kicked something small and round that flung off the edge. My gut begged me not to look down, but my stubborn curiosity ignored it. Looking down, my mind reeled at the endless number of root bridges that twisted and formed as far as my eye could see.

"Let us hurry now. There are those who would not see us through, and our destination is just there," Kyrie whispered, pointing. There was a black hole in the side of a trunk some yards away, gaping and uninviting.

"What do you mean?"

"I don't know what you'd call them, but they cry out in the abyss, and if you make enough noise, they come to feast." Kyrie's words sent a chill down my back. I wasn't entirely certain what he meant by that, but the idea of it seemed too horrendous to entertain. The sooner we freed ourselves from this strange place, the better I'd feel.

I glanced behind me, comforted that Neferíl and Olbi were still following us. Olbi kept them a fair distance away, though.

I halted when Kyrie did. Tension rolled off him in waves, and I followed his gaze as it settled on the path before us.

A small dragon stood there, its claws digging into the roots as half of its body curled off the side. Its wings were out, its scales shining a vibrant blue, and it stared at us with such sentient intelligence that I felt the urge to drop to my knees and bow. Its face was long and thin, with whiskers trailing from its snout, and it parted its maw, revealing several rows of sharp teeth. Its sudden appearance made my skin crawl, made something inside me crawl, like my soul was attempting to liberate itself from its fleshy prison.

It spoke in a language I did not understand. Its presence overwhelmed my mind with such force that I whimpered, my legs giving out beneath me. Kyrie held me upright by tucking his free hand under my arm, but even his hands shook as the dragon lowered its head and studied us with great intent.

"*Human*," the voice purred. I was finally able to understand it; it was as if it had plucked my language from my head and was speaking it back to me. "*We don't see many humans walk these paths. It's curious. Most curious.*"

"We won't be able to pass until it's been given something," Kyrie whispered beside me. "That is what cries out in the abyss. Some call them World Eaters. Others call them dragons. Many whisper of them as gods. They swim through the space between worlds and claim whatever they want. We will do well not to offend it."

As the dragon snaked its head forward, its gaze bore a fair bit of amusement. Heat rolled off its body, and as it drew closer, that strange feeling flourished again in my chest. It wasn't painful, not really, but it was like an itch I could not scratch or a weight that pressed underneath my skin that I could not alleviate.

"Stay still," Kyrie said as the dragon stopped a foot or so from my face. The hot air from its exhalation brushed against my skin, and I steeled myself, chasing the fear away. It stared at me with swirling green eyes.

It inhaled deeply, sniffing the air in front of me, then grew incredibly still before it flinched away. Turning its long body to leave, it said, "*You have been touched by another god, human. You may pass.*"

Its words rattled around in my head as it pushed itself off the path and stretched its wings, soaring away into the void. The further it got, the less wound up I felt, my chest untangling from that strange feeling that had plagued me the moment the dragon had landed.

"What did he take from you?" Kyrie asked, his voice laced with concern as he studied me over with his eyes. "Sometimes it's small, like a memory. Other times it's a piece of your soul."

I shook my head, rattled. *Touched by another god?* My mind instantly flickered to the vision I'd had when the witch had taken me. Had that dragon spoken of the one I'd had in my vision? I swallowed the lump of panic in my throat and shook my head again. "I don't know what he took. He did not say." I pointed to the path in front of us. "It doesn't matter anyway. The way is free."

Kyrie nodded slowly, his hand still in mine as he led us forward. "The way through might feel strange—like the way here. Just keep walking forward, and you'll find yourself back home."

It was already strange, like we were wading through honey or quicksand. My legs were heavier every time I took a step, and I stared at the great hole of blackness that was etched into the tree trunk with bated breath. I did not fear. I was a wolf. I was a wolf.

"You first. I'll be right behind. Go quickly once I let go," Kyrie said, and then he let go of my hand. The difference was immediate. The air swelled around me, and every inhalation was as if I were underwater. It gave me little chance to prepare, so I stepped forward and climbed into the hole.

Darkness swallowed me, but the air lightened, and I gasped, my chest aching as the reprieve from such heaviness ailed me. I massaged my chest and blinked several times as I peered through the darkness. No matter how long I looked or how much I strained my eyes, the darkness was endless, all-consuming.

I took a step forward.

Then another.

On the third step, something sharp curled in my belly and tugged me forward.

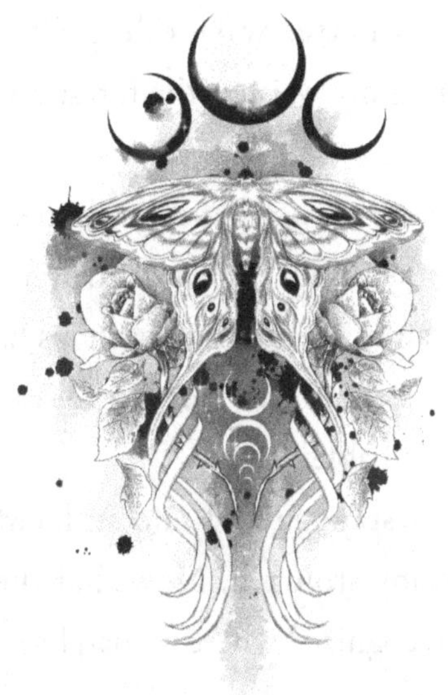

# TWENTY

## *Neferit*

A WARM BREEZE TRAILED through the air and brushed my face as I slipped through the hole in the tree. We stood before another great lake, though this one was less grand than the one we'd just left, and light filtered through the trees. Olbi appeared not two seconds after I did, muttering and groaning about how uncomfortable it was to walk between worlds.

The leaves on the tree were a deep vibrant green. I groaned, clutching my waist as the forest refused to stop spinning.

Róis was already on her hands and knees, vomiting. Rushing over to her, Olbi pulled her hair away from her face. A few feet away, Kyrie stood with his hands clasped behind his back as he stared out at the sea of trees, his expression indescribable.

"We shouldn't stay here," I said suddenly, my heart plummeting to my stomach. Now that the world had righted itself, I recognized where we had been spat out.

Eirwyn's court.

The elven king of the south. My relations with him had always been fragile. I had never met another faerie with so much pride and arrogance, but I had always admired his love and devotion to his court. He'd been ruling for far longer than I had, and I could only hope that our presence in his realm was going unnoticed.

"This place is as beautiful as it has always been," Kyrie said softly, a strange tone to his voice. "I sense no sickness here."

"That's because we're not in my court. The plague has not touched the land here," I said, reaching down to tug

Róis to her feet. She jerked away, her face pale and slick with sweat. She'd stopped purging her stomach, but the look she gave me was murderous as I smiled sweetly down at her.

"We're trespassing though. If we don't leave now, Eirwyn will send his guard after us."

"Is there a root where the Rot originates?" Kyrie asked. "If so, I would love to see it for myself. Perhaps I can figure out a way to soothe its pain."

"We haven't been able to locate where it's coming from," I said as I let go of Róis and backed away. She wiped her mouth with the back of her hand and shuddered, collecting herself as I hurried over to Kyrie. He seemed apprehensive and on edge, his eyes flickering around the tree line. "It started by infecting the souls of the forest." I waved my hands around, gesturing to the trees. "Elvira screams out in pain, and I know the humans are to blame."

"Oh?" Kyrie's curiosity tinged his tone, and I nodded.

"A long time ago, there were no courts, just spirits of the forest. Then the humans came and tore down the forest's trees and killed the spirits that dwelled inside. The only reason I know of it is because sometimes the forest sings of it."

I pressed my palm to the trunk of a nearby tree, my skin mirroring its color as I marveled at our shared beauty. All living things were carved in the likeness of nature, and I couldn't help the pride I felt at being so close to it. The tree's heartbeat was slow and steady beneath my fingertips, and I also felt its simplistic joy, its quiet peace.

"This way," I said, leading us through the trees. We needed to keep moving until the trees turned from green to red to gold, marking my court's territory.

Silence passed between us for a time before I spoke again.

"Humans came and began cutting down the trees for their villages. They didn't realize they were touching a different world, and they feared the forest spirits and the wild fae the first time they contacted them." Sympathetic pain pressed against my chest, and I spared a glance over at Róis. She watched me warily as she pulled Olbi into her arms.

"The forest retaliated, of course. Each tree has a soul, an essence of life coursing through it. They are emotions in their rawest form. Sometimes they will offer you protection if they deem you worthy. But if you offend them, their grudge holds strong, and you will never see the end of their wrath. The forest thought it only fair that if the humans were going to cut down its trees, then they could trade the souls of their children."

"Nature demands balance," Kyrie agreed.

I nodded. "It is how the court faeries came to be, or so our scribes have written it in our history. We were all human once, kidnapped by the spirits of the forest and forced to eat its food and drink until we were of the forest too."

"How old were you when you were taken?" Kyrie asked.

I blinked. "I don't recall." My memories of my human life were hazy, like a dream of another lifetime. I had devoted myself to my court because the forest had deemed me fit to rule. The queen before me had saved me from a forest's wrath when she hadn't had to do any such thing. She'd been the closest thing I'd had to a mother for some time but had rejoined the forest spirits when I'd been naught more than a child. There had never been time to mourn the loss of my human life. "I must have been young, though. I remember growing up here."

Kyrie hummed in response, and I moved forward, content with ending the conversation. Whenever I was reminded of my humanity, the world grew heavy, and the weight on my shoulders became a burden. I used to ask the faeries that had raised me in the castle if any of the humans had ever returned to their world, but they'd always told me it was impossible once a human ate too much of the fae's food.

"Your soul is tethered to the forest now, Miss," one of my maids had told me while she was braiding my hair. "If you were to leave for a long time, you would either be driven insane, or you would simply fade away."

Those words had haunted me growing up, so I had shoved my humanity away, tucked it in the back of my mind, and let it fade from memory.

We walked until the endless sea of green began to turn into crisp reds and oranges. My court was just ahead. The hold on my lungs lessened, and relief loosened my shoulders.

"See something," Olbi said. "Just there."

Something shuffled, a shadow that disappeared behind a tree, and my relief vanished.

We were too late.

"They're here," I said, tilting my chin up as a grim smile crossed my face.

Eirwyn's guards slipped out from behind the trees at the edge of our courts, and they held their spears and glaives out to stop us. I resolved myself, knowing I was now going to have to speak to the Elf King of the South.

# TWENTY-ONE
## *Róis*

T HE SUN WAS SO bright here, an endless spring. They led us through gardens before a massive castle, and the flowers were in full bloom as they grew around small grassy pathways. I'd heard stories of the Elf King, of his generous nature and his kindness towards humans due to a treaty forged between him and the southern kingdom of Kahl, but those had been rumors from the kingdoms in the south, rumors that the north had scoffed at as their babies had been ripped from their arms and the faeries had come for them in the night.

Neferíl was silent beside me as tension radiated from her. My chest tightened, keeping me on edge. I tucked Olbi closer, his presence bringing me some sense of calm. The two faeries that led us through the trails kept their faces forward and did not look at me. They were achingly beautiful, which only urged on my rage and the affirmation that looks were so often deceiving. Nothing so evil deserved such beauty.

Kyrie walked behind me, and Olbi stared at the guards with a furious expression. "Olbi dares them to hurt Caretaker," he muttered. "Olbi will throw apples at their heads if they poke him with sharp stick."

I knew better than to speak, so I remained silent. The castle before us was so unlike Neferíl's. It was like one giant greenhouse with grey stone between the glass, half-covered in the slow crawl of vines. The trees around the castle grew naturally, as if they were co-existing with the building, and the flowers were almost an overabundance as they trailed through the front gate. Faeries of the court flitted about the gardens, and they all halted to stare as we passed, their eyes trained on Neferíl, who walked with grace and ignored them.

My heart leapt to my throat as I locked eyes with a white tiger that lounged on a stone bench, its eyes ever watchful. It was a beautiful creature, its tail dangling over the bench and twitching in a playful manner. I tightened my hands to fists. I would not let my fear fester lest it consume me.

The tiger did not move; it merely stared.

The castle was huge, larger than any I'd seen. My little village was not near any large cities with castles, but I liked to imagine some of the northern castles in the human world were this large. I was like a child again, unable to contain my simplistic curiosity as the guards pushed open the doors and led us inside.

The inside of the castle was much of the same as it was outside. Nature grew freely within, climbing up the walls and growing in small formations on the floor. I peered up, sucking in a breath as my gaze was met with the sight of a ceiling made completely of glass. Sun cascaded through in an untamed warmth, and once more, I missed my dagger. The guards had wrangled it from me when they'd stopped us at the border, and this place was far too beautiful to be a place of kindness.

A hummingbird zipped past my ear, fleeing up the half-circle set of stairs we were climbing, which led to an ornate door made of dark wood. Carved into the door was a visage of woodland creatures weaving around trees. Small white gems dotted starlight at the top of the door, and they twinkled against the rays of the sun.

The guards spoke as the door was pushed open, their voices soft and lilting. The language sounded almost akin to songbirds, similar to Neferíl's but not quite.

We entered the throne room to find the king sitting on a throne of glass. The sun passed through it, reflecting a sea of color about the room. Grass dotted the floor, stifling the sound beneath my feet, and birds flew about, making homes in the trees that lined the walls. There was no roof here, and warmth graced my cheeks.

The king watched us approach in the same manner that tiger had outside. He was sprawled haphazardly on his throne, one leg kicked up over one arm. A crown of golden leaves and sun rays sat upon his fair head; his eyes were a golden-blue. A magnificent male white lion rested at the king's feet, his tail flickering in his sleep and his head resting on the king's other foot.

We halted at the foot of the small set of stairs that led up to his throne, and for quite some time, no one spoke. Neferíl never looked away from the king, her lips pursed. Finally, after several painstaking moments of staring at each other, the king's lips split into a radiant smile, and he straightened. The lion lifted his head, his golden eyes displayed for but a moment as the king readjusted and then he laid his head back down.

He spoke, his attention on Neferíl as he gestured to me. Olbi wiggled out of my grasp to cling to Kyrie's leg. The room was absent of guards, which was strange. If I found some kind of weapon, I knew I could reach the king. The lion would kill me, but if I was quick...

The king approached, stepping over the lion, which did not move. He walked down the stairs with a fluidity not possessed by humans, and he wore a long, flowing white tunic edged with golden threads. It matched his hair, a honey-white gold with pieces of it twisted into intricate braids. He drew close enough I could see that almost each one of his fingers bore a ring, the most prominent being a silver lion's head on his right ring finger. In his left hand was a clear glass full of golden liquid, which he offered to me.

It looked like faerie wine, and I didn't reach out for it immediately. My instincts screamed at me, as they had when Neferíl had offered me the blackberries. *Do not eat their food. Do not drink their wine. If you are running from them, find running water. Only iron can harm them. If you know their true name, you can use it against them.* I glanced over at Neferíl for guidance despite myself, despite knowing I could not trust her either.

Neferíl frowned, then gave the slightest of nods.

The king remained silent through the exchange, and as I took the glass from him, my hand brushed his fingers. I was shocked to find how warm they were, so similar to a human touch. I had always known faeries to be cold.

I tipped the glass back. The wine moved slowly, like it shared the consistency of honey, but it tasted of a citrus fruit I'd sampled only once, when a trader had come through Farmere with exotic fruits of the southern coasts. A hint of spice hit at the end, almost like cinnamon, and I found myself enjoying it immensely, forgetting my fear of what consequences I'd face from drinking it.

"Good little human," the king purred, tugging the glass away once I finished. The room slanted as dizziness took hold, but I was elated to be able to understand those around me once more. It was only the third time I'd sampled their food or drink, but it ferried me too close to nature. I almost understood the birds that sang to each other above, and I felt the lion's contentment. Neferíl's heartbeat sat in my chest like it was my own.

Did the faeries sense these things all the time?

I needed to be careful. Each time I gave in and ate their food or sampled their drink, I gave them a bit of my humanity.

He offered another glass of wine to Kyrie, who held up his hand and shook his head. "I can understand you just fine."

The king tilted his head as a peculiar expression crossed his face. "I do not recognize you, and yet... you bare similarities to my people." He leaned forward, his fingers grazing over Kyrie's cheek as he pulled the druid's hair back, revealing the point of his ear. "Most curious. I would have remembered a face like yours."

"You will not harm them, Eirwyn," Neferíl demanded. Eirwyn turned away from Kyrie, sighing at his empty glass. "I have claimed her blood. You know of the Old Ways."

King Eirwyn was at her side so quickly that my mind shuddered, and he snarled, pulling his lips back over his teeth. The king's canines were sharp, wickedly so. *Just like mine*, I realized. *I wonder if he filed them to be that way or if he was born with them?*

"Do not speak to me of the Olde Ways, Neferíl. I have been king far longer than you, long before when you stumbled into the woods naught more than the *filth* that stands there," he hissed, throwing his hand in my direction.

My brow furrowed. The queen hadn't always lived in the forest?

Neferíl trembled with rage.

"The forest may have accepted you as their queen, but do not fret, Nef. I have not forgotten the way you scorned my offers for a joined kingdom. Our courts were one a long time ago, after all." He straightened, sliding his hand over the edge of his open tunic to smooth a wrinkle in it before returning slowly to his throne.

"Is this treatment because I did not accept your proposal for marriage?" The queen spoke quietly, so quietly the hair on the nape of my neck stood up straight.

The king scoffed and reached down to trail his fingers through the lion's mane. "I have had quite some time to cope with that silly little rejection. No—but fret not, my lady. No harm will come to your sweet little fawn." His eyes raked over me. They were such an impossible color, like the deepest parts of the ocean mingled with the brightest gold of the sun. "I can taste the Forest Father's influence on her." His eyes flickered between Kyrie and I, and his grin was slow to return, wolfish in nature. "Upon both. You have brought me such a beautiful gift. Now go. My guards will take you to your rooms."

My eyes flashed in surprise. "We won't be taken to the dungeon?"

Eirwyn waved his hand in dismissal as two guards appeared, awaiting his signal. "Of course not. My land may be a kingdom of beasts, but you have not brought any

harm upon my people. Besides –" His grin gleamed against his golden skin. "The queen and I are not at war. It would be insulting to condemn her to my dungeons." He glanced at one of his guards. "Take them to one of the rooms in the guest ward. Take those two" –he pointed at Kyrie and Olbi– "to the King's Ward. I'm very interested in making this one's acquaintance and have much to ask him." His gaze burned as it met mine. "Make sure the human has much to eat and drink. We must be able to understand one another."

He contented himself with other things then, leaving us to the mercy of the guards. Neferíl was gifted with the honor of walking first, and she did so proudly, making sure her head was held high. I hated myself in this moment for admiring her grace and beauty, and I gave a small wave to Olbi as they were led in the opposite direction.

The hallway we were led down was open and airy. One wall was decorated with beautiful windows that reached from floor to ceiling, their panes decorated with ornate dark woodwork of swirling designs. Doors lined the other side of the hall, but we were led up the stairs and to a door at the end on the right. The statue of a rearing tiger stood guard at the end, and the faerie guard gestured.

"Your room. We will return with food and drink. In the meantime, you are required to remain inside." She stepped out of the way as Neferíl pushed open the door. The room was magnificent in its grandeur, with a sitting room that led out to a balcony. Just like the rest of the house, the ceiling was made of glass, and the retreating sun cast an ethereal glow about it. A fireplace sat nestled before a few seats, devoid of flames.

As we padded into the bedroom, the door shut and clicked behind me. When I tried to turn the handle, it would not open, and I let out a small breath of frustration. I was naked without my dagger and once more at the mercy of the queen should Neferíl decide her oath fulfilled. I wouldn't go without a fight, but my fear betrayed me in the sweat at my palms.

"I do not intend to kill you here, little thorn." Neferíl's voice made me jump, but I hid it behind a veiled expression. It was frustrating, knowing the queen could hear my heart beating frantically, could sense the quickening of my breath.

"Why did you protect me? After the witch..." I swallowed, my fingers grazing over my waist, where the ghost of the witch's wound echoed despite its healed state.

A strange look came over Neferíl at the question. Something flickered in her gaze: anger, confusion, and a hint of something I could not grasp. Faeries, I had found, were difficult to read. They did a better job at hiding their emotions than humans did. Even humans like me, who tucked my emotions behind a wall of steel.

"I couldn't—" Neferíl's voice took a softer tone, as if she didn't trust herself to speak. Silence echoed through the room, and something beckoned me to reach out and lay a hand on Neferíl's arm.

But Neferíl didn't give me the chance as she lowered her head and slipped her gaze behind a mask of indifference. "I swore an oath," she said coldly. "The life of my people depends on it."

I remained silent. Words would not change our fate. Despite not being confined to the dungeons, the king had imprisoned us nonetheless.

I turned to pace as Neferíl trailed out onto the balcony. The sun was on its journey to set, casting a brilliant array of golds and pinks over the treetops, and my mind refused to quiet. I had prepared for years to enter the woods and slay all the faeries I met. I had lived and breathed that notion until I'd recited it like a mantra in my sleep. I just needed to get to the Grove. I needed to find my sister, heal the forest, and return home. I fled to the bedroom, where my mouth dried.

There was only one bed.

"You will take it. Faeries have no need to sleep," Neferíl said from behind me. I turned to find her plucking a blackberry from one of the trays. Meat and cheeses complimented the fruit, and several decanters sparkled with wine.

"Fine," I said, reaching out to run my fingers along the door's frame. A hidden door settled in the lip, and I pulled it out, eager to face a bit of privacy for the first time since having stepped foot in Elvira. The queen's hard gaze was the last thing I saw before the door touched the other side of the door frame, and I was granted silence.

Sleep beckoned me, but I refused, fearing that sleep would only bring a death sentence. My waist ached where the witch had pierced me with the blade. I desperately wanted a bath—there was a beautifully ornate tub nestled in the corner—but I did not trust my surroundings. Getting in a state of undress was the last thing I needed. Being without my weapon left me vulnerable enough.

I crawled atop the bed instead, noting with fierce joy that the blanket was made of some sort of animal. As I slipped beneath it, its white pelt was exceptionally warm and soft. It felt like I hadn't slept in years.

Pressing my back against the headboard, I dug my fingers into my palm and chased away my sleepiness. If I wished to survive, I'd need to keep my wits about me and figure out a way to sneak off.

*Tomorrow*, I thought, my eyes growing heavy despite my inner turmoil to stay conscious. *I'll try to make sense of the castle tomorrow. Perhaps I'll be able to find my dagger.*

As sleep won, I dreamed of home, of the brush of mountain air and sea salt. I dreamed of a world free from fear.

# TWENTY-TWO
## Róis

THE WORLD WAS DARK. *Creaking limbs scraped against the wall of my home just outside my window, beckoning and teasing. I was a slave to my fear, a slave to my sister's as she stared at me with wide eyes from across the room. Beside her, at the window, a pair of large luminescent eyes peered at me from the shadows.*

*"Monster," I wailed, stumbling out from under the covers. "Papa, there's a monster outside." I barely made it to my door when my sister's screams pierced the air, when something with long, thin fingers curled around my arm*

*and yanked me back. I cried out in terror as it slammed me against the windowsill, my back thumping painfully against the wood.*

*"No, Róis. No, no, no," Sister cried, reaching out to grab my hand. "Do not let the monsters take you away."*

I woke suddenly, a whimpering cry fleeing my lips as my eyes darted up and met Neferíl, who was half-sheathed by darkness. She stood near the bed, and as she drew forward, I flinched away, gasping as white-hot pain burned through my recently healed wound. "Stay away from me," I seethed, pressing my hand to my waist.

The flicker of concern that had crossed Neferíl's face disappeared behind a wall of rage and disgust. "The king requires our audience," she said, speaking quietly through clenched teeth. "He does not tolerate tardiness." She eyed the tub. "I recommend freshening up."

I shook my head. "The king will have me as I am," I hissed. The lingering fear from the nightmare still chased the strength from my limps as I dragged myself out of bed. I tried to ignore the grime that had collected under my fingernails and the grease that forced my hair out in odd directions. A bath was needed, yes, but I'd rather smell foul than have faeries come for me while I was naked.

Neferíl's laugh was bitter. "Stop fretting, little thorn. We're in the king's court now. If the king finds you unfit for his halls... he will see to it." Her face softened, so strange to see after it had been so full of sharp lines. "I will stand just outside. No one will come for you. I promise. "

My eyes flashed in distrust, but I knew Neferíl wasn't lying. She couldn't, and I sensed the bonds of the oath forged strong between us. After a moment, I nodded.

"The water here should aid in your healing too," Neferíl said, looking at my waist. "Whatever evil lingers from the hag, it will help." After a curt nod, she left the room and pulled the door shut behind her.

As I drew close, water filled the tub, and soft curls of steam ascended from its surface. *In and out, quick as you can*, I thought, tentatively stepping over the lip and slipping into the water.

It was warm but not unbearably so as I lowered myself down until only my face stayed dried. The bath chased away any lingering stiffness from my nightmare, and I relaxed against the wall of the tub as the warmth pulled the aches from my muscles and forced my knots to relax.

"Little thorn," the queen said after I'd been relaxing for some time. "The king's guard has come." I shot up, spilling water over the side of the tub.

*It is a good thing*, I told myself. I had been getting too comfortable in the water. The warmth had brought on a deceitful sense of comfort, and my midsection no longer ached from my wound. Pulling myself out of the tub, I looked down to see the wound on my midsection had turned into little more than an angry red scar. It no longer ached, and I recalled the soft and gentle stroke of the queen's fingers as she'd grazed them over the wound. I shivered, ignoring the blare of heat that settled at my core.

*She is wicked*, I thought angrily to myself. *She wants to kill me.*

Still, I couldn't shake the softness that had been in her eyes when she'd thought I was dying. The quiet desperation in them when she'd protected me from the witch's wrath.

My heart squeezed. Salia had never looked at me like that.

Padding over to the chair, I shoved those feelings aside as I studied the clothes that had been left for me. A simple white tunic and black pants. *Thank the Moon Mother*, I thought. I would have been horrified if they had left me a dress.

Pulling the shirt over my head, I nearly shivered at how soft the fabric was against my skin. The southern cities were known for their silks, yet their clothes still paled in comparison to this shirt's comfort.

After tugging the pants on, I searched the room for a weapon of any kind. There didn't seem to be anything I could use against them, however, so I curled my fingers into fists as I took a steadying breath. I would use my teeth if I had to.

Sliding the door open, I found Neferíl waiting on the balcony. She was staring down at the grounds below, her gaze far off. Unlike me, they had dressed her suitable to her title. Her dress was black with gold threads trailing along the edges of her neckline and the sheen sleeves that went up to her wrists. Her back was left bare, and I took a moment to stare at the wings splayed across the queen's shoulder blades.

"Do all fae have wings?" I asked. The effects of the faerie wine from the night before still left the world vibrant and colorful, and a golden hue echoed off the queen's wings in a regal sort of beauty.

"Just my court," the queen said simply as she turned. It was almost envious, how gracefully she moved. "And only some do." She didn't elaborate after that, and I didn't ask. It didn't matter anyhow. I only needed her to lead me to their god's grove so that he might heal the Rot that infested the land and I could find a way to return home.

"Have you figured out how we're going to get out of here?" My question sent a chill down my spine, as if the very walls were listening. With the fae, anything was possible, and the queen gave me a stern look before walking to the door.

"We're esteemed guests of the king. We will leave when he dismisses us."

It was strange, seeing the queen so *submissive*. She'd been anything but since the moment I'd met her, but something about the king was making her anxious. If the faerie queen was anxious, what right did I have to my confidence?

The door opened, and the two guards from before appeared. They were so tall and thin that it was nearly alien. Their long hair was pinned straight and tucked neatly behind pointed ears. Each of them wielded a glaive tucked against their sides, and while they wore no helm, the gleam of their plated armor shone brightly in the light.

"Follow us to the king," was all they said before leading us out of the room.

The halls were much more occupied than they had been the night before, with faeries trailing through and muttering to each other behind slender fingers. Much like before, I was the afterthought of a conversation, their gazes on the queen as the guards led us back to the throne room. Birds sang from the branches near the top of the room, and somewhere was the soft bumbling of a creek tucked just out of sight. *I thought they didn't like running water?* It was as if the king's palace was not a palace at all but merely an extension of nature.

King Eirwyn sat upon his throne. His hair was tied back today, woven in intricate braids and curls. His eyes gleamed blue-gold, and when he grinned, his canines poised dangerously. "Come closer," he commanded. "We have much to discuss."

The lion was absent from the king's feet, but several large cats napped in various spots of the room. As we drew closer, the king stood, gesturing to a small table off to the side at the bottom of the stairs. "I'm having breakfast delivered as we speak, so sit. You can tell me why there are some of your scouts trespassing at the outskirts of my kingdom."

The queen flinched, but it was so slight that I doubted anyone saw it but me.

"My people were instructed to pull back behind my walls. No one, not even my scouts, should be anywhere near the borders," the queen said shortly. Her gaze was accusatory. Did she think the king was lying? What benefit would he get from doing so?

"Sit." The king's command was not optional as it slipped from his lips in a quiet sort of anger. His gaze melted to molten gold as he stalked down the steps, elegant like the large cats that patrolled through the flora of the room. If I couldn't see the glass walls poking through the trees, I might have thought we were still outside.

I sat after a moment's hesitation, wondering where Kyrie and Olbi were and if they were okay. The queen slipped delicately into her chair, and as the king sat, several faeries approached, dressed in beautifully woven clothing that elevated their beauty. They were so beautiful they were almost painful to look at. I swallowed the lump growing in my throat as I pressed my fingers to the edge of the table to ground myself.

The faeries floundered about the table, slipping plates of food and goblets of drink in front of the three of us. The king sat lazily but somehow still managed to look regal. I wondered if human royals were able to achieve such grace. I'd never been to the large cities to see the royal families for myself, but somehow, I doubted it.

"I will give you one more chance to tell me the truth. One. If you fail me again, well…" He sighed, picking up a grape and studying it for a moment before popping it into his mouth. "You know I don't like to be disappointed." He gave the queen a pointed look as he chewed slowly and gestured to the plate in front of me.

"I must insist you eat," he said, his voice lacking the warmth from the day before. "It gets terribly annoying when we cannot understand each other."

My hold on the edge of the table tightened. I could feel it—the effects of the faerie wine and their food. I stood at the edge of a cliff and threatened to topple over it. If I had too much, I would never be able to return home. The magic that sang through me deemed it so. My blood would be too poisoned by the forest to flourish anywhere else.

I'd become a faerie just like them.

Still, I sat in a cave of lions. If I were to scorn the king's wishes, I wouldn't exist *anywhere*. So I plucked a piece of bread from the plate in front of me and pulled it apart before slipping a bite into my mouth. I was nearly disgusted with how delicious it was, but I ate ravenously, as if I hadn't eaten in days. Sometimes it felt that way.

"Excellent." The king's smile was cold. "Now–" He turned to the queen. "An explanation."

Neferíl sighed as she picked up a fork and a knife to cut at the meat on her plate. "I have been away from my court for quite some time. The man you ferried away, the druid that came with us, can attest to that. It was *his* world we found ourselves in after our little thorn sent us there on accident." Stabbing the meat with her fork, Neferíl took a tentative bite. "If there are scouts on your borders that you are so concerned about, Eirwyn, I would implore to ask why? Do you have something to hide?"

Her words clung to the air with implication. My gaze darted between the two of them as I remained silent, focusing hard on the food in front of me. I sat among two otherworldly beings; it would be foolish for me to intrude.

"No." His smile widened as he took a bite from a tomato. The inside seeped out between his lips, dribbling down his chin. He ignored it, staring at Neferíl with a challenging expression. "Why would I have anything to hide?"

Eirwyn didn't appear as if he was hiding anything. He was far more relaxed than Neferíl, with an easygoing smile and relaxed shoulders as he dabbed at his mouth with a napkin and straightened in his seat. "You are the one that suffers with the unwillingness to work together. Tell me, Your Majesty, do you not trust me?" He pressed a hand to his chest, mocking offense. "Your distrust wounds me. Your *lies* wound me."

"She's not lying." The words left me before I could think to stop them, and both fae turned towards me. Neferíl's eyes flashed dangerously, a warning in her expression, and a flicker of ire passed over Eirwyn's face before it was tucked neatly behind a wall of curiosity.

"Oh, do share, little human," he said, his words a low purr.

I steadied my courage. Little Wolf was what my father called me. I would not submit to the whims of lions.

"The forest is rotting. Surely, you've seen signs of it even this far south?" My gaze passed between the two of them, and I continued before I could be interrupted, "We're on our way to the Sacred Grove to plea with the Forest Father. My hope is that he will liberate the sickness that ails this wood."

Eirwyn leaned forward, threading his fingers together thoughtfully as he rested his chin on them. "What does a human care for the trifles of the fair folk?"

Sircha's words rang heavily in my head. *Kill the queen.* The longer I was in Elvira, however, the less that seemed like the right path. It did not feel like killing the queen would cure the Rot. It didn't even seem like they were the cause of the Rot, like I'd assumed. I jutted my chin up sharply. "The fae are fleeing the forest in their sickness. It is only a matter of time before they infect my village. My elders have sent me to learn and aid in whatever way I can."

Eirwyn sighed and called over a nearby servant. The faerie flitted forward with a glass decanter in her hands, the golden liquid inside twinkling with temptation. I found myself watching the decanter move, my hands itching to reach out and grab it. I refrained, horrified at its pull, and the faerie tilted the decanter against the lip of the king's goblet.

"If you are truly on a quest to seek the Eldertree, I will not stop you. I cannot. It's written in the Olde Ways that safe passage will be given. However –" His gaze darkened, and he paused to drink deeply from his goblet. "If unrest is taking place in your court, Neferíl, I will demand order. You brought order to the Unseelie Court when you took the throne, but old wounds are not easily forgotten. Our treaty stands yet, but I've spilled Unseelie blood before. I will do so again if it is for the best interest of my court." He let the threat sink into the air, and the queen scowled.

Tossing her hair back, she straightened in her chair. "As would I, Your Majesty. My intention was never to cause discourse between our people. Perhaps if you provided aid—"

"I'm afraid that's not possible. If I had the spare resources, you know I would." He turned back towards his food, and the queen's rage thickened the air. It was palpable, and I inhaled deeply as my own eyes flickered down to my plate.

"We suffer a sickness of our own." My gaze darted up again, meeting the king's expression as it sought mine. His fingers picked at the food on his plate, and he stared at me with a haunted look. "But your Rot has not reached here."

"Your Majesty." A faerie stepped inside the throne room, his expression apologetic as it darted between us.

"Most apologies for the interruption, but there is someone here to see the queen," he said, his eyes flickering to Neferíl.

"Tell them they're not taking any visitors," Eirwyn said, waving his hand in dismissal.

"It's the queen's general, sire, but she—" He hesitated as fear flickered across his face. "She is not well."

# TWENTY-THREE
## *Róis*

T HE TABLE SHUDDERED, AND porcelain clanked as Neferíl stood, a trace of distress crossing her face before disappearing. "I need to see her, and I need Kyrie to meet us." Her gaze hardened; her lips pursed. "I will beg if I have to."

"No need." But her words seemed to satisfy Eirwyn. "Bring her in, and fetch Kyrie from his room."

"Forgive me, Your Majesty." The faerie swallowed thickly as he darted from foot to foot in a restless nature. "No one wishes to go near her. She's not *well*, my king."

Eirwyn's face twisted as annoyance made itself a home in his expression, and he stood abruptly. His goblet tipped over, spilling wine all over the food. I remained still despite my instincts telling me to bare my teeth, and Eirwyn composed himself by tugging on his tunic and turning to Neferíl.

"Come then. We will go greet her. You too," he said, waving at me to stand. "Cannot let a human roam the palace by herself." He reached down to press a finger under my chin, then tugged upwards, forcing my gaze to meet his. Where some might be attracted to his unnatural beauty, I saw him for what he truly was: a dangerous monster. Eirwyn wielded his beauty like a blade, and, to me, that was more dangerous than anyone with a sword. A weapon was merely that: a weapon. Beauty could be used to deceive. Beauty was a mask.

"Unless you'd like to be escorted back to the room?" His voice was soft like velvet, and I gave a slight shake of my head. I did bare my teeth at him then. Consequences be damned. I would not be scared into submission.

"Right then." He pulled away, and I stood reluctantly, sneaking a glance at Neferíl. Worry trailed off her, and her fists shook at her sides as the faerie led us from the room. I could tell she was struggling to refrain from pushing past.

The faerie led us down the stairs, past the whispering hands of other court members and glittering eyes. The effects of the food and wine made everything extra vibrant, and even after all the times I'd been forced to indulge, I was wholly unprepared for it. Nor was I prepared for the tingling in the tips of my fingers or how light my step now was.

As we neared the courtyard, the air began to feel different. A sharp sweetness coated my tongue, and the faeries flitted about anxiously, darting away as we stepped foot into the front gardens.

Rhi stood at the other end. She was hunched over with her arms around her waist. Her eyes darted up as we approached, and Neferíl's earlier calm and control shattered at the sight of her general's ruined state.

The Rot was different than I'd seen before. It was moving slower, like normal rot in the forest might. Dotting her arms and legs, it puckered like a dark rash, and mushrooms had sprouted in jagged lines up to her fingers and the side of her face.

"General," Neferíl whispered in a horrified tone, reaching her hand out.

"Do not come near me, Your Majesty." Rhi whimpered, her eyes glossed over with pain. My heart squeezed painfully for the faerie despite my aversions. No one deserved such a fate.

Neferíl halted, her shoulders square and tense. Even Eirwyn was silent, his brow furrowed as everyone gave Rhi a wide space. The large cats prowled at the edge of the garden, their ears pressed flat against their skulls and their tail flickering in distress.

"I had to—" Rhi moaned, clutching her stomach. "I had to get here to warn you. Oh, it *hurts*."

Neferíl turned quickly on her heel and strode up until she was inches from Eirwyn's face. "The druid. I need him. *Now*."

Eirwyn nodded faintly and snapped his fingers, then turned to whisper in a faerie's ear as she materialized. She was gone quicker than she'd arrived. The queen turned back to Rhi, who breathed shallowly and was looking worser with every second that passed. There was no telling how long we'd been gone, how long she'd been infected. The faeries I'd seen touched by the Rot had deteriorated quickly. It was surprising that Rhi was still alive.

"Warn me about what, Rhi?" Neferíl's voice was soft and full of concern as she paced a safe distance from Rhi. The rest of the faeries were silent.

"She's taken over. I think it's been her plan all along. I think..." She gulped. "I think she..." She collapsed, her eyes rolling into the back of her head as more mushrooms pushed through her skin, and other parts rotted away to reveal the gleam of bone.

"Eirwyn, I'll never ask a single thing from you again if you'll just get me the druid," Neferíl cried out, her voice breaking as she paced at the edge of where Rhi had fallen. Conflicting emotions danced in her eyes as if she fought not to doom herself by approaching Rhi anyway.

"I have sent for him," was all Eirwyn said. The wait for Kyrie was agonizing, but he finally came. His eyes lit with concern, and his gaze found Rhi.

"Oh," he said, uttering something in a different language as he rushed forward. "You were all wise not to approach." He halted a few feet away, inhaling sharply. "I cannot treat it, but I can put her to sleep. Preserve her body for a short time. I believe your blood, Róis, can save her." He hesitated. "If you're not willing, there are other potions I can try, not magic." He looked uncertain as he studied her wounds, but he didn't look hopeful. I clamped my fingers around my wrist as the Rot on my arm burned, its pain flourishing for the first time since I'd gotten it. My lungs rattled suddenly, and I wondered if the Rot was growing there too.

"My blood? I don't think—"

"Do it," Neferíl demanded, her brow pressed in worry. Tears stained her cheeks; it was the first time I'd seen her cry, and she mirrored the same horror that had been on my face when Salia had died.

Still, I hesitated. I had spent my entire life hating the fae. The *fiagaila* taught me of their evil and wicked ways, incapable of pain or fear. My time spent with Neferíl and the other fae was unraveling all of that.

I nodded. Despite my better judgment, I nodded. "I'll save her if I can."

Eirwyn watched on silently, his mouth drawn in a faint frown. It was as if time stayed suspended as Kyrie and I knelt next to Rhi, who was crying and thrashing about. The mushrooms had stopped growing on her skin, but half of her jaw was exposed from where the plague had rotted away the skin on her cheek.

Kyrie hummed, and a soft green glow rose from his skin as he trailed a finger over Rhi but never quite touching her. A thin sheen of sweat dotted his brow. "This magic is wicked," he said, his voice barely a whisper. "Whatever the cause, it needs to be stopped."

His magic tugged on mine like it was beckoning it forth, and I turned to look back at Eirwyn.

"I need a knife. Something small will do."

Eirwyn scoffed and raised his head high. "Why would I—"

"We're deep within your court," I sneered. "What can a little human do to you when surrounded by your people?"

After a moment, he nodded, and one of his guards approached and offered me a small knife that had been strapped to her side. The hilt was very light, made of golden and white metal, and the blade itself was sharp and translucent.

A soft voice compelled me to turn and plunge the blade into the king, but I ignored it. Taking a deep breath, I slid the blade across my right palm.

The pain was sharp, and my heart roared in my ears as blood collected like a well in the center of my palm. I ignored the whispered shock that traveled through the fae as they flitted about the courtyard, scooting closer.

"Having her ingest it might be the best course if we can get her still enough to drink," Kyrie said. "But I fear touching her will lead to me contracting the Rot myself."

I pressed my left hand to her chest to pin her to the ground as I tipped my other hand against her lips. She struggled for a moment before pressing her mouth to my hand. Drinking deeply, she pulled the blood from my wound. Something flourished through me at the sensation, and the Rot began to disappear from Rhi's arms. The skin regrew over her cheek, and though the Rot did not disappear entirely, it receded, like it was going dormant.

Rhi's eyes fluttered as she slipped into an unconscious state, and I slumped, suddenly exhausted.

"Magnificent," Kyrie whispered. He stared at me, and I met his gaze despite the embarrassment I felt due to his scrutiny. "Your magic is raw like that of my home. If I didn't know any better, I'd say you come from a family of druids."

"My father is a healer, but he works primarily with herbs," I said as if that offered an explanation. Father had never spoken much of his family either.

Now that Rhi was unconscious, her face had smoothed out and was free of pain and worry. The Rot had taken much, but my blood seemed to be healing her.

Neferíl drew closer, her face twisted. "How did you do that?"

"I don't know." My blood hadn't done anything like that before. What had changed? My thoughts couldn't help but linger back on the dragon in the other realm. *You have been touched by a god.*

"It's unclear what will happen to your general now that Róis' blood is in her veins, but she seems to be stable for now. Still, she shouldn't be moved much," Kyrie said.

"We have a spare wing she can stay in." Eirwyn finally spoke as he strode forward. "The druid will stay near her and tend to her while the two of you..." He sniffed, studying his nails. "Will make your way to the Sacred Grove post haste. I will not have this plague touching my lands." He paused, his gaze flicking quickly to meet Neferíl's. "She spoke strangely before her collapse. Who is 'she' that she spoke of?"

Neferíl shrugged. "I do not know, but if someone has assumed my place in my stead, their rule will be short-lived."

Eirwyn's face softened as he stepped forward and rested a hand on Neferíl's shoulder. "While we wait for your general to wake and enlighten us, I will send scouts to your lands and see if we cannot find out what has occurred in your absence."

Neferíl nodded stiffly as Eirwyn pulled away and spoke quickly to an armored faerie nearby. The gardens were cast into a state of whispering panic, and Kyrie rose to his feet after checking on Rhi. His face was apologetic as he turned to me.

"It isn't safe for any of the fae to go near her," he explained. "Just in case the Rot is still contagious. It would be better for you to carry her whenever Eirwyn is ready to move her."

I nodded, and while everyone was distracted, I slipped the small knife I had used to cut my palm up the sleeve of my shirt. The wound on my hand ached, but it had thankfully stopped bleeding.

Eirwyn snapped his fingers. "Come. I will show you where to take her."

"We'll leave on the marrow, Eirwyn," Neferíl said as I bent over Rhi. She didn't look older than her early twenties, but I knew better. The fae were deceptive. Who knew how old she really was? Her hair was a coiled mess around her face, and I took care not to touch her wounds or rattle her too much as I picked her up. She was light, and I carried her with little trouble as Eirwyn soothed a few fae nearby.

"She cannot die," Neferíl said quietly. "Losing her would be a devastating blow to my court."

"I promise to do everything I can to ensure her body fights it off," Kyrie said, tucking a loose strand of hair behind his ear. "Just do not be led astray. I do not think Róis' magic cured it."

"The Grove is only a few days' travel from here," Neferíl said.

A sense of relief and horror coursed through me at the thought. The queen's oath only protected me until we stepped foot in the Grove. I stared at her wearily. Perhaps

Rhi's sickened state would protect me a little while longer. If not, I would do whatever I must.

Still, I despaired. I didn't want to die.

*Perhaps the Forest Father will show us a way.* He had to.

Eirwyn turned back to us as the gardens cleared, leaving the area empty except for the king, queen, Kyrie, and me, holding Rhi.

My fate was in the Forest Father's hands now.

"Come," Eirwyn said, smiling radiantly at Kyrie. "It seems like you'll be getting a room upgrade, my little druid," he said as we ascended the stairs.

Kyrie didn't reply.

Eirwyn led us down a hall on our right after we entered his castle. At the furthest door on the right, he opened it, revealing a large room with a velvet-clad bed taking up a large part of the opposite wall. Like much of the castle, the walls were translucent, letting the sun in. Vines climbed the walls, and long, thin flowers hung from the ceiling. I padded over to the bed and laid Rhi gently across it.

"No one will enter this room unless you're the druid. Not unless I permit it." There was no room for suggestion in the king's voice as Neferíl brushed past me to stand next to the bed. I searched her gaze but could not discern the feeling in them, and I turned to see Eirwyn watching on with ill-tamed curiosity before he went to the door.

"I will send someone to escort you back to your rooms." He left without another word, and Kyrie trailed over to the plant life in the room, muttering excitedly under his breath, looking like he'd been gifted with whatever he'd need for his healing.

"The king must have done this on purpose," Kyrie said quietly, turning to stare at us as his fingers ghosted the leaves of a large plant. "There are many potions I can make with these plants to alleviate her pain while you two are away."

"I'm sure you know, but keep away from that corner," I said, gesturing to the vibrant purple and black flowers trailing up the wall. "The nectar from those flowers will paralyze you for hours with a mere touch." My father had used it once or twice to keep someone still when he'd needed to stitch up a wound.

"There is something similar in Vilanthris," Kyrie said, eyeing the corner with some interest. "Though it's rarely used for healing purposes."

I refrained from shuddering at the thought. There were many nefarious reasons a person could use that flower for.

"Time to return to your rooms," a voice called out from the other side of the door. I turned and was greeted by a female faerie with a deceptively kind smile and large dark eyes. Her fingers were pressed to the door, holding it open, and she gestured at us impatiently. "Come now. The missus deserves some rest to preserve her strength."

Neferíl forced herself away from the bed and hid her stress behind a smile when I met her gaze. Her eyes couldn't hide it though. I'd always been good at seeing past masks, and I frowned. I wanted to tell her we'd find a way to cure Rhi, that we'd find a cure for the Rot, but I stayed silent. There was nothing in moments like this that would change the fact that Rhi would die if we didn't find a way to cure her. My silence remained as I watched the faerie lead Kyrie to the room on the left of Rhi's.

"Our majesty wants you close to the girl, should anything happen," the faerie explained, showing Kyrie to his room. "Your goblin will be brought to here soon."

"His name is Olbi," Kyrie said sternly.

The faerie lowered her head. "My apologies. Olbi will be brought to this room after the ball."

"Ball?" the queen asked sharply.

The faerie nodded. "It is the king's wish to celebrate the coming of summer. He has deemed you all to be treated as guests and says you are welcome to attend before your departure should you wish."

Ire cut through me. Faeries were dying in the northern part of the forest, and the king was throwing a ball. It didn't seem fitting, but it didn't surprise me.

I grinned widely at the faerie, revealing the flash of my pointed canines. She mirrored me with a set of her own, and we both stilled, a silent challenge of who would back down first.

Eventually, she turned, but my satisfaction was short-lived as Kyrie pressed a hand to my shoulder. I flinched as my instincts screamed at me to strike out, and Kyrie's expression turned sheepish.

"Take this. If there is a source of water in the grove you travel to, there's a good chance it holds some sort of magical healing. Soak this pendant in it. The magical properties of this stone will draw the water in and trap it inside. It could help Rhi." He held it out to me, but it was the queen who took it, studying it closely before slipping it over her head. It gleamed a bright, vibrant green against her skin, and I stared at it for a time before my gaze rose to meet Neferíl's, then darted away.

"Take us back to our room," the queen demanded suddenly, and I took one last look at Kyrie before we were shuffled away. I had this strange feeling in my gut.

Will I ever see him again?

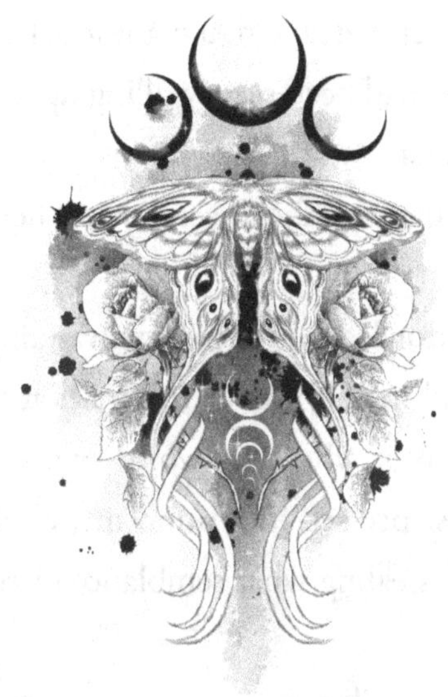

# TWENTY-FOUR

## *Neferit*

THE MOMENT THE DOOR of our room closed behind us, I collapsed. I couldn't remember the last time I'd cried. When I'd been a human, perhaps. The reason why evaded me after all these years. A bully at school or maybe a sickness I hadn't been able to curb. Maybe it had been the day my parents had thrown me into the woods as a child offering.

I couldn't remember, and that made it all harder, like the dam in my chest had been slowly filling up over the years, never able to burst.

Rhi's appearance and the uncertainty of her fate was the tipping point.

I vaguely acknowledged the human standing in the corner, but I found myself unable to care that she watched on awkwardly. Not when the world swirled, not when the whole forest pressed in around me, choking the air from my lungs, stealing what semblance of control I still carried...

A sob rattled my rib cage.

*Oh dear, sweet Rhi.*

She was my right hand, the one who acted as my reason. We'd grown together from children to women, had gossiped about other court members, and had snuck around the castle to perform harmless pranks when the bore of the court had grown too overwhelming. Without her...

I wailed, my hands reaching up to clutch at my braids. I tugged on them as if the small pain that wrought would stop the weight in my chest from crushing my heart. It didn't do any such thing. Rather, it just turned the anxiety into a beast, a beast with claws that dug at my throat as if desperate to get out. I stood abruptly, grabbed the nearest object, and flung it as hard as I could against a wall. Whatever it was, it shattered, the noise barely registering as I moved on to the next thing. And the next and the next and the next and the next and the next...

Hands grabbed mine, and I snarled, attempting to tug away. I was blind by my grief. Great wells of tears boiled over and trailed down my cheeks. The grasp on my hands was strong, and Róis' face swam into view.

Her sadness clung to her expression, the same sadness that pierced me now. The same fear. The same understanding. It was the understanding that broke me. The flicker of it in Róis' eyes pulled me down and leveled me against the chaos inside.

"You shouldn't be here," I whispered, trying to stop the great trembling my body had fallen prey to. I tried to tug my hands away again, but this time it was more lackluster, and I was acutely aware of how warm Róis' skin was, how soft. "I'm going to kill you."

I whispered it in the air like a promise.

Still, Róis stayed, her thumbs moving gently across the back of my hands. The movement was strangely calming, and I inhaled sharply, shuddering against my despair.

"I lost someone to it," Róis said quietly, her hands tightening on mine. "Just before I came here. It wasn't the same, not quite, but we were attacked by one of the infected faeries, and she died." The grief in her eyes was so tangible, so tangled within her own expression, I could almost taste it. *Almost*. It mingled with my own, bred on familiarity, and another wave of tears cascaded down my cheeks.

"That's why, if it comes to it, I have made peace with dying. If that's what is needed to save someone else from this cursed Rot, then I will gladly do it." She spoke with such fierce determination, but still, no one wanted to die, not truly. My eyes flickered over Róis' face, searching for the truth or any hidden agenda. There was nothing in there that betrayed that, and a small passing observation washed over me: she'd make a great queen.

I danced away from the thought even as Róis nodded. "We'll save her," she said.

My heart squeezed painfully at the thought of killing her now when she was willing to help me, but Rhi's face swam in the forefront of my mind. If I needed to rid the forest of the Rot, I'd do it.

"Thank you," I said. Now that I'd finished crying, I just felt hollow, my head full of bees as I swayed in the middle of the room. The floor was covered in broken porcelain and feathers from ripped pillows, and I eyed the ruin with little shame. It was cathartic to have destroyed something of Eirwyn's. I doubted he'd notice.

Róis shook her head, her eyes shining. "I told myself when I entered this forest that I'd gladly die for my people."

Her words tugged at me. Could I do it were the roles reversed? Could I stand on the cliffside of fate and take the plummet? Could I sacrifice myself for my people?

*Yes*, I decided. *I could.*

I became acutely aware of how close Róis was to me. She wasn't flinching away or baring her teeth. She had a thin dusting of freckles across her nose and cheeks, and there was a faint scar at her right temple, hidden almost always behind the wild untamed mess of curls that was her hair. Her lips were thin but not overtly so, and my gaze lingered on them for a moment too long. When my eyes darted up to hers, she was studying me with a soft, questioning expression.

"Excuse me."

Róis jerked away from me with a hard and conflicting expression on her face. I straightened my spine and steadied my breath, then turned to meet the gaze of the faerie that had opened the door to our room.

He didn't appear at all surprised, disgusted, or embarrassed for having interrupted. The people of my court thought it ill will to have any sort of relations with a human, but Eirwyn's people did so all the time, so it came as no surprise when the faerie guard ignored what he'd seen and laid the clothes he had in his arms on the chair just inside the door.

"Your attire for the evening. The king's servants are finishing the last of the preparations for the feast, and then I will escort you to the ballroom. He urges you to prepare for the evening now." His fingers grazed the door as he stepped back into the hall. "I will be waiting right outside."

As the door clicked shut behind him, Róis brushed past me without looking at me and tugged one of the articles of clothing off the chair. I opened my mouth to say something, but she was already fleeing the common room and sliding the bedroom door closed behind her.

I stood in the middle of the room, my face warm from crying, my lips tingling from the almost kiss. I raised my fingers to my mouth as I slowly spiralled back down to reality, and I shook my head to compose myself.

I was a queen. The queen. I had no business kissing a human.

I repeated those words to myself as I slipped around the couch and danced over the broken cups and teapots scattered about the floor until I stood over the chair and admired the dress that had been laid out for me. It was a deep, brilliant red with open shoulders and a low back and embellished with swirls of gold that spiraled throughout. The dress would hug me in all of the right places, and the low back would let me display my wings, which meant Eirwyn hadn't forgotten how important it was for my people to be able to do so. For all of his less than desirable tendencies, the king was a good man and honored the respectful nature between the two courts. I would honor him in return. It was the least I could do for his accommodation of Rhi.

As I pulled on the dress, my thoughts strayed back to the almost kiss. I felt my cheeks heat, and I steeled myself against the way my heart thundered in my chest. I wanted to kiss her, but I couldn't. Not if I was going to kill her.

I ran my hands along my waist to smooth out the wrinkles as I stepped up to the mirror, which was surprisingly unbroken from my earlier distress. I was tall and slender, and the dress had a slit up the side that revealed my leg as I stepped forward. I admired the way the gold seemed to shine in the fabric, a contrast against the dark red.

My thoughts wandered to what Rhi had said before she'd collapsed. If someone was trying to usurp me, I'd have their head the moment I was able to return home. My people loved me and would rally behind me the moment I returned. I clenched my fists so hard my hands shook. I had no doubts about anyone, no inklings as to who might want my throne. My eyes trailed up to greet Róis' as she reappeared.

"There's masks for us," Róis said, tearing me away from my thoughts. She raised two of them and offered one to me. She'd reclaimed her composure after our earlier intimacy and seemed content to act like it hadn't happened. Which was fine by me...even if my eyes failed to resist drinking in the sight of her.

Instead of a dress, she wore pants and a vest, both made of deep velvet. The pants and vest were a dark red, and the long-sleeved shirt beneath was white gold, almost but not quite matching the gold in my dress. My outfit complimented hers almost exquisitely, and I cursed Eirwyn for his antics. I *knew* what he was doing and cursed his amusement of it.

I held my hand out and took the mask she offered. It matched my dress and was simple in design, same as Róis'. A knock came at the door as soon as we slipped them on, and I turned to answer as Róis hovered near the bedroom. Her nervous energy swam over me as I greeted the faerie guard from before.

"It is time," was all he said before leading us down the hall.

I took a deep breath and then followed.

# TWENTY-FIVE
## *Neferíl*

"QUEEN NEFERÍL AND RÓIS." I gave a sharp look at the announcer as we entered the royal gardens. Humans only got their names announced if they were attending a party *with* a faerie escort. Eirwyn's doing, no doubt.

My ire died as quickly as it had been forged as the magic of the gardens washed over me. I had expected one of Eirwyn's grand balls, not the tea party that seemed to be going on, but it did not lack in lavish nature. Faeries sat at circular tables set about the gardens, drinking wine or tea and eating pastries.

I plucked a glass of faerie wine from a table as I passed. It felt good to have my wings out. Many stared as I walked past. Eirwyn's people knew better than to scorn me even if the tension between our two courts was high.

Róis hugged the edge of the gardens and tugged her arms to herself. I couldn't blame her unease. Despite the handful of humans lingering about, many of them had positive interactions with Eirwyn's faeries. Róis had only ever known pain. Perhaps I could show her that not all fae were cruel. That she had only ever known the wrath of the forest. She had warmed to Olbi. Perhaps...

I downed my wine.

I was going to have to get properly drunk to forget that idea.

Eirwyn's cats wandered freely through the soft grass of the gardens, their movements lazy as their tails flitted about behind them. Eirwyn's lion rested where it usually did: next to Eirwyn, who sat on a small throne that had been set up at the end of a long rectangular table full of food and drink. The king's gaze sought mine from behind the white-gold mask he wore. He gestured for me to join him, so I wove through the crowds of dancing faeries until I stood next to him. He leaned an elbow on the arm of his chair and stared out at his gathering.

"I hope you have news," I said to him.

"You really know how to have fun," he said sarcastically, and I scowled behind my mask.

"I'll be sure to hold court balls when my land isn't over-run with Rot." My eyes trailed over the crowd. Their lives were so easy, unburdened by the darkness that rested on mine and Eirwyn's shoulders. As I stared out at the laughing fae, at the drinking and the dancing, a bitter realization struck: Rhi was in a different part of the castle, fighting for her life against a plague that wanted to kill her.

"Your throne has been claimed by a woman who calls herself Deirdre."

I stilled. "Is that so?" I fought to keep my voice light as my insides grew cold. My eyes sought out Róis as she conversed with a dark-haired elf. Kyrie, perhaps? I couldn't tell behind the mask.

"Are you familiar?" Eirwyn asked simply, his fingers dancing in small patterns as he stared out into the crowd.

I nodded. "The forest brought her to me some time ago. She was determined to free her daughter from this 'wicked place,' but I had never seen her daughter in my court. 'Course, she couldn't return to her human world, and she took some time to grow used to a life here. I was under the assumption she'd adapted." She'd also been the one to tell me of the prophecy, the one where I had to kill Róis. That knowledge danced at the edge of my tongue, but I silenced it before it could leave my lips. The Rot might not be that bad in Eirwyn's court, but if he was desperate to end it, he could kill her before I found out the truth about everything. The words of the rotting faerie who'd attacked us before we fell into Vilanthris come back to me.

*"Kill her so we can all rot."*

"You assumed wrong," Eirwyn said, pulling me out of my thoughts. He straightened in his chair, and his lion yawned and raised his head to rest in the king's lap. Eirwyn stroked the lion's head absentmindedly, but his expression was cold as he turned to me. "Our courts are expected to coexist, as is the ways of Olde, but when I reached out to Dierdre to formally accept a peaceful unity between us, she sent my messenger back. Do you know what he looked like?"

My stomach plummeted and then rose to my throat as I shook my head.

Eirwyn blinked slowly, his frown deepening. "She infected him with Rot, killed him, and returned him in pieces. We still haven't found all of him, but he's left little pockets of Rot in my court."

"Eirwyn—"

"If my court suffers from your lack of judgment, I *will* forsake the Olde Ways, and we will no longer know peace, I can promise you that. If you are to go and plea before the Forest Father, then you must leave. Now."

My gaze hardened. "You do not command me. You are not my king."

Eirwyn's eyes burned as he stood, and his lion yawned as he moved to follow. "And you are no longer a queen it seems. Just a courtless faerie with the entire fate of this forest resting on your shoulders. On hers," he said, pointing to Róis. "If you do not go and soon, I will drag her there myself, and I won't be pleasant about it. You can enjoy a few hours of the party, but then I want you to leave... tonight."

His threat clung to the air long after he left my side. Many of the fae parted and greeted him fondly as he passed. He paused to grab a glass of wine before he stopped where Kyrie and Róis stood near the windows.

The cold chill of horror crept through me. My hands wouldn't stop shaking no matter how much I willed them to still, and the gardens became a blur as the world spun.

It felt like rocks sat on my chest, and I closed my eyes, counting backwards from twenty.

Dierdre's betrayal cut deep. She'd come to my court long after I'd been named queen, and I had seen a lot of myself in her: her anger, her sense of betrayal. I'd gone to her more often than any of the other seers for advice and a peek into the future.

My loyalty had all been for naught.

Squaring my shoulders, I opened my eyes. The gardens had stopped spinning, and the soft gentle melody of the music wafted over me, calming my racing thoughts.

Stealing another glass of wine from the table, I drowned it as I approached Róis. Eirwyn and Kyrie spoke quietly some feet away. "We need to talk." I nodded towards the door. "Eirwyn's gardens continue through the trees over there. We can take a walk."

A blush climbed its way onto Róis' cheeks, and my gaze darkened. I wondered if she would deny me.

Finally, Róis nodded, her face unable to shield her curiosity. Gripping her glass, she followed me down a path towards the trees.

"Róis," I said after a moment, grabbing her wrist before she could ferry herself too far away for me to reach. "Can you tell me what the human world is like?"

A strange look crossed Róis' face. "Why?" She paused as if remembering something. "Eirwyn said something—that you came to the forest, that you were human once. Is that true?"

I ran my wine around my glass and watched it swirl. "My court... we do not take human babies from your village, nor are we responsible for their change. We could send them back, yes, but the forest marks all who enter. Any returned humans would be stolen back by the forest spirits, and we would be punished for having helped them.

"I don't remember my life as a human. I was a baby when my parents abandoned me in the woods, when the faeries of my court found me. I remember my younger years being in the castle, and I remember the moment I realized I was a part of the forest. We don't take human babies—" I swallowed thickly, looking up to gauge Róis' reaction. "The spirits of the forest do it to restore balance every time one of your people chops down a tree or steals food or water from the woods."

Róis clenched her fist and said nothing, though frustration and anger crossed her face. She drew back her lips, revealing the gleam of sharpened canines, and she sighed, running a hand through the mess of her hair. "I know faeries can't lie. It's a shame there can't be a call for peace, a way for us to live aside one another in harmony."

"A shame," I agreed. Silence filled the air between us, and I tilted my glass up to finish the last of my wine. Fireflies danced about the trees, filling the gardens with tranquil peace, and I tucked a braid behind my head, staring at Róis gently. "So...what is it like? The human world?"

"Loud," Róis said, shrugging. "Chaotic. Bloody. We love to fight among ourselves. I think the kingdoms are warring. Who knows what the reason is, but it's likely over something trivial and easy to mend." She hesitated. "But we're also full of life and love, and we care very deeply."

I sighed, a small wistful sound. So similar to the fae. So different.

Perhaps it was the wine. Perhaps it was the tension from earlier. Perhaps it was simply the way she looked as she did now... so human, with all of its raw emotion.

Without thinking, I moved forward, ripped our masks off, and crashed my lips against hers.

She was warm, warmer than any fae, and I felt the flutter of her heartbeat as she shoved me away and pinned me up against a tree. A knife was pressed to my throat, the same knife she'd used to cut her palm and save Rhi's life, and her eyes were wide and bright as she searched through my expression, her breath heavy against my mouth.

And then she was kissing me back, the sharp of the blade still poised dangerously at my neck, and I fell into the kiss as it tore me away from the stress and grief over the recent days.

Róis tasted of faerie wine, sweet and citrus, as I bit down and sucked on her lower lip, my hands coming down to grab at her hips and tug her closer. I almost welcomed her to pierce me with the blade if only for the chance to get closer as a fire woke inside me, as it forged fires in the lower halls of my belly.

She pulled away, her breath heavy, her eyes shining. "What...I..." she shook her head as if it were clearing her head. "That shouldn't...you're..."

"I apologize." I wasn't the least bit sorry, not as warmth hummed through me, chasing away every darkness of my life, but I apologized regardless, seeing the confusion that tinged her gaze. "My mind is muddled with wine. I received the worst of news, and I haven't been thinking straight."

Róis' brow furrowed. "What news?"

I wasn't sure whether to share the news of my court with her. She was a human and did not care for the trifles of the faerie courts. Still, I had no one else to talk to, no one else to tell. Rhi was the only one I'd ever talked to about these things, and she was unconscious.

"Eirwyn's scouts reported someone has stolen my throne from me." My voice was steadier than I felt, and Róis' gaze flashed in shock.

"What?"

"The traitor's a seer I thought I could trust. She goes by Deirdre, though I do not know her true name." Most court faeries never gave out their true names even to other faeries for a name granted power.

Róis' face paled. "Deirdre? That was my mother's name."

I opened my mouth in shock. A chill rolled down my back, alarm bells went off in my head, and I stepped forward, pressing Róis against the trunk of a tree as I scanned the gardens for any sign of danger.

Her breath caught, and she shifted against me.

"What are you doing?" Róis asked in a low, raspy tone. Her fingers grazed my waist as she gave a small shove, but there was no strength to it, and I ignored it with ease.

"Something is wrong," I whispered. The air was too thick, drenched with trepidation. A scent, sickeningly sweet, clung to the air, and, off in the distance, shouts echoed.

Alarm crossed both of our faces as we turned towards the main party. A shadow blotted out the moon, and the trees whispered anxiously, the quietness of their breath passing through each other as their branches ruffled. I pulled away from Róis, and we rushed back towards the main gardens.

Faeries were fleeing the party in a flurried panic. Every time I tried to stop one to demand answers, they brushed past me, their eyes wild with fear. Frustrated, I pushed past them until I noticed Olbi and Kyrie near the wing leading to Rhi's room.

"What is happening?" I asked, my voice laced with concern. Eirwyn held rule over the warmth of the Seelie Court, and yet his castle was currently bone cold like it was sitting on the edge of a storm. Eirwyn himself was nowhere to be seen, and Olbi's ears laid flat against his skull as he shook his head and muttered to himself. Even Kyrie looked concerned as he gestured for us to follow him.

"Quickly," he said, and I glanced back at Róis before doing so.

He led us to Rhi's room, and my heart plummeted as we neared the door, which was ajar. Sickness clung to the air, the same feeling of destitution that infected places where the Rot flourished, and Kyrie hesitated for a moment before he stepped aside and allowed us to enter first.

Róis inhaled sharply behind me.

The room had been torn apart.

Something had shredded the blankets on the bed, and the plants that had grown up the walls and over the ceiling were all rotten and dead. Bulbous yellow pus balls grew where flowers once had, and the air was dim with a thin layer of spores. I wasn't sure it was even safe to be in the room, but I ignored that as my eyes landed on Rhi's bed.

In the middle sat a single red rose.

# TWENTY-SIX

## *Róis*

"We must go. Now," Neferíl said, turning to brush past me. "Someone has her."

I trembled. I hadn't noticed I was until Neferíl's arm grazed mine, but I shook from head to toe. Violently. So violently my teeth clashed against each other, and the shock of everything came crashing down.

"Who? What do you mean?" I asked, following Neferíl from the room.

"Sister, wait—" I halted at the door as a lump of horror formed in my throat, and I turned to meet the gaze of my sister, who sat cross-legged in the center of Rhi's bed. She twirled the rose in her hand, studying the thorns that pricked her skin. A thin bead of blood collected at her thumb, and she stared up at me with wide eyes. She looked terrible, like a sickness was rotting her insides. Her hair hadn't been washed in days, and decay tinged her skin. Her eyes were shiny and bright, her cheeks red with fever.

"Sister? How did you get in here?" I asked, drawing closer.

"Who are you? Do you know who took her?" Neferíl halted, her gaze traveling between us as her gaze hardened in shock. "What is this? Some kind of trick?"

I shook my head, stepping up to shield my sister from the queen's wrath. "She's my sister. She's sick, just like this forest. I was going to the Forest Father to beg him to heal her." *And kill you there if need be.* Words I did not dare speak.

"She was taken to the Grove. A seer took her," Sister said, her voice rattling as she coughed. She gripped the rose tightly as blood ran down her arm. I reached out to gently pry the flower from her grasp. She did not struggle, and I took the rose from her with ease as Kyrie and Olbi entered the room.

Sister cried out, clutching her stomach. "There's a dark thing inside of me, and I know it's rotting the forest. It hurts. Oh, it *hurts*." Tears slid down her cheeks, and my heart squeezed.

"We need to leave." Neferíl's eyes were molten as they bore into me, and Kyrie stepped forward, his face twisted with worry.

"Róis, she's..." His gaze flickered to Sister as she rocked back and forth on the bed, holding her head in her hands. He lowered his voice as Olbi stared on and then the myrlír scurried over to the wall, where he began counting the cracks that had formed in the glass with erratic movements.

"She is drenched in something dark. You didn't tell me you were a twin."

I stared at him and then at her. "I didn't see a reason to. Sister was taken so long ago by this forest; I don't even remember her name."

"Twins are powerful, Róis. It's important. Especially—especially this," he said, gesturing between my sister and I. "I think I might know why this is happening, but I need more time, and the king isn't going to like her being here."

"Sister, how did you get inside?" I asked, turning back to her. "You said a seer took Rhi?"

Sister nodded solemnly as she stopped rocking. She stared up at me with a wide gaze. "She did. She has her. Said she's going to bleed her if we don't come."

"There is no time for this." Neferíl swept out of the room, and I wanted to follow her, but I stopped myself, focusing on Sister.

"Go to the Grove," she whispered, her eyes shining with tears. "She's there. Mother is there." And with that, she disappeared in a puff of black spores, a stain left behind on the bed where she'd sat. The room was thick with an awful stench, and my eyes watered as I looked at Kyrie, who gestured for me to follow him out.

I was vaguely aware I was still shaking, but it was swept aside as a torrent of grief and shock paved through me. Mother was behind all this?

"Something is wrong. You must be careful. Your sister—" Kyrie swallowed thickly, hesitating. "She is not right. I fear the Grove is a trap."

I nodded. "It's definitely a trap, but I'm afraid I have no choice." I curled my fingers into fists and found my courage as I gave him a faint smile. Turning, I moved down the hall.

I found Neferíl at the front of the castle with Eirwyn at her side, his eyes bridled with rage. His mask had been discarded, and the castle was empty and foreboding, as if a great tragedy had struck it. Even Eirwyn's cats were absent, and my eyes remained bound to Neferíl as I approached. She was unable to stand still, pacing with her hands clasped tightly in front of her. The moment I arrived, she bounced forward, her face twisting in anxious rage.

"The queen has informed me of what's happened. How was she able to get past the guards?" Eirwyn's hair was in disarray, his braids torn from their usual uniformed twists, and he pushed past Neferíl to speak with the guards at the front door.

"Do you think Rhi was truly taken to the Grove?" I asked.

Neferíl shook her head. "If so, I do not know how Dierdre found its location. Only court fae are granted knowledge of that. No seer has ever seen it either. It is a place of great power, and only those deemed worthy by the Forest Father can step into his sacred home. No, I do not think

Rhi has been taken there, but if we don't leave for the Grove immediately, there's no telling what will happen."

I coughed, the sound rattling around in my lungs. Exhaustion caressed me like a lover, its gentle touch beckoning me to relinquish control, but I resisted, knowing there was still much to be done.

Soon, I'd have all the time in the world to sleep.

Neferíl looked ragged; tears stained her cheeks, but she held her head proudly as she stepped up to me. Her gaze flickered to me, to the way my throat clicked when I breathed. Ever since I'd helped heal Rhi, I'd been feeling it: a growing sickness inside of me, like the Rot was spreading quick.

"Something doesn't feel right..."

"This rot has already infected the castle long enough for my liking," Eirwyn said, approaching once more. "You will go to the Forest Father, and you will not return until you have been granted some answers."

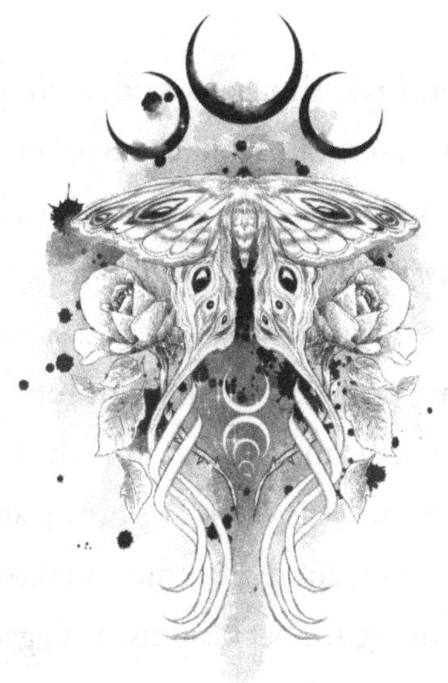

# TWENTY-SEVEN
## *Neferil*

Róis AND I IMMEDIATELY returned to our rooms to change back into our normal attire. The human tugged on her clothes frantically, and something broke inside me, seeing Róis so manic. She looked and moved as I felt, her hands shaking as she grabbed and clipped her dagger to her belt. It was only when I drew forward, my hands reaching out for her, that she stopped, her eyes wide with emotion.

"Do not fret, little thorn," I said, sliding my fingers down her arms, careful to avoid the Rot on her arm, and threaded them with hers. I was surprised she let me. *Careful. You're drawing too close to the flame.* "We will find a cure for whatever plagues your sister." I stared at the Rot fester against her skin, wondering, not for the first time, why it hadn't infected me when she touched me with it.

"I cannot lose her. Not when I've only just found her." Róis' words were raw, an edge of emotion that spoke to me and thickened the space between us. I tugged her closer, my lips pulled back as I bared my teeth.

"The Forest Father cannot ignore such a rotten disease. Not if he wants his beloved forest to remain standing."

Róis seemed unconvinced, and who could blame her? How could someone as powerful as a god let darkness like this fester? My heart ached bitterly at the thought, at everyone my court had lost.

"We will do everything we can," I said again, more firmly this time. The sickness was more apparent in Róis now. It lined her arms and darkened the underside of her expression. Her breath rattled when she inhaled, and exhaustion had made a home in her face. A part of me knew I should not be so near, but another part of me did not care.

"I believe you. Your people are the ones getting hurt the most by this infestation," Róis said, not quite able to meet my eyes. "From the beginning, you've made it clear you'll do whatever it takes to ensure the safety of your home."

My hands loosened around Róis'. "Of course." The rest of the words lodged themselves in my throat. *But that's not the only reason.* I wanted to speak them, wanted to tell Róis about the growing fire in my chest, about the river of emotion that swelled in my throat, but I couldn't liberate it from the prison of my mouth. My heart thundered like waves against a shoreline.

I offered a weak smile instead. "We're both in agreement then. The ones we love must be saved."

Róis' jaw pulsed as I tugged my hands away and turned to move towards the door.

"Neferíl, wait."

As soon as I turned back, Róis crashed into me. It was strange to be taken by surprise by a human, and my eyes flickered with shock as Róis' body pressed up against mine, pushing me against the door. Her mouth sought mine out in hopeless desperation.

She was warm, just as before, only this time it was more so, her hunger for me deepening as she threaded her fingers through mine and forced my arms above my head.

I had never been kissed like this before. Róis was inexperienced and sloppy, but she was passionate and kissed me with everything that she had, eager to devour me, and I gave way, matching her with my own desire. I was a moth to the flames, and the fires of passion swirled around me, burning away all rational thought. I rolled my hips forward. My tongue darted out, and I tasted a hint of honey wine on her lips.

*More. More. More.* I craved more, to be closer, to feel her beneath my fingers. The flame forged brighter in my chest. She pulled away, gasping for air, but I chased her with my lips. She dropped her hold on my hands, and I tasted her desire and sickness in the air, mingled together like a curse. I pulled away this time.

My hand flew to my mouth. Would I get sick? Had she kissed me with the intention of forcing the Rot upon me? I didn't feel it clawing inside me, but time would tell. I bit down on my bottom lip so hard I tasted blood as it beaded against my skin. Frustration squeezed my lungs. I was such a fool. What if Graeir wouldn't show me the way to the grove because of my infection? What if I had just ruined my chance to save my people?

"We have to go," Róis said, her tone brimmed with regret. Her eyes flickered to the bedroom, her expression hungering, but I knew. We had people counting on us to get to the Grove, to seek out the Eldertree.

Róis' eyes were sad as I nodded. Pulling the door open behind me, I stepped into the empty hall. Only time would tell if I had made a terrible mistake.

Our walk through the woods was the most peaceful it had been in a very long time. Eirwyn's court had always bred a semblance of comfort, the quiet of a warm summer's day. My skin still crawled though. Like something was waiting just beyond the haze of heat. A quiet malice tucked away, lurking.

Róis' sister showed up again two days into the journey. After an initial tension, it was decided she would travel with us in hopes that the Forest Father could cure her. Both sisters weren't doing so well. We had to stop many times due to a violent coughing episode or general fatigue, and at one point, Róis' sister grew so frail, Róis had to carry her, hefting her onto her back but making no complaint as we trailed through the trees.

"Do you want to take a break?" I asked, noticing Róis' laboured breathing and the way she clung to the trees as we passed by. Sweat coated her brow, and her sister's head rested on her shoulder, her eyes shut and her breathing shallow.

Róis shook her head. "How close are we?"

I looked around. Even the court faeries chosen by the Forest Father were never told the actual location of the Sacred Grove, but we were granted with an innate sense of where to go. I couldn't imagine we had much further to travel.

"Perhaps a day, if that." I watched Róis struggle to heft her sister more securely atop her back. The dedication Róis had to her sister despite having not seen her for most of her life was admirable. "I wish I could share the burden."

Róis gazed sideways at me and shook her head. "Too dangerous," was all she said before pushing forward silently. I let her go, watching her struggle over the uneven terrain of the forest. I sighed but said nothing else until we broke through a cluster of trees. I halted, alongside her, my breath catching in my throat.

There was only a small break in the trees before a massive grove rose up before us. It was much like the grove Olbi had taken us to meet Elahir in the other world, only on a much grander scale, with the trees clustered so closely together, they forged a natural wall, and in front of them was a line of druids who stood tall, ever watchful.

My stomach clenched. It was time.

# TWENTY-EIGHT
## *Róis*

THE DRUIDS WATCHED US approach as they stood in a line, each of their faces covered in deer skull masks. I had lowered my sister to the ground, and I threaded our fingers together as I pulled her towards the grove with Neferíl at our side. The queen had been silent these past few hours, save for a couple of words here and there, and her eyes were bridled with some uncertain emotion. I had been too worried about my sister's worsening condition to have checked in on the queen even though my eyes had darted over to her several times throughout our travels.

I looked at the druids now. Their unyielding nature and silence was jarring. "Please," I said. "Please let us through. My sister is sick. She has something rotting inside of her. We need the Forest Father's aid." Desperation sat at the back of my throat. It hungered and clawed as my eyes darted to each druid, but they did not respond behind their masks. They each wore their own light green cloak that swept over their shoulders and covered just how bulky each of them were; I wasn't even entirely sure *what* they were. Human? Fae? Or perhaps something else entirely.

"Who are you talking to?" Sister whispered, her fingers brushing my arm. "I don't see anyone..."

One of them stepped forward, using a gnarled branch-like staff to steady himself. The wind grew still, the forest cast into an uncanny silence as the druid stared down at me, the black orbs where the deer's eyes would have been boring into me.

"Open your eyes, earth child." The druid's voice curled through me, like earth pressing down on my lungs. I squeezed my sister's hand and pulled my lips back over my teeth in frustration.

"What do you mean? My eyes are open."

The druid reached out, his hand smooth, golden-brown, and slender as his thumb moved towards my forehead. *"Open your eyes."* The moment his finger pressed against my skin, my stomach lurched, and then a different sight sat before me. I blinked. All the druids before me were dying, covered by moss or blackened with rot. One had his mask torn away. His hair, long and blond, was plastered against the side of his face as blood coated his cheek. He heaved, his chest rattling wetly, and then he exhaled as spores exploded from his chest.

"Get back," Neferíl warned, tugging me away by my arm. "Where did they come from?"

"I don't—" I looked around. There were at least eight of them, now dead, but the way into the grove was clear for us to pass through. A warning hung in the air, thick as smoke, and I glanced to Neferíl for guidance. "I don't know. When we approached, they were just standing there. One of them told me to, 'Open my eyes', and when he touched me, this happened."

"I didn't see anything until this," Sister said, gesturing to the gruesome scene before us before coughing violently. "Oh, sister. Please. It *hurts*. Can we hurry?"

"Don't," I said sharply as Neferíl moved to help. "I don't know how you have made it so long without infection –" The forest lurched as vertigo struck me, and I pressed my hands to my knees, shivering from the chills that rolled down my spine.

"Do not be ridiculous. Both of you can hardly stand. If the Forest Father is gracious enough to heal both of you, he can heal me too," Neferíl said, grabbing me under the arm and hoisting me up. I was broader than she was—she was such a slender thing—but she slung my arm over her shoulders and bore my weight with ease. Then she tucked my sister into the crook of her arm on her free side. "Some terrible thing must have happened if all the druids are dead. Your sister is right; we need to hurry."

I leaned heavily against her as we moved towards the mouth of the grove. We stepped around the dead bodies of the druids, and a part of me despaired. Staring down into the blank eyes of one as I passed, I set my jaw. I couldn't get distracted from the real reason we were here: freeing the forest of this rot.

As we stepped into the grove, everything lightened. The sun broke through the trees, and the grove was relatively clear, full of soft grass and pockets of small ponds. Tall, massive trees dotted the clearing here and there, and I realized quickly that this was the same grove I had stood in after being attacked by the witch.

Wild, breathless laughter seeped from Sister's lips the moment we stepped into the grove. She pulled away from us violently. It was so violent that she fell onto the ground and rolled away. I cried out in concern.

She landed on her hands and knees, and when she looked up, her face was free of the pain that had lingered there since I'd found her again. "Foolish bitch." She spat at the ground as she stood, her eyes glittering with disgust. "You led us right where we needed to go."

"What—" The revelation sank in slowly, followed closely by the cold grip of horror.

Neferíl was still as stone beside me, and I still clung to her as if she were a lifeline as Sister paced before us, her fingers twitching. She stared out at the grove where a large tree, larger than the others, stood with its gnarled branches and ethereal fruits. Before it, a dragon with antlers sat, its wings folded in as it regarded us with silent interest.

My eyes locked with the dragon, and my stomach rolled. My soul shuddered, like it was desperately trying to tear itself free of my skeleton, and Neferíl trembled beside me.

My mind rebelled at the knowledge that I was staring at the god from my vision, and though it begged me to look away, I could not. My eyes stayed locked with the several alien eyes that dotted its head.

It dipped its head knowingly, and only then was I freed from the shackles of its gaze. I gasped and lowered my eyes immediately. When had I started crying? I shook as

Neferíl tightened her arm around my wrist. Sister heaved and stared at us angrily.

"We're here, Sister," I said, still weeping. My chest was hollow like I'd looked at something so otherworldly and beautiful that nothing else would ever compare. "We can heal you."

"Róis," Neferíl said softly. "I don't think—"

"I've always had this rotting thing inside of me. It wasn't the forest that infected me." Laughter spilled from Sister's lips, her eyes wild with manic glee. "But the forest kept figuring out how to heal itself. I could never get the Rot to spread very far." Red beaded against her mouth as she grinned, where the skin peeled apart.

"Much like you, sweet sister," she said bitterly as all the joy faded from her face. "I thought simply getting near you would kill you, but the Forest Father gifted you with life." She wailed. "Life, life, life while I rot."

"That doesn't matter. We can heal you," I said again with more determination. I was no longer crying, but the tips of my fingers tingled, and I was so incredibly tired like I could lay down in the soft grass tickling my ankles and never get up again. It would be so easy…

"No." The word was uttered from my sister's tongue with pure malice, her eyes lit with rage. "No, no, no. My insides have always been ugly, but with you and the Forest

Father dead and rotting, the world can join me in this darkness. That is what she said."

"Who?" I asked.

"Hello, Róis."

The voice sank into me as I turned, and I stared, horrified, into the eyes of my mother.

"Thank you for bringing her to me, Lil." It was the first time I'd heard my sister's name since I'd forgotten it, but the moment it was spoken, it found its way back to me like a long-lost dream. It entered me so suddenly that I started to cry again. *Liliana*. Lil had been a sickly child, and I remembered...I *remembered*. I would bring her white lilies from the nearby meadows with my father to cheer her up when she'd been bedridden.

"You were supposed to be taken." Lil's words turned cold as the grove went silent, and her eyes darkened when I met hers. "The forest was meant to take you so that you could soothe its rage. The Forest Father put his life inside us and blessed our mother when we were in her womb." A quick glance at Mother's face told me she had told Lil this, and I held onto Neferíl, grateful for her unyielding strength at this moment.

Lil moaned, wrapping her arms around her stomach. "He also put in his death, all of his rotten disease." Skin flaked off her cheek, exposing a stark patch of new skin as it floated away.

"You two weren't supposed to be twins," Mother said, her eyes bright with rage. Neferíl stiffened beneath me as Mother tugged something roughly behind her. She had Rhi by the hair.

"I don't understand," I said.

Mother sneered. "If the magic had flowed through one child instead of two, balance would have been maintained. Now, your sister's magic is too chaotic, too destructive, too rotten."

Neferíl started forward, shaking with rage, but Mother's grip on Rhi tightened, and Rhi cried out, causing Neferíl to stop in her tracks.

"You will not move closer," Mother warned. "I told you to kill her. How disappointing and unsurprising that you would fail." Mother's back straightened, and she turned her attention back to me. "As I was saying... nature has a fucked-up humor," she said bitterly. I could do nothing but stare, my fingers itching to dart to the dagger at my side. Betrayal sang a sad tune through my veins, poisoning my lungs and pressing against my chest. I didn't want to believe it. Sweet, beautiful Lil... And my mother, both traitors.

"That night, do you remember it, sweet sister?" Lil cocked her head to the side and stalked closer. Neferíl's grasp around me tightened protectively as she backed us away. "The night the monsters came for you?"

*Long spindly fingers. High-pitched screeches in the dark. Large luminescent eyes in the window. The soft whimpers of children too scared to move from their bed.*

The memories flickered through my mind unbidden, and I hardened my gaze. "It wasn't my fault she threw you to them instead," I snarled, flinging my hand towards Mother. "It wasn't my *fault*." My voice broke at the end, guilt replacing my betrayal as the hate for my mother was reforged in the flames of despair.

"No, perhaps not," Lil said, her voice deceptively soft and calm for the way her skin blistered and rotted. "I tried to kill her the moment she threw herself into the forest to serve her guilt-ridden penance. I wanted to see her body rot beneath my fingertips, but no. Mother was very persuasive and instead convinced me to open my eyes."

I winced.

"The forest didn't mean to take me. Greedy little thing, this place," Lil said, the corners of her eyes stained with tears, her chest rattling while she breathed. "It didn't, but it did, and what a mistake that was."

"Enough," Neferíl said. "You blame a fate that was laid before you the moment you were born. It's not for your sister to bear."

"It doesn't matter." Lil sneered and turned on her heel, walking back towards the Forest Father, who watched on silently. "Nothing will matter when the Forest Father is dead."

Neferíl stiffened under me, and I shoved myself away from her as Mother tugged Rhi close. I unsheathed my dagger at my hip and forced my vision to steady as everything swayed. *Keep it together, Róis.*

"Rhi has nothing to do with this. Let her go," Neferíl said, her eyes flickering from my mother to Rhi in her arms. Rhi was conscious, but her eyes were glassed over, and her breathing was laboured. I was pleased to see, though, that my magic was keeping the Rot at bay.

"Ah, ah, ah. Not until you carry out the prophecy," Mother said, and I spared a questioning glance Neferíl's way. Her expression warred between conflicting emotions, then hardened.

"Go and take care of your sister, Róis. I must have a conversation with your mother."

I didn't argue, turning away to chase after my sister as my dagger gleamed in the sunlight. Would I be able to do it? Strike out at my own sister? Kill her?

*Your sister died the day she was taken.*

The thought stayed heavy in my mind as I neared her, weighing down my arm as I lashed at her. She flinched out of the way with ease, then dodged the strike of my dagger as I aimed again, this time for her waist. She was deceptively quick, and it became a dance of her dodging my attacks and me striking out quicker than I'd ever had before.

"Wanna see who gets to the Forest Father first?" Lil sneered, disappearing in a puff of black spores. My heart lurched, and I turned to Neferíl, who had pulled out her sword.

"Go," Neferíl said. She stood tall as she stared down my mother, who smiled wickedly at the Unseelie queen.

I hesitated. Just long enough to memorize each part of Neferíl's face. To take in the honey hue sprinkled throughout her expression as she looked at me. The way my heart ached at the thought that this might be the last time I looked at her. How had it come to this?

"Go," she urged again. This time, I complied, turning on my heel and chasing after Lil, towards the towering dragon in the distance.

# TWENTY-NINE

## *Neferil*

"WHY DO YOU WANT her dead?" I asked Deirdre. "I don't understand why a mother would want to kill her daughter."

Deidre smiled; her teeth blackened with rot. "If Róis dies, there will be no one to save you all from the Rot. The forest will finally wither and die, and the humans will be safe from your wickedness."

I didn't want to believe her but seers were fae. Seers cannot lie.

Deidre's head lolled to the side, and she took a small step forward. "One more chance, Your Majesty. One more chance to kill the girl."

The seer's warning was ignored. Killing Róis would not stop the forest from rotting. That much I knew. It would not stop her from killing Rhi. It would not do anything but strip the forest of any chance of healing from this disease.

My gaze met Rhi's, her eyes unfocused and lethargic. The faintest of nods came from her, and my chest tightened painfully.

That was her blessing for me to do whatever must be done.

There would be time for tears later.

"I will not."

The seer's eyes darkened as Rhi used what energy she had to lash out with her magic. Vines and plants grew from the ground, whipping out to strike out at Dierdre. Crying out, Róis' mother dropped Rhi to the ground. The forest rose up to encase Rhi, to keep her safe, and I did not hesitate as I swung my sword through the air to cut through the seer.

"Your people have abandoned you. They will never forgive a traitorous queen that harbors a human." Dierdre's lip curled as she flinched away. "Don't worry, Your Majesty. I will rule them kindly." Behind her, the dead druids from before shuddered to life. Some of their deer masks had been cracked, exposing decayed flesh underneath, and they approached with sickles and spears in their hands.

They came at me without mercy as the seer stumbled away, her eyes wild with glee. I couldn't get to her before she slipped away, and I found myself barely dodging the druids' blades as they moved as one. They moved with exceptional speed despite their reanimated state, and I felt the weight of their attacks without pause.

They attacked silently, their feet not even making a sound. They came at me at once, forcing me to retreat as they pressed down on me. I lashed out, wounding one with my blade, and yellow, sap-like blood secreted from a line formed on the druid's arm. He continued forward as if he didn't feel the injury at all.

My eyes darted behind him, and I despaired. The seer had fled, and there was no way I was going to be able to fend them all off. Not when they were already dead and were refusing to die again. Not when they attacked as one. I refused to look back, to see if Róis had caught up with her sister, but I hoped she had. The fate of the forest depended on it.

*Foolish*, I thought to myself. I had let the words of the seer sway me so much that I had almost cut down the one person who could cure the forest. Turned out, it was her sister who had to die. Cut a sickness out at its root; that root was Lil.

I hissed as a spear pierced my shoulder. The druid who wielded it stared at me with sullen, dead eyes. I gasped as she retreated, taking her spear with her, and pain flourished through me, quick and sharp.

I struck out, satisfied when I managed to strike down one of the druids, but the others took his place, and I darted around a tree to avoid them.

*Come, Nef. Think.*

A low howl echoed throughout the grove. I peeked my head around to see a large wolf approaching, its lips curled back over bared teeth as it snarled. Atop its back sat Olbi, his eyes shining as he clung to the wolf's back.

The wolf shot forward as the druids turned, but they weren't quick enough. The wolf lunged at them and flung Olbi from its back. He landed on the shoulders of a druid, and with his fingers drenched in yellow spores, he dug them into the druid's face. The corpse withered away until Olbi was on the ground, and he ran up to me.

"Olbi and Kyrie followed. Olbi and Kyrie want to help." I turned my head to the wolf as he ripped through the corpses of the reanimated druids, suddenly realizing who that was.

"That's Kyrie?" I asked.

Olbi nodded. "Well, he's a druid, ain't he? Go find her. We'll take care of this."

I glanced over at the mound that had tucked Rhi away from the fighting. Some fae used such things to protect themselves from the wrath of the forest. I knew she would be safe until I found Róis, so I turned on my heel and ran deeper into the grove.

# THIRTY

## *Róis*

"Lil, wait!"

I raced through the trees after her, but my sister had grown quick during her time in Elvira, and she eluded me easily. A soft hum graced the trees, a gentle noise that deceived me into thinking the forest was peaceful and comforting. A part of me begged me to lie down in the soft grass and sleep. I was so, so very tired.

I resisted even when the air grew thicker, even when the very blood in my veins heated like it was boiling beneath my skin. Panic sat at the bottom of my throat, and my eyes flickered in and out of focus as I halted just before the Forest Father's resting form.

He was massive, so much larger than I had comprehended before. Warmth radiated from him, the points of his antlers reaching out into the tree line as he lowered his head to stare at me. His face was angular and thin, his wings tall and triangular as they tucked against his sides.

Lil stood before him, staring up at him with a mixture of fascination and disgust. Her hair had clumped around her face, and she tugged at it, ignoring the strands that came out in her hands.

"Lil, please don't touch him," I begged. It hurt, being so close to a god. It was as if my soul had caught fire, like it wanted to pry itself from my flesh and greet the dragon bare. The world tilted as I dropped to my knees, and the grass tickled my legs beneath me. Lil didn't seem affected by the Forest Father's nearness, but I could tell by the way she twitched and writhed, she wasn't completely free from it.

"Quiet," she hissed without turning. "You're about to witness the death of a god."

I needed to fight it. Whatever shackled me to the ground, whatever power the god held over me, I had to fight it like my sister was. The Forest Father did not move, watching us tirelessly behind intelligent eyes, and I cursed him for it.

*Do something*, I thought angrily. *You foolish god. She's going to kill you.*

I dug my fingers into the grass and ground my teeth together as tears fell down my cheeks. We'd been wrong. Lil was sick, but she wasn't innocent. I felt it now, felt her rage, her despair, the rotting thing inside of her. Every time she had gotten sick as a child, I had always been there to hold her hand.

Not this time.

Forcing myself to my feet, I took one shaky step forward. It was like walking through wet sand, like my feet were stuck in the grass as I pulled them up. The forest was silent save for the steady breathing of the Forest Father before us, and I curled my fingers into shaking fists as I drew closer to my sister.

"Remember when you were little, and you got sick a lot? I would bring you lilies because they reminded me of your name..." My voice was no louder than a whisper as my eyes trained onto the back of Lil's head. She was reaching for the Forest Father's snout, but her hand stilled at my words.

"Or when Father went to comfort Mother after you got worse, and I snuck into our room to hold your hand and sing you the lullabies Mother should have sung in my stead?" My throat threatened to close, swollen by emotion, but I tossed those feelings aside as I reached my hand out towards Lil's. "Or the sick dog someone had left outside for dead. How you helped nurse it back to health? You're not evil, Lil. You're not. Don't let this sickness poison you."

Spittle flew from her mouth as she laughed. "Poison me? It's too late. I'm rotten." She shook her head as she turned to look at me, her eyes bright and flush with sickness. "You're too late, Róis. The darkness swallowed me long ago. That little girl you remember? She's nothing but a ghost."

She was right. I saw it in her eyes. The sister I'd known as a young child was dead. I was foolish for thinking otherwise.

"Stop."

I blinked as the word wrapped around us like silk. Neferíl stepped into the clearing as several vibrant orbs floated aimlessly through the clearing. Even the Forest Father, in all his grandeur, had a soft blue glow that carved through his antlers, his face, and dotted his body.

It was all too pretty to feel real.

It was almost sickening, the relief I felt when I locked eyes with Neferíl. I did not know if I had the strength to stop my sister, but Neferíl had promised me. She'd promised she'd do what needed to be done.

"No," Lil snarled, turning to push back towards the Forest Father. "I've come too far to be stopped now." Neferíl appeared in front of her before she could move. The moth hilt of her sword glowed light blue in the moonlight as she moved to strike Lil down.

My heart beat painfully inside my chest, two words forming despite the conflicting emotions suffocating me. "Wait, no."

My sister was too quick and dodged her attack with ease. She moved to infect Neferíl, but the queen evaded my sister in turn. I launched myself forward to help, but Lil evaded both of our attacks. It went that way for a while before she twisted around to reach the Forest Father.

The forest withered and died beneath Lil's feet, only to reforge and bloom beneath mine as we danced around each other.

Lil grabbed her hair and shouted, sending us all stumbling back.

"Stop. Just stop and stay where you are," she snarled, her eyes bright with madness. I looked down as I tried to move forward but found my feet sinking down into wet mud.

Before too long, Neferíl and I were stuck up to our waists on muddy ground as Lil turned back towards the

Forest Father. Neferíl's sword arm stuck out, her exclamations carrying through the grove as I snarled in frustration.

"Don't do this. Forest Father, stop this. Fight back; do something." My voice cracked as I pleaded with Lil and the Forest Father, who just stared and stared and stared...

Lil ignored me, bounding forward and splaying her hand across the Forest Father's snout.

Everything went silent then—an ugly silence that rippled out through the trees and strangled the noise from all the birds and bugs. The world turned grey then as all the vibrancy from the grove was stripped away. Nature growing near the Forest Father decayed and rotted.

Wails shattered the silence, the high-pitched cries of wisps that rushed past me as they came to aid the heart of the forest.

But it was too late.

The Forest Father's head slammed against the ground as Lil's rot blossomed over his face and traveled to the rest of his body. It flourished through him, sinking into his skin, which then flaked off and trailed away into the night sky.

A sob rattled my lungs as the Forest Father took one last shuddering breath and died.

"Why didn't you fight back?" Neferíl wailed, beating her free hand against the ground as she struggled against her shackles. "Why the *fuck* didn't you fight back?"

The forest spirits began to disintegrate as they touched the rotting soil beneath the Forest Father's feet. Their cries crashed against the trees as they perished. Lil had fallen to her knees, her back towards us. Her shoulders bounced, and I wasn't certain whether she laughed or cried, but the sight of her and the knowledge of what she had done filled me so utterly and full of rage that I couldn't swallow it—not this time.

It filled me up and boiled over as I pried myself from the earth. I dragged myself through the mud, then the grass, stumbling towards my sister. My rage was ugly. My rage was dark and thick and boiled my blood as it rose up to infect my lungs. My rage was a storm as I drew my blade and shoved it through my sister's chest.

She didn't try to stop me as I pierced her soft flesh nor when I shoved it straight through to her heart.

Her head fell back against my shoulder as her breathing turned ragged. She stared up at me blankly, her gaze hard lines. I saw no trace of the Lil I knew, but she reached up to press her fingers to my cheek.

"The rotting thing inside me... It's gone." Relief struck her so fiercely it squeezed against my heart as I drew a shallow breath and pried my dagger from her chest. I held Lil as she cried out in pain, as her breathing grew more labored.

"It's inside you now, sweet sister." Her voice was naught but a whisper that sent a chill through me. "I see them, Róis. I see the valley of white lilies. They're so beautiful. Róis, I'm, I'm so—" She shuddered and then her eyes stopped seeing, and her fingers fell from my cheek.

All my rage went silent and paved the way for my grief.

*I'm sorry, Lil. I failed you. I'm so, so sorry.*

"Róis," Neferíl's voice broke from behind me. "We have to go." I looked up as the forest started to die. Rot and death spread across the trees and grass at alarming speeds, killing wherever it touched. My throat constricted painfully as I made eye contact with Neferíl.

My chest ached. It felt like there were cobwebs in my lungs as I struggled to breathe, as the Rot climbed up my arms and peeled back the skin at my fingertips. Pain flickered at the edge of my consciousness as I set my sister on the ground and rose unsteadily to my feet.

*"It's inside you now, sweet sister."*

"I think I can fix this," I whispered. Neferíl moved forward, her eyes bright with fear. The sky darkened, the moon tucked behind clouds, and the wind whipped around my face as Neferíl reached out for me.

I let her embrace me. I wanted to hate her, wanted to push her away, yet pull her closer. Her skin was warm, her beating heart against my chest a thread of life as death surrounded us. I didn't want to let go, so I clung to her as if my life depended on it. I was so, so weak. If I didn't move now, I never would.

"I-I have to try." I whispered the words against the skin of her shoulder before ghosting several small kisses there. "I think I can save him. It's like a knot in my stomach. My magic was gifted to me by him. I think I can return it."

"What will happen to you? I thought surely, with Lil's death, the Rot would go. I...I don't—" Neferíl's voice was raw, and I noticed with horror that the Rot had begun to pepper her skin.

I leaned in and kissed her, knowing it would be the last time I could. I kissed her until I knew that if I didn't pull away, I never would.

So I did. I pulled away and turned. The Forest Father's corpse was little but bone, the grove naught but a husk of its former beauty as all the trees stood black and rotting.

Pulling Lil's body over to the Forest Father, I looked up at the dead god before me. There were still flickers of that strange magic permeating from him. It tugged at my soul, begging me to liberate the magic from my bones and return it to nature. I resisted, just as I resisted the urge to look back at Neferíl. If I looked back at her, I would lose my courage.

So, I steeled myself against my fear. I thought of home, of my little village near the sea. I thought of Father, of his tender hands, who only wanted to heal people. I thought of Salia, of her sweet voice singing softly as she freed me from the shackles of another nightmare. I thought of our little safe haven, tainted now by Salia's death. I thought of the forest, of how Neferíl–

Pain flourished down my spine as I was thrust forward. I looked down to see my blood coating a blade that had pierced my belly. What an ugly red it was. I choked, a startled sob rattling my throat as I looked up.

"I'm sorry," Neferíl whispered from behind me. "I'm sorry. The seers were right, after all. I thought we had to kill Lil, but the forest is still dying. I must try. Real gods require blood." Her voice trembled, and I could tell she was crying, but my shock paved the way for relief. All my fighting was over.

Deep down, I had known Neferíl would put her people first. My heart swelled from the betrayal, but I understood.

"Don't cry," I wanted to say, but blood gurgled up and poured out of my mouth instead. My hands dangled uselessly at my sides, and a vague desire to defend myself flickered through me.

I couldn't. I didn't.

As Neferíl pried her sword from my waist, I fell forward and bled on the Forest Father. Life began to blossom along the ground where I lay, and I finally shut my eyes.

I could finally rest.

# THIRTY-ONE
## Róis

I THOUGHT I'D DREAM of something after I died, or that I would be swallowed up by an endless void of nothing and float up until I met the light of Nymera's domain. Perhaps there I'd be a twinkling light in the sky, ever watchful of the earth beneath me. Or perhaps Mother Moon would let me be the ocean. There was something about the sea that radiated beauty and power.

But no. No, I was *aware*, like I had just woken from a pleasant nap on a summer's day. Whatever I was lying on was soft and warm, and I nuzzled in deeper like I could fade away in comfort.

The soft call of conversation dragged me from that dream, though, as pain radiated from my waist, and the memories flooded back.

Lil had betrayed us and killed the Forest Father despite our best efforts to stop her. And then...

I'd died.

Neferíl had killed me.

My eyes shot open, and for a moment, I thought I might be back home in my little cottage by the sea. Everything that had transpired in the forest was hazy like a dream, but no. I woke in a familiar room in a familiar bed, the one we'd stayed in in Eirwyn's castle. It was daytime, the sun's beams casting through the window, and I relished the warmth. Death's chill began to recede as I blinked blearily at my surroundings.

Olbi howled from where he sat at the bottom of the bed, his ears bouncing comically atop his head. "Oh, she's awake! You were right, Neferíl. Your faith in the Forest Father was just. Oh, I must go and find Kyrie. I must, I must!" His excitement caused the bed to bounce, and I struggled not to get ill. My head spinning, I pressed back against my pillow. He left quickly, his small form disappearing through the door to the sitting room. In his absence, silence encompassed the bedroom.

"I understand if you hate me," a voice said quietly from my left. I flinched, my gaze meeting Neferíl's as her brow pinched with conflicting emotions. She looked at war with herself, struggling against guilt and pride. My stomach plummeted at the sight of her, and I warred all on my own.

She had killed me, stabbed me in the back. Her betrayal cut deeper than any blade, but I had prepared myself to die. I had known the Forest Father's resurrection wouldn't come with my survival, so how could I blame Neferíl for having ensured it? A small part of me was relieved that I hadn't had to do it myself, that the choice had been freed from my hands. Another part of me begged me to get away from her hands, resting on the bed, to flinch away from her as if she were dangerous.

*She is. She's a faerie. That part hasn't changed.*

"What happened?" I asked, my voice hoarse as I struggled to sit up in bed. I gave up after a moment but bared my teeth at Neferíl when she attempted to aid me.

She stopped, then pulled her hands away as she straightened in her chair. "After you..." She cleared her throat and turned her head, staring out into the sitting room. "I stood there and a part of me knew. When Lil died, when the forest continued to rot, it made sense. The seer's words made..." Neferíl trembled. "Twins. You two. One soul, two bodies..."

Her implications forced a chill down my spine. Of course, it made sense now. Mother was only ever supposed to have one child. When my sister had died, it hadn't killed the rot, not when it'd existed inside me too. My death had been written in stone the moment my sister and I had been born.

"After you died," Neferíl continued, this time meeting my eyes, "something strange happened. Lil's body decayed rapidly and turned into spores that sank into you." Neferíl stared at me, her eyes questioning. "You stayed the same though, even as life grew from your blood, even as the green of the trees returned, and the Forest Father drew new breath. After that, he touched your wound with his snout and healed it."

I wanted to sob. My sacrifice had worked. The Forest Father was alive. Tears sprang from the corners of my eyes, and I nodded. "I would do it again. I would save the forest again. I was prepared to do it myself."

I hissed as something screamed inside me, a new hurt, a darkness that brushed up against the life of my magic. It felt the same as Sister's rot had, a small taste of her decay. I whimpered quietly. It *hurt*.

"I'm so sorry I stabbed you," Neferíl said, staring at the blanket where my waist was, mistaking the cause of my pain to be from my injury.

The Rot-like darkness faded so quickly that I thought I might have imagined it. The pain from my injuries was fresh enough to cause some imaginary things, after all. I shivered beneath my blanket but reached a hand out to brush against Neferíl's, ignoring the way my stomach clenched in fear.

*She won't hurt you. She will. Get closer. Stay back.*

Taking her hand in mine, I studied it for a moment. Her fingers were so long and thin, elegant and dark compared to mine–short blunt fingers and light skin. "I'm not going home, am I?" I asked quietly, ignoring her apology. I couldn't forgive her. Not when the betrayal stitched itself into my lungs.

Neferíl was silent for a long time. I knew. Somewhere deep down, I knew what her response would be. I understood her still despite not having had any berries or faerie wine for a while. I'd felt the change course through me. I didn't feel like a human anymore. I never truly had in the first place. Not really.

Neferíl shook her head. "I'm afraid not."

I opened my mouth to speak, tears shining in my eyes, but a lump choked the words from my throat as a knock came on the door. I would never see my father again. I would never live in my little home by the ocean. My village was safe, but the consequences left a hole in my chest, an aching loss that I'd never recover.

Neferíl's eyes were sad as she pulled away and trailed over to the door. Olbi and Kyrie pushed their way through, and Kyrie's expression carried a sense of relief as he hurried over.

"When they brought you to me, I thought you were dead. Neferíl said you had been stabbed." He glanced up to meet Neferíl's eyes, and I quickly wiped my tears away as I steeled myself against the plethora of news.

*Stay strong, little wolf. You just saved the world.* I repeated the words in my head until I believed them.

"I'm glad to see you're awake," Kyrie said more gently, his hand resting on my shoulder. "Rhi is making a remarkable recovery as well, thanks to your sacrifice. I've never seen anything like it."

Olbi crawled his way back onto the bed, where he sat at the end, eating a shiny red apple. I smiled weakly. My home was lost to me, but perhaps I'd found another one in the dark forest I'd feared my entire life.

Perhaps I wasn't done here. Perhaps I could continue to soothe the forest of its rage. Something inside me spoke the truth. I was meant to be here.

"My mother?" I was almost afraid to ask.

Neferíl's ire slipped over her face like poison. "Sits on my throne and has proclaimed herself a queen of my court. She uses fear to hold my people hostage. I intend to take back what is mine." Her words clung to the air like a promise. "Until then, Eirwyn has graciously opened his home to us for as long as we need it."

I bit my lip, my stomach rolling at the implications. I hadn't thought about where I'd go now that I was barred from leaving the forest, much less that it would be among those I'd spent my entire life training to hunt and kill.

I nodded, suddenly exhausted.

"We'll let you rest," Kyrie whispered, squeezing my shoulder before stepping away. "Olbi and I have decided to remain here. We have grown to like the safety of these woods despite its troubles, so we'll talk again when you're feeling better."

As they left, Neferíl turned to leave as well, stopping only when I reached out a hand and grabbed her wrist.

"Wait." The lump had reappeared in my throat. My heart slammed against my ribs as she stopped and turned. "Stay with me," I said before my courage could leave me, before her betrayal could silence my voice. "I don't want you to go."

A strange look crossed Neferíl's face, a mixture of adoration and guilt, but she nodded and slipped into the bed with me. Soon we were entangled with one another, her head on my shoulder.

All was silent for a time.

"Little thorn?"

I didn't remember having closed my eyes, but I must have fallen asleep because when I woke, it was dark and Neferíl was hovering above me, her lips inches from my own. A longing pierced me. I could reach up and meet her lips with mine, but I didn't know if I wanted to, didn't know if I'd be able to pull away if I started.

"Your Majesty?" It was the first time I'd used her title without any trace of mocking. It was also the first time I'd noticed flecks of gold in her eyes.

"Do you forgive me?"

"No." My confession slipped from me without hesitation, my vulnerability bare as it lay across my face for her to see.

"Could you learn to forgive me?" Her words ghosted my face, and I suppressed the urge to shiver. Could I forgive her? The wound in my chest ached in reminder, and I gave a slight shake of my head, my expression hardening.

"Maybe." It was the only promise I could give her.

"I promise no harm shall come to you by my hand ever again." Like her oath before, magic wove over my skin and solidified her promise so fiercely, I shook. "I promise no harm shall come to you by my court so long as I draw breath in my lungs."

"I will hold you to your oath," I said, searching her eyes for any sign of deceit. Faeries couldn't lie, but they could trick.

Her thumb ghosted my lower lip as she trailed her hand down to curl around my throat. *Faeries are dangerous.* Still, my mind screamed as my body flooded with desire and fought against the warning bells that were going off in my head.

"I'm depending on it," she uttered.

*She's going to kill you.*

She kissed me.

*Faeries don't have hearts.*

Her heart fluttered against my hand as I pressed my palm to her chest. I curled my fingers around her shirt and tugged her closer, suddenly insistent. I kissed her like I was suffocating. Desire pressed low in my stomach, and I gasped as her tongue slipped into my mouth to stake its claim. Her free hand danced down and slipped under my shirt, careful not to go anywhere near my wound.

"I want you, little thorn," she whispered, her voice dark and low as she pulled away. Her wings had come out, large and beautiful and a luminescent blue in the dim darkness of the room. I trembled beneath the heat of her gaze. "I've ached to know what you taste like."

"Please," I begged, and that was all the permission she needed to press a lingering kiss to my lips as she slowly dragged my shirt up until she couldn't anymore. Pulling away, she helped me take it off.

"I'll be gentle," she promised, staring down at me with a molten expression. I was desperate for her touch as I writhed beneath her, unable to contain the desire as it flowed through me. Every kiss she left on my skin was like a small flame had been ignited, and I didn't hold back the soft moans as she kissed sensitive spots, as her tongue danced lightly across my exposed flesh. I didn't even know such feelings could come from feather touches, but she drew them out of me until I was a mess under her careful touch, until her kisses had reached my waistline. She slowly freed me from the shackles of my pants until I was naked before her.

As she descended, my quiet whimpers turned into moans, and I let go.

As I watched the sun rise for the first time since I'd entered the forest, I felt peace. Neferíl slept soundly beside me, and I nearly laughed at her soft snoring. Faeries might not need sleep, but they still seemed to indulge in it.

It was calming, having woken without any trace of nightmares, no sleep paralysis chaining me to my bed. I'd woke up rested; even the pain from my wound had been gone. When I'd checked under my dressings, there hadn't even been a wound. Just another shiny scar to remind me of everything I'd been through.

As I stared out at dawn, a lightness consumed me. I was free, free for the first time in my life. No more anger, no more pain, no more...

I shifted as pain smarted up my right arm. Neferíl stirred in her sleep from my movement, and I forced myself to still until she did. Her braids were flung over her face and shoulders. She looked so young when she was asleep, unburdened by responsibility, and I stole a moment to memorize her face.

More pain echoed in my fingers, so I pulled my hand out from under the blanket. I held it up to the window, bathing it in light.

My breath caught in my throat.

My fingers were rotting.

*"Róis."*

Neferíl's voice caught me off guard, and I tried to hide my hand from her. "Show me," she said, reaching out to curl her fingers around my wrist. She studied my blackened fingers for quite some time. My breath caught as they tingled. Then the black rot faded until my fingers were healed.

"I don't understand," she said.

But my sister's words washed through me, unbidden. *It's inside you now, sweet sister.*

"I think I'm infected now," I whispered, pushing away from Neferíl and stumbling out of bed. If I truly was rotting, the last thing I wanted to do was infect Neferíl with it. "I think it happened when my sister died." Horror clung to me like a second skin, the chill of the room ghosting against my bare skin. I moved to the floor, where my clothes had been scattered in my insistence to rid myself of them. I pulled them back on haphazardly, stumbling towards the sitting room.

"Little thorn, where are you going?"

I ignored her. If I was sick, then I needed to leave before the forest began rotting anew. My heart pounded in my chest, making me dizzy. I'd thought this nightmare was over, but I'd been wrong. I was always wrong.

"Róis, look at me."

My head snapped over to her as she draped the blanket around her shoulders. She leaned forward, the sun highlighting the determination in her expression.

"I think I know where we need to go to get you the help you need. The Forest Father was content not providing any answers, but his seers, his druids, are sprinkled throughout Elvira." She nodded as if affirming her own words. "We'll go to them. We'll find out what's happening before it gets bad."

My head swam. "Kyrie's a druid, isn't he?" I asked softly. "If we're going to see druids, I want him to come with us."

Neferíl nodded. "Of course. We'll figure this out. The fate of the realm depends on it."

I still despaired, but I trusted her words. If I knew anything about Neferíl, queen of the Unseelie Court, it was that she cared for her people.

Above all, she would make sure they were safe.

She was right.

We would figure it out.

But my aching fingers promised otherwise.

# Acknowledgements

I want to give the biggest thank you to the child in me. I've been obsessed with Celtic mythology for as long as I can remember. I'm talkin' long nights and years of extensive research on faeries and all the myth that surrounded them. That obsession never went away, and I finally got to write a story about my love for those stories and beliefs. I owed it to little me to build this world, and I hope you all loved it as much as I loved creating it.

Big thanks to Miranda, my editor. I just simply would not be the writer I am today without her. She's constantly pushing me to be the best version of myself, and I couldn't imagine my books being the way they are without her insight. Endless gratitude.

Biggest of thanks to the people who backed the kickstarter for this title. Without your support, this book would have taken much longer to come to fruition. Among those who backed, I want to thank: Bailey Nicole, Sam Vermillion, C. Attard, Catherine Holmes, Meg Mordros, Christina, Cara Reasner, Alexandra Corrsin, Ross Bishop, Ashley, Maggie Laigaie, Sarah, Justise Briones, Kristen Altmann, Sacha Black, Amaryllis Jeanne Quilliou, Self Spectrum, Allan Haimes, Bianca Tatjana, Kevin Chang, Danika, Jonathan Brown, Mason, Sean Brimm, Amber, Zelda Knight, Jess McKelden, Isabel B., Lorenzo G., Eron Wyngarde, SD Simper, Connor Teinert, Rebecca Hampsher, Kassie H, Sarah Albrecht, Jessica S. Taylor, Chris M, Diane, Skylar Charbeneau, Lily Blackthorn, Louise Morelli, Chris Whiteley, Quinn Elena, Anna Bissonette, Shannon, Efren Perez, Katie N., Rose Boss, Paul Douglas, Paris J., Tia Ledvina, FoxDenDenizen, Kela, Katie, Elizabeth Hosea-Small, Nena, Molly S., Rachel Spina, Kira, Lily G, Amanda Nalley, Kevin Chafe, Rachael Rooklin, Claire Wickham-Eade, Maddie Barreda, and everyone else that aided me in my kickstarter journey.

Big ol' thanks to the people who got to listen to ALL of my ramblings when these stories are still in their early stages. *A Flower's Fatal Thorn* was a big step for me. Misfits is my soul project, but the groundwork was laid before me; I just had to fill in the muscles and bones of that story. *A Flower's Fatal Thorn* is 100% mine. And I feared that it wasn't going to be loved in the same way Misfits has been. But to people like Katie, Tia, Miranda, and Ellie, who have read and screamed about their love for this story (even in its bare bones), I am forever grateful.

Thank you, as always, to the reader. I truly wouldn't be where I am today without you. I'm so so grateful. □

# What now?

If you liked *A Flower's Fatal Thorn* and feel so inclined, **reviews** are so helpful for an indie authors journey. Whether it be on Amazon, Goodreads, Storygraph, or your socials, I'm grateful to anyone who takes the time to review. You'll never find me bullying anyone who doesn't like my books, but please don't tag me in any reviews where anything negative/critical might be said. The reviews are for the readers, after all and I put a lot of work into this story. Feel free to tag me in any positive reviews, though! And if you'd like to keep up to date with my work, make sure to follow me on instagram or tiktok at @jordandugdaleauthor. Until next time. □